EVERYTHING I
THOUGHT I KNEW

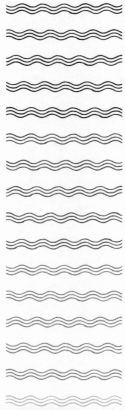

EVERYTHING
I THOUGHT
I KNEW

Shannon
Takaoka

CANDLEWICK PRESS

First edition 2020

Library of Congress Catalog Card Number pending
ISBN 978-1-5362-0776-7

20 21 22 23 24 25 LBM 10 9 8 7 6 5 4 3 2 1

Printed in Melrose Park, IL, USA

This book was typeset in Minion Pro.

Candlewick Press
99 Dover Street
Somerville, Massachusetts 02144

www.candlewick.com

For Emi, Evan, and Scott,
who always believed in me

 **BROKEN**

Here's one of the many things I thought I knew that turns out to be wrong: you need to fall in love to end up with a broken heart.

That's not how it was for me. At least not at first.

Sometimes things—glass, eggs, hearts—just break, and there's no way to put them back to their exact, original form. You can't stir the cream out of your coffee. A broken plate, even if you glue it, will always have cracks. This is just basic physics, or, more specifically, the second law of thermodynamics. Not to nerd out on you too much.

But I'm already getting ahead of myself, which I tend to do, because my brain never seems to want to slow down and just *be still*. There's too much going on in there, especially now. So let's rewind a bit and begin with the moment the universe decided to start messing with all my assumptions and well-laid plans, big-time.

October 14 at 3:45 p.m.

It's the fall of my senior year.

I'm running.

"Damn, it's hot," I say to Emma as we round the curve at the far side of our high school's track. The lane lines vibrate ahead of me in the heat. Halloween is a few weeks away, and it must be more than eighty degrees, at least.

Emma, her auburn ponytail smooth and perfect, looks like she's barely broken a sweat. "Is it?" she asks. "Feels pretty good to me." A warm spell, typical for the San Francisco Bay Area in the fall, has brought us beach weather in the middle of a month packed with college application submissions, after-school practices, and, as always, piles of homework. The result: we won't, in fact, be hanging at the beach. Cross-country is basically the only time I get to breathe outdoor air.

We're doing intervals today, and Emma's pace seems faster than usual. As soon as we are side by side, she pulls ahead. I have to push myself to catch her. I push, she pulls. She pulls, I push. This is starting to annoy me, even though it's what Emma and I always do when we practice together—we compete.

She pulls ahead again. I try to focus on increasing my pace.

Focus, Chloe, focus.

But all I can think about is water.

I didn't drink enough before practice.

I didn't drink *any* water, actually. I got held up leaving seventh period because I needed to talk to Ms. Breece about my paper proposal for AP Physics and had barely enough time to pull on my running shoes. My proposal is going to be late, which Ms. Breece made sure to note is "unlike you, Chloe," which is true, I guess, but it got me thinking about what really, honestly *is* "like me," because sometimes, or maybe even *all the time*, I'm stumped on that one. Which got me stressing again about my college application essays and whether they are mind-numbingly boring, and, by extension, if *I* am mind-numbingly boring. Which resulted in me forgetting to fill up my water bottle. This is starting to seem like kind of a big mistake, now that my mouth has gone dry and I'm dizzy and feeling like I might be about to throw up all over my shoes.

I turn to Emma. Her mouth is moving, but I only hear her last few words.

". . . don't you think?" she asks. "Chloe?" Cross-country is when we catch up on anything we didn't get to talk about at lunch. The pop quiz we weren't expecting in Calc. Weekend plans. Emma's ongoing analysis of her five-minute conversation with Liam Morales about *Catch-22* — *Was it an excuse to talk to her? Or did he just need some quick info from someone who actually read the book?* — a topic that, for my own reasons, I really don't want to analyze anyway. But I must

3

have zoned out for a few seconds, or minutes, because I have no idea what she just said.

"Think about what?" I barely have enough breath to get out the words, so I slow to a light jog as Emma pulls ahead of me for the third—or is it fourth?—time. Instead of pushing, I just stop. My heart is thumping hard.

Thump thumpthumpthumpthumpthumpthumpthump. It's all I can hear. *Thumpthumpthumpthumpthump.*

Emma turns around. "Chloe?"

The lane lines ahead of me look wrong. They're not just vibrating, they're rippling. Like those wave graphs in my physics textbook. The whole field around us is rippling. *Are we having an earthquake?* I look toward Emma, also rippling, who has now stopped running too and is staring at me, eyes wide.

"Chloe, are you okay?"

My chest feels like it's being crushed. My ears are on fire. Sweat is running down my face and my back, soaking my shirt.

Not okay, I think.

Definitely not okay. But I can't say the words.

And then the world that's spinning, spinning, spinning like a top gets tipped over, me with it. The last thing I see is the brilliant blue of the October sky overhead.

When I open my eyes, my mom is there, and I can tell immediately that she's been crying. Her face is puffy and red. Next to her, my dad is pale, like someone drained the blood out of him.

"Mom?"

"Hi, sweetie." She grabs my hand.

Machines whir all around me. A tube is fitted under my nose. Oxygen, I'm assuming. Electrodes are attached to my chest under a thin fabric gown and there's an IV in my right arm. I'm in a hospital, obviously. But not dead. So that's encouraging, at least.

"Mom, what happened?" I whisper. My chest hurts. I still feel like I don't have enough air in my lungs, and it's hard for me to talk. She and my dad look at each other in that way they do sometimes when I ask a question they don't really want to answer. Like when I was five and asked them if they were going to die someday too after we held a backyard funeral for my recently departed hamster, Nugget.

I can tell my mom is holding back tears as she struggles to keep a neutral face. She clutches my hand with both of hers.

"It's your heart, Chloe. There's something wrong with your heart."

My heart?

How can there be something wrong with my heart? Heart problems are for big-bellied old men. For people who eat greasy cheeseburgers and fries all the time and never exercise. For people who smoke. Not for just-turned-seventeen-year-old girls. Not for vegetarians who run five miles almost every day after school. Not for people like me.

I turn from my mom to my dad. Dad's the science teacher of the family; maybe he's the one who should cover this. But he's still as silent as the grave, which is highly unusual for him. And alarming to me.

"Dr. Ahmadi says it's a defect," my mom explains. "One that we didn't know about until now. He will be here shortly to go over everything with us."

"Who's Dr. Ahmadi?" I ask.

Nothing that's happening right now is making any sense. *Why didn't they call Dr. Curtis?* I wonder. She knows me. I know her. She's been my doctor since I was a baby.

"Dr. Ahmadi is a cardiac surgeon," my mom says. "He's a specialist."

The word *surgeon* gets my attention.

Surgery seems serious. *Heart* surgery, extremely serious. But it can't be anything that bad. I was *fine* when I left the house this morning. Wasn't I? Plus, I don't have time for any surgery. Not now. Not in the next-to-last semester of my senior year. Not with midterms coming up in a few weeks and college applications due. I try to take a deep breath to calm myself down, but I just end up inhaling a horrible plastic-y smell from the oxygen tube and it freaks me out even more. Why are they giving me oxygen?

"Do I need surgery?" I ask, my chest already tightening up in anticipation of the answer.

My mom and dad look at each other again, and I really want to shake them this time, because I know they know

I hate it when they treat me like a baby who can't handle uncomfortable information. If there's something important going on, I want to know what it is. I like to have answers.

But before I can ask another question, there's a knock at the door.

"Hello?"

A man wearing green surgical scrubs appears in the doorway and my mom and dad stand up.

"Please come in," my mom says. "She's awake."

A smile spreads across his face as he walks toward me.

"Nice to meet you, Chloe. I'm Dr. Ahmadi."

According to Dr. Ahmadi, here's what (not who) is responsible for breaking my heart:

Arrhythmogenic Right Ventricular Dysplasia. ARVD for short.

It's a rare form of cardiomyopathy—a cellular defect—and it's been slowly killing the muscle tissue of my right ventricle, probably for years. Maybe since I was born. The resulting scars are now making it hard for my heart to do what it's supposed to do. Like beat hard enough to oxygenate my blood. Which is not exactly something a pint of Ben & Jerry's and an ugly cry is going to fix.

ARVD is why I collapsed on my high school's track. Why I have been feeling so tired and out of breath recently.

Why I'm going to need a new heart.

And it's why, if I don't get one soon, I'm going to die.

I'm going to die before I turn eighteen. I'm going to die before I graduate high school. Before I get to go to college, visit Tokyo, climb the Eiffel Tower, fall in love, own a dog, and become the first scientist to confirm the existence of life on another planet. *Oh my god*, I think. *What else?* I don't even know all the things that I want to do, to see, to taste, hear, and touch, because I assumed I had plenty of time to figure it out. A lifetime of it.

Dr. Ahmadi tells us that, based on my condition and my age, the chances are good that I'll be given a priority position on the transplant waiting list.

And then we will be in the very awkward, awful situation of hoping that someone who is not me might die instead.

So I can live.

⧼⧼⧼ STRANGE DAYS ⧽⧽⧽

Somewhere—close by? far away?—I hear an alarm. Is it a
hospital monitor, alerting nurses to come running? Or is it
the phone on my nightstand, in my bedroom, at home? I'm
stuck again in that weird in-between place that bridges asleep
and awake, where I'm not sure if I can trust my senses.

Is what's happening right now *really* happening, or is it
a dream?

Where am I?

What am I supposed to be doing today?

I never got stuck like this *before*. Before everything that
happened with my heart, I always woke up with a plan, hardly
remembering my dreams. My brain would already be busy
preparing for the day ahead: the French quiz scheduled for

first period, the English paper that I needed to revise during study hall, the cross-country meet after school.

But now, I sometimes struggle to ground myself. *Am I in my room, or someplace else?* Sometimes I forget *when* it is, forget that it's morning and not night, that it's almost summer and not fall, that more than eight months have passed and I'm not still running side by side with Emma in the second week of October during our senior year. Sometimes . . . sometimes I open my eyes and wonder, for many more seconds than is comfortable, if I'm living or if I'm dead.

Spoiler alert: I'm still alive. My heart? Not so much.

Now I have a new one, and a lot of things are different. Not just different—*strange.*

The most obvious is the scar. It runs from the top of my collarbone to my abdomen and makes me feel like the Bride of Frankenstein, who, as you may know, was also brought back to life using borrowed parts. This is why, technically speaking, I guess I shouldn't even call it a "new" heart.

If I want to be 100 percent accurate, it's recycled.

Repurposed.

Reanimated.

One that previously belonged to someone else.

Until a fog-shrouded night this past December—one week before Christmas—when it was extracted from my donor's still-warm body and transplanted into mine.

We both had run into some serious bad luck.

My luck, as we know, turned south that day I collapsed

during cross-country practice. And two months later, a trauma of some sort rendered my donor's head pretty much kaput.

Healthy heart. Dead brain. An ideal match for a patient on the list.

A patient like me.

True story: The national transplant waiting list is the only list I've ever made it to the top of for failing rather than succeeding. My heart was getting a big fat F in keeping me alive, and that's one consideration that moves you to the front of the line. Minors also generally get priority over older people, who have less of their lives ahead of them, I suppose. How much you have in common with your donor determines the rest. Blood types need to be compatible. Proximity is also important, since hearts, in particular, have a limited shelf life. My donor had O positive blood, just like me. We also lived within thirty miles of each other, which is how, on the night I got the call, I was able to be in surgery, buzz saw poised over my sternum, within minutes of my partner-in-bad-luck's official pronouncement of death.

And now we're not partners in anything anymore. It's just me left standing, trying to wrap my head around everything that's different, and strange, and not like how I'd thought.

So what else? In addition to the scar, there are a *lot* of pills. Pills to take in the morning. Pills to take at night. Pills that I can't forget or else I'll break this heart too, and then I'll be back on that horrible list, waiting again for someone who is not me to die. Or not waiting, if it's me who does the dying. This is why my mom makes me carry around one of those plastic dispensers with a tiny compartment for each day of the week, just like my grandma.

I also used to run all the time, but now I don't. I used to be a vegetarian, but now I'm not. I used to have every minute of my life scheduled, but now I have hours, sometimes whole days, where I do nothing but watch back-to-back episodes of *Parks and Recreation* and *The Walking Dead* and leaf through the stack of comics I bought at the used bookstore downtown.

I used to never have nightmares.

But the most different thing of all, especially for everyone who knew me *before*, is that I'm now a high school dropout. Well, sort of. I missed more than half of my senior year, so I'm making it up in summer school, which is full of actual dropouts, like Jane Kessler, who tells me she flunked trig; and Brian Felder, who didn't graduate because he had to go to one of those rehab camps for *World of Warcraft* addicts. So instead of doing a research-lab summer internship like I'd planned, I've been spending my weekdays in the nearly empty school library, staring blankly at an open Google doc and pretending to make headway on the essay I need to turn in about *The Grapes of Wrath*. Normally, this is something I could probably wrap up with one hand tied behind my back, but the "Symbolism of the Turtle in Chapter Three" is eluding me. Does anyone really *care* why John Steinbeck wrote about a turtle crossing the road? I know I sure don't. Not at the moment, anyway, which is not . . . like me.

I hear my mom in the hallway and prepare the smile I will put on when she pops her head into my room to make sure I'm up. She's weirdly cheerful and helicopter-like and overenthusiastic these days, which is yet another thing that's different. I don't have the heart (no pun intended) to tell her I'm not all that excited to get out of bed. That I don't want to take another handful of pills, or write my AP English essay about symbolic turtles, or start dealing with the college acceptances stacked on my desk, which, due to my "special circumstances," can be deferred a semester while I complete the credits I need to graduate. That I feel like a stranger in my own skin.

In fact, though I haven't mentioned this to her or my dad or anybody else, I'm not all that excited about anything these days—except for one thing: at three o'clock, I surf.

≋ HEADS AND HEARTS ≋

A slimy piece of seaweed tangles around my ankle and I shake it off, simultaneously shaking some feeling back into my numb toes. Even with the wetsuit on, the coldness of the water is always a shock at first—the ocean spray like tiny needles pelting my face. Paddling my board over the swells, I keep my eyes on Kai's head bobbing up and down about ten yards ahead of me and try to forget the fact that most of my weight is resting on a breastbone that not so long ago was sawed in half. It almost feels like the scar is tingling beneath my suit.

My parents would freak if they knew I was out here, putting my recently restored life into the hands of this guy I barely know. I SPECIALIZE IN BEGINNERS read the ad I found pinned to a bulletin board in a nearby surf shop a few weeks ago—a shop I had finally ventured into after spending more than a few afternoons surveying all the action from the beach.

Initially, I'd been hanging out there to escape Senior Week. To avoid everyone trying to convince me to come to the senior picnic and the senior-faculty dodgeball game and the night where all the seniors spray-paint their names on the Wall—a cement barrier that holds up the hill behind campus. I was invited to everything, of course, even though I wasn't officially graduating. But feigning excitement about my classmates' upcoming parties and travel plans and college start dates when I was days away from reporting to summer school? Hard pass. So instead, I got in my car, which lately is one of the few things that makes my brain stop buzzing, and I drove until I reached the coast. Watching the waves, alone, with my feet buried in the cool sand, was so much better than attending Senior Pajama Day. And once I started studying the surfers paddling out and gliding like water gods over the waves, I couldn't stop. Had I really never noticed how mesmerizing they are before? I guess not, because if you had told "before Chloe" that she'd be attempting to surf, she would have said you were dreaming. She'd have warned you that the waves here are too powerful. The water is too cold. That there are sharks lurking nearby that might mistake you for a seal.

The truth is that, until I first connected with Kai, I'd never more than waded into the water north of the Golden Gate. But now . . . *now* I'd much rather be freezing my butt off and paddling like a madwoman than be safe on solid ground. Even if my arms feel like rubber and my last attempt to stand up on the board left me struggling through the shallows, tossed around like an empty bottle sucked up from the shore. Strangely, my usual cautionary reflex seems to have malfunctioned. I'm not worried that I might drown, or break a limb, or get eaten by a great white. I only want to skim across the top of the water effortlessly, like Kai. And I'm going to keep eating sand until I find the wave that will take me out of my head and make me more at home with this new heart. If only for a minute.

Kai doesn't know about my heart transplant, of course. The full wetsuit covers my scar. The only thing he knows about me at all is that I want to learn to surf. And I don't know a whole lot about him, aside from the fact that he seems like he was born riding a wave. He doesn't talk much.

After I catch up to him, we float on our boards and wait.

And wait. It's a sunless day. The sky above is milky white, covered by a thick layer of fog, and the water is a hard steel gray. The wind whips at my face, its scent sharp with salt and brine.

"Heads up," he says, as a promising wave rolls toward us.

I position myself on my board—not too far forward, not too far back—and start paddling into the wave like he's taught me, my arms burning from the effort. It feels like I'm going nowhere. Then I remember how he's always warning me about beginners wasting energy by paddling too shallow, and with all my strength, I reach into the water as deeply as I can.

Right, left. Right, left. Right, left. My board rises with the wave. I can't see where Kai is at the moment, but I hear him yell, "Pop up!" as it starts to break. The heart in my chest is pounding. We've practiced pop-ups a bunch of times on the sand, but I haven't yet managed to stay standing on the water. Will today be the day?

Kai's advice echoes in my head. *Don't grab the rails.* I place my hands under my chest and push up. *Back foot first.* I slide my back foot out from under me and then launch my front foot forward. *Make sure your knees are bent.* I twist sideways as I come up to standing, knees still bent, aaaaannnd . . . pitch forward, headfirst, into the ocean.

Damn it!

I surface as the wave rushes past, its momentum roaring in my ears, pulling me and my board with it. *Damn it, damn it, damn it.* Our hour is almost up today. Which means there won't be time for me to try to catch another wave. About ten seconds later, I see Kai passing by on the next one, riding it all the way in and hopping off with ease. *Great.* Now I also get to struggle out of the water like a flopping sea lion while he watches.

He's standing in the sand with his board planted next to him, his black hair dripping, as I trudge out of the surf.

"You looked at your feet," he says.

I nod, still breathing hard.

"You need to look ahead, in the direction you want to go," he explains. "It'll help you keep your balance. Also—"

"I was leaning too far forward."

"Uh . . . yeah. You were leaning."

He only has a lot to say when it's about technique.

We make eye contact and my face warms up, which is equal parts embarrassing and annoying. Sometimes I wish I had found an instructor who was less "surfer." I mean, I know this is kind of a cliché and all, but guys who surf are very, very . . . *fit*. Kai included. He also has nice lips. It's a little distracting.

"Okay," I say, sighing. "Look ahead, don't lean forward. Anything else I'm messing up?"

Kai leans down on one knee and detaches me from the ankle leash.

"Don't get so frustrated," he says as he pulls at the Velcro on the cuff, which I really didn't need help with because it comes off super easy. "You're doing great for someone who's never surfed before. A lot of people quit as soon as they have a bad wipeout."

So far, bad wipeouts are my middle name.

"Well, I'm not going to quit, but I do have sand in places where I never thought I'd have sand," I say. "How does that even happen if I'm wearing a wetsuit?"

Kai ignores my question and looks up at me. "Where'd you get this leash?"

"Same place I bought the board," I tell him.

"It's cheap. If it snaps and you lose your board, you'll have to swim all the way in," he says. "I'll bring a better one for you next week."

He's still on one knee and I almost blurt out, "Are you about to propose?"—but I stop myself. Making flirty jokes with a boy I've only known for a few weeks is *definitely* not something I did *before*. Besides, we don't really have a joke-cracking relationship. Most of the time, Kai is all business. So what I actually say is, "Okay, thanks. I'll bring some extra cash."

He stands. "No need. You can borrow one of mine. See you next week."

I nod. "Next week." I pick up my board and start walking toward the path that leads to the parking lot, but I pause to call over my shoulder. "I'm catching one next time. Even if I have to stay out there till I can't feel my toes."

"Hmm. If you can't feel your toes, how are you going to keep your balance?" Kai raises his eyebrows as if he has just imparted some deep wisdom.

Well, okay. That was *kind of* a joke, so maybe he's not *all* business.

〰〰 THE TUNNEL 〰〰

When we were younger, Emma used to tell me that if you died in your dreams, you'd never wake up. "Think about it," she said. "If someone is trying to kill you or you're falling through the sky, you always wake up before." Before the hunter unleashes his arrow. Before your body slams into the ground.

Even though I was skeptical of anything superstitious, Emma's certainty spooked me. "Dream your death, and you're screwed."

But now I know this can't be true. Because for the last few weeks, I've died over and over again in my dreams. Every single night.

It always starts with me speeding toward the black mouth of a tunnel on a motorcycle. I wear a heavy leather jacket, steel-toed boots, and a helmet. Air rushes through the seams on my face shield and bright yellow lights streak by, blurring into a single fluorescent line. I lean into a curve and, as I'm pulling out of it, I see a Christmas tree, tied with twine, lying across the lane. I swerve, slide, hear the echoing screech of tires behind me. Time slows for a few brief seconds as I am sent flying. There is broken glass. There is the acrid smell of burning rubber. Oil-stained pavement rushes up to meet me, filling my field of vision. The last thing I hear is a loud, sickening crack as blood washes over my eyes.

And then there is nothing.

A nothing so complete and empty that I know without a doubt that I am dead.

Until the phone on my nightstand sounds its alarm, ushering in another day.

I jolt up in bed, heart hammering, and silence my alarm. *It's okay,* I think. *You're okay. You're in your room. In your bed. Not dead.* It's the "nothing" part of the dream that's the worst. Worse than the crack as my head hits the pavement. Worse than all the blood. Is that what death is really like? Like *nothing?* It's terrifying to think that in one instant you're seeing and smelling and feeling and hearing and thinking and then in the next you're just this . . . void. Even though I'm sweating, the thought makes me shiver. And my head hurts like hell. Almost like it really did just slam into the pavement.

There's a knock on my door, and a nanosecond later, my

mom pops her head into my room. I always used to protest when she wouldn't wait for my "permission" to enter, but now I cut her more slack. All the heart drama has put her through the wringer.

"Are you awake in here?" she asks.

"Yep, I'm up," I say.

Mom gives me a closer look and the little worry line between her eyebrows deepens.

"Everything okay?"

My pulse is still racing from the dream, so I take a deep, calming breath. "I'm fine," I lie, not wanting to get her all worked up over a nightmare.

She sets a glass of water down on my nightstand and sits at the edge of my bed. "You look a little pale."

"Mom, I'm *fine.*"

"Okay," she says, standing back up, giving me "my space." "Don't forget your pills."

"Yes, Mom."

Making sure I take my medication has become her number-one mission in life. She pauses in the doorway again on her way out.

"Dad wants to stop for lunch in the city after your appointment. Any thoughts on where you'd like to go?"

Oh, boy. I knew they were going to make a big deal out of this.

"I still don't understand why you both need to come," I say, throwing off my covers and swinging my legs out of bed.

"Don't be silly, Chloe. Your six-month appointment is a big deal! We should celebrate, don't you think?"

I should want to, right? Today is my six-month postoperative checkup. Six months since my original model heart was removed and replaced by another. Now that I have reached this milestone, and provided that the heart biopsy that I must submit to this morning looks good, I will no longer have to see my cardiac surgeon every few weeks. It also means that I'm supposed to be able to get back to most "normal activities," whatever that means.

The thing is, taking a gazillion pills a day doesn't exactly feel normal. Neither does going to school in the summer or my constant compulsion to just get in my car and drive *fast, fast, fast*, or the weird memory issues I've been having—*for how long now? weeks? months?*—or my now-nightly death dream. And the least normal thing of all? The constant, ever-present, can't-get-away-from-it-not-even-for-a-second awareness of someone *else's* original model heart beating inside *my* chest. *Thump.* Does it sound different? *Thump, thump.* Does it speed up faster? Does it skip in a way that's unlike the one that used to be mine?

I wish I could tell my mom and dad that it feels strange to celebrate. That *everything* feels strange.

After showering, I pull on a pair of jeans and find a sweater to wear over my T-shirt. It's always so cold in the hospital. Before heading out to the kitchen, I take a quick look at myself in the mirror on my closet door, just to make sure it's still me looking back. Same brown eyes. Same constellation of freckles on my cheeks. Same not-quite-manageable hair. Still me.

At least, it appears to be. Aside from the *thump*.

Thump, thump.

QUESTIONS

From the moment that I could talk, I wanted to know *why* about everything.

Why do people need to eat?

Why do my fingers wrinkle in the bath?

Why don't we get burnt up by the sun?

Mostly because I was curious. It was fun to ask questions and learn the answers. But a part of me also really *needed* to know. Explanations were comforting, especially when delivered by my science-teacher dad:

"Your fingers wrinkle in the bath to help you grip things in the water. The water tells your brain that things might get slippery, so your brain sends a message back to your fingers that makes the skin on them shrivel up a bit, so that it's easier to hold things that are wet. They'll go back to normal in a little while, after you dry off. No worries."

My five-year-old self had been studying the puckered skin on my fingers and was relieved to hear that it wouldn't stay that way.

"Or maybe you are actually an old woman named Gertrude disguised as my daughter," he couldn't help adding, looking into my eyes and squinting as he wrapped me in my pink butterfly towel. "What have you done with my Chloe?"

"Stop it, Daddy." I giggled. "It's me, it's me!"

"Gertrude" became our little joke for the next couple of days—*Gertrude, could you please pass the salt? How was school today, Gertrude?*—until I moved on to another *why*, and another, and another.

By age ten, the questions I asked didn't always have simple explanations.

Why are we here?

What happens to you when you die?

How big is the universe, anyway?

I remember folding myself into the three-way mirror at Macy's while my mom was busy with zippers and hangers, watching my reflection repeat and repeat and repeat into what seemed like an infinite number of Chloes in an infinite number of dressing rooms. I wondered: Would we all leave the dressing room and go home to the same house, the same parents, the same life? Or would some Chloes take a left when they stepped out of the frame while the rest of us took a right? And then what? How many combinations of lefts, rights, ups, and downs could there possibly be? Was there a Chloe headed to a fancy restaurant for dinner? One about to get hit by a bus while crossing the street?

"Do you think other versions of us exist?" I'd asked my mom. "Like in other realities or something?"

"I think you watch way too much *Doctor Who*," my mom had answered. "I can't see the mirror, Chloe. This is the last dress, I promise."

Reluctantly, I moved out of her way, still daydreaming about what all the other Chloes were doing. It had to be something more exciting than watching their moms try on fifteen black dresses that all looked the same.

I don't know exactly when I stopped asking so many questions. But by high school, I was convinced that right answers are what *really* matter. You can't get bogged down questioning everything or risk being wrong when every test, homework assignment, and pop quiz has the power to add or shave a fraction of a percentage from that all-important GPA. So I made sure that I studied hard enough to earn As on all my tests. I selected AP courses and after-school activities based on which ones would look best on my college application submissions. I went to the library. I volunteered. I signed up. This rigorous attention to detail had a singular purpose, of course: a résumé competitive enough to earn me a spot at a great school. By the fall of my senior year, high school graduation seemed like it would be a formality—I just needed to show up, follow through on my final assignments, and claim my place near the top of the class.

And yet, there was a small part of me that still wondered . . . *Why?* Why had my childhood curiosity given way to caution? Why did I worry so much about saying the wrong thing or making a mistake? And, despite my successes, why did I sometimes feel like my life was not entirely my own?

But I pushed those questions aside. Because everything was on track. Everything was going according to plan. Until the thing happened that was definitely *not* on my to-do list: a failing heart.

And now here I am. Instead of having lunch with my fellow summer interns or shopping for dorm room supplies with my mom, I'm sitting on an exam table at the UCSF cardiothoracic surgery center, freezing in a crinkling paper gown. It figures that in the one circumstance that my actual life depends on acing a test, no amount of studying will make a difference. Instead, all I can do is wait for Dr. Ahmadi to appear so he can tell me if my latest circulatory grade makes the cut.

I've banished my mom and dad to the front lobby, mainly because I can't stand it when my dad gets anxious and starts to pace. But also, I'd like a little time to absorb the news if the report isn't good. I have no reason to believe that it won't be, but if recent experience has taught me anything, it's that the absolute shittiest worst-case scenario can happen when you least expect it. I hear footsteps in the hall outside and sit up straighter, adjusting the plastic tie on the gown.

When Dr. Ahmadi walks in the room, he looks as happy as my parents did when I got a near-perfect score on my SATs. "Looking good, Chloe!" he says, as he holds up my most recent heart biopsy and EKG results. He hands me a piece of graph paper that maps the electrical activity of my transplanted heart. To most people, it probably looks like a bunch of squiggly lines, but I've viewed enough EKGs by now to understand what I'm seeing. I trace my finger over the pattern of low peaks interspersed with steep upside-down Vs. It's showing a "normal sinus rhythm," which means this heart is doing exactly what it's supposed to do: pumping blood into my lungs and out to the rest of my body without making a fuss. Zero drama is pretty much the best you can ask for when it comes to a heart.

"All functioning appears to be normal and there are no signs of rejection, although you'll need to continue on the immunosuppressants indefinitely, of course," says Dr. Ahmadi. "But for now, things really look good. How do you feel about that?"

I feel relieved, of course, but maybe not as relieved as my parents will be—especially my dad, who, if he were in the room right now, would probably crush Dr. Ahmadi with one of his bear hugs.

But *weird* is the word that comes to mind first. I feel weird. Physically, things are getting back on track. My body feels stronger every day. I notice it for sure when I'm out paddling in the waves with Kai, although I'm not going to tell Dr. Ahmadi or my parents about that. I don't have any chest pain. This is all objectively very good news, yet I can't shake the feeling that something is not right.

I study Dr. Ahmadi's kind face, still young-looking despite the fact that his hair is flecked with gray. His calm manner has often reassured me, especially on the night when I was whisked into the operating room for my transplant, an entire team of doctors and nurses jogging along beside me. Maybe he will have a simple explanation if I tell him what's going on with me now. Because sometimes my head seems even more messed up than my old, defective heart.

There's something wrong with my memory, for one thing. In the last few weeks—or maybe longer—I've been feeling like I've lost places, events, even people, from my life before. I keep seeing these fragments that my mind can't seem to fully download and piece together. Didn't I once fall out of a tree? Why can't I remember when? Or where? There are faces that I recall, but not names. Scenes that appear in my brain without any other context that I'm unable to anchor to a fixed place or time: a windswept hillside blanketed with wild lavender. A blue house. A thin woman wearing a knit cap. I can tell you that the woman's eyes are beautiful—a tropical water color that's somewhere between green and blue; that her cap is charcoal gray; that she wears tiny, delicate gold hoops in her ears, but I don't remember *who* she is.

These gaps in my memory, or whatever they are, are scaring me. And I haven't mentioned them to my mom or dad yet because I don't want to scare them. But I'm wondering: Could my brain somehow have been damaged during those weeks I spent connected to an oxygen tank, never feeling like I had enough? Have I forgotten key moments from my old life?

Then there's the latest thing: the nightmares. And the headaches that come after.

And it's not just my memory. It's my mood that feels off. Shouldn't I feel happy? Shouldn't I feel *#blessed*? This recycled heart, after all, has saved me. There will be more birthdays. College. Travel. A *life*. If I tell Dr. Ahmadi that I often have an overwhelming desire to reach in and rip it out, pulsing and dripping—a bloody hole in my chest seeming preferable to a piece of someone else pumping away in there—will he think I'm ungrateful? A terrible person? Or will he smile his easy smile and tell me it's all normal and nothing to worry about?

In the end, I decide not to say anything about any of it. I don't want any more tests. No more blood draws. No more machines scanning parts of my body. Today, I'm officially free of all that. My parents are free of all that. For a little longer than usual, at least. Dr. Ahmadi types a few notes on his tablet and stands up. "Okay, then! I'll run out to give your folks a quick update while you change. And keep the copy of the

31

EKG—you might want to frame it." He smiles. "We'll see you in four months. Until then, call us if you're experiencing any pain, shortness of breath, nausea . . . well, you know the drill. Or call us if you just need to talk."

I know he means this, and if I thought it would help to unload on anyone, he'd be the person I'd choose. But cardiac surgeons are busy, and the last thing I want to do is get everybody all worked up over nothing. My brain is probably just a little scattered from all the meds I have to take. And I have a normal EKG in my hand that tells me I *should* be celebrating. So I'm just going to make my parents happy and post this on our fridge under that ridiculous MY CHILD IS AN HONOR STUDENT AT OAK VALLEY HIGH magnet that my dad purchased at the school's fund-raising auction because he thought it was hilarious.

In my most cheerful, everything-is-fine voice, I echo Dr. Ahmadi with a "See you in four months!" as he slips out the door.

≋ THE RIDE ≋

If you surf, having a solid understanding of physics is useful. Waves, after all, are one of the best examples of physics in action: energy (wind) moving through matter (water). And if you can get a sense of the origin, intensity, and direction of the energy part, and how the tides and the type of break interact with it, you'll have an idea of how the water is going to behave. Before I figured this out, I thought catching waves had more to do with luck than anything else. But now I know why Kai is always going on about "checking the surf report." Turns out you can apply some science to surfing.

"Let's go!" I barely stop after finding Kai on the beach when I arrive, eager to get out before the tide changes.

"Hold up," he says, picking up his backpack to retrieve the ankle leash he promised to bring for me last week. "Let's swap this for the one you have. So you don't take anyone's head off out there."

Ankle leashes do more than just ensure that you won't lose your board in the surf. They also protect the other surfers around you, especially the more experienced ones from the amateurs. A runaway board can result in a whole lot of stitches for anyone in its path.

Kai hands over the leash and I lay my board down, squatting while I remove the one that's already attached. "Thanks," I say.

"They're a little tricky. Want me to get it?"

I shake my head. "I can do it." He stands back in a posture that looks as though he expects me to ask for help at any minute. I line up the two ends of the leash string, tie an overhand knot, and push one end through the plug on my board. Then I attach the cord and fasten the cuff at my ankle.

"Ready!" I say, standing up.

"Huh," he says. "Usually takes me a couple of tries to get that right."

I shrug. "I once earned a Girl Scout badge for tying knots."

He nods and squints at me. "Of course you did."

I squint back. "What's that supposed to mean?"

"Nothing. You just . . . seem like the kind of person who might excel at Girl Scouting."

I raise my eyebrows.

"I mean, you level up fast." Kai rakes his hand through his hair and shakes his head. "Never mind."

"Waves should be good today, right?" I ask, changing the subject. "I saw that the swell interval is supposed to be long." A longer interval between waves means that each one accumulates more energy and peels longer, which makes for a better ride.

"Take a look," he says, nodding toward the horizon, where a handful of surfers are already lined up, waiting. I watch one pop up and sail across the face of a wave. "The report helps, but nothing's better than your own eyes."

"Looks good," I confirm.

He nods. "Let's go, then."

As we paddle out, I'm having a harder time getting through the white water than I did last week. Although the waves look long and clean farther out, they are breaking hard on the beach. Kai is ahead of me, and I watch what he does, mirroring his movements. He's paddling strong and sure, propelling himself directly into the oncoming waves. The trick is to generate enough momentum to push through the impact zone without getting rolled off your board. I dig deep into the water, trying to pick up as much speed as I possibly can. The spray stings my face, and now I can't see Kai at all—he's lost behind the roiling wall of foam that's surging toward me. I push up hard on my rails and throw all of my weight forward. White water rushes past as I *push, paddle, push, paddle,* and then I'm through the worst of it, denying the ocean its first opportunity to screw with my surfing plans today. Now I just need to keep it that way.

Kai twists his head around up ahead to make sure I'm still behind him and gives a quick thumbs-up with his right hand. We join the lineup.

"You okay?" he asks as I paddle up next to him, my eyes taking in the size of the swells. They look pretty damn huge up close and I feel like we are floating in a giant bowl of water. All I can see is ocean ahead and ocean behind and the blue-gray sky up above.

"Yeah," I say, more confident than I feel.

Kai looks a tiny bit anxious as well, which I know is not because he's worried for himself. I've already seen him surf waves bigger than these. Is he worried that he's got me into a situation that I might not be able to handle?

His eyes connect with mine. "If you can't get up, just hang on to your board and paddle back in with the wave."

Yep, I think. *He's already expecting me to wipe out. Again.*

I watch the surfers ahead of us as they race for incoming waves, pop up, and then take off toward the shore. Not one has fallen. *I'm not going to be the only one who does,* I tell myself.

Another wave sweeps toward us, rising and rising and rising till it begins to cast a shadow over our heads. This is the one.

The one I'm going to catch.

"It's yours!" Kai yells and, as soon as I hear that, I launch.

Left, right, left, right, left, right. I paddle harder than I've ever paddled before and get myself into position, the nose of my board pointing toward the beach. I wait until it begins to lift under me. Now I just need to hang on for the right moment. Which is . . . *now.*

Now!

I place my hands underneath my chest and pop up, so shocked to be standing that I almost topple off again, like last week. The board wobbles slightly, but this time I regain my balance and then, *holy shit*, I'm surfing, actually really surfing, on my own, for the first time ever.

The wave that I've caught is a big one. Bigger even than it seemed when I watched it gather itself up, before I perched myself near the summit of its rising, racing, liquid surface. It whisks me toward the shore, and I feel as though I'm no longer in the water, but flying above it, like a pelican or a gull. Everything looks, and feels, different from this perspective as the scale and scope of the world multiplies, expanding in all directions. The ocean. The beach. The sky. For a split second, I can even see behind the sand dunes, glimpsing the roofline of pastel-painted storefronts that line the road beyond them. I inhale, filling my lungs with salt air, which has got to be some kind of enhanced, extra-intense version of oxygen, because I've never felt more awake and alive. My board rises higher.

And higher.

And higher.

Too high.

There's a surfing term for what happens when the lip of a wave crashes beneath you. It's called "going over the falls."

I imagine it in slow motion, but really it's only milliseconds before I'm tossed from water to air. My board slips out from under me, my foot yanked with it by my new (and hopefully improved) ankle leash. Unlike last week's tumble, I come down hard and fast with this wave. The ocean alternately muffles sound and then roars around me as I surface, briefly, only to be pushed back under. I struggle up again, gasping for breath. As I do, my head hits something hard. Or something hard hits my head. I can't tell which.

And suddenly, the death dream is all I can think about. The one where my head smashes into the pavement and my skull cracks. The world, huge and wide and open just seconds ago, is closing in, confusing my senses. It's dead quiet. The water feels thick and heavy, so thick that I am caught, suspended like a specimen in a jar, unable to move my limbs. I can't tell up from down, right from left. As the metallic taste of blood fills my mouth, along with what seems like gallons of salt water, I frantically try to conjure up Kai's words of advice for when you are pinned under a wave: *stay calm.*

Stay calm.

I force myself to open my eyes so I can try to get my bearings. But what I see doesn't make any sense. Instead of murky water, I see a silver-gray pit bull with a scar above its eye. I see a different beach, a different break, and clear water lit up by the sun. I see a woman lying in a hospital bed, tubes everywhere. *Is she the woman I remember? The one wearing the knit cap?* I see a cypress tree, a porch swing, an EKG. I see the tunnel from my dream, the motorcycle crash, blood washing over my eyes. Then everything goes blank.

"Chloe."

A dark silhouette moves into my view, encircled by a white halo of light. I wonder if I'm in the hospital again. Or maybe I never left in the first place. Maybe I never made it to the top of the list and there never was a heart. Maybe I'm dead and all the surfing lessons are just a figment of my disjointed, oxygen-deprived imagination.

"Chloe," the silhouette says, louder this time, moving in. The blurred edges start to come into focus and a familiar face emerges. Hazel eyes. Black hair dangling, wet, over warm brown skin. Lips dusted with sand. This is no Angel of Death. It's Kai. And this time, he looks more than a little anxious.

I stare at him.

"Are you okay?" he asks. "God, I feel like an asshole."

"What? Why?" I push up to my elbows and Kai sits back on his heels next to me. I look out toward the pounding surf, watch the edge of the water bubble up over the coarse sand and then retreat. It's cold and windy and I'm shivering, but I am on the beach and very much alive. *How did I even get here?* I wonder.

"Your board," he says, frowning. "You got cracked really hard by your board. Maybe we should call—"

"No!" I say, louder than I mean to. We are not calling *anybody*. No professionals. No hospital. The last thing I want is for my parents to get wind of what I've been up to these last few Wednesday afternoons, when they think I've been at the library catching up on summer school assignments. So far they know nothing about my new and dangerous hobby. And, for now, I want to keep it that way.

My tongue throbs and I realize I must have bitten it, but otherwise I feel all right. Heart is beating. Head is . . . the same. But something seems strange in an out-of-sequence kind of way, like this movie I watched with my dad one afternoon in the hospital, about a guy with a weird amnesia condition who has to write everything that happens to him on Post-it notes. *Was there a dog on the beach with us?* If there was, it's gone now. *Who was that woman in the hospital? Is she the same one that I'm sure I know but can't remember?*

"I'm okay." I shut the weirdness out of my mind and focus my eyes on Kai, who looks relieved that I'm at least speaking and moving and hopefully not about to ruin his surf lesson business. "Why do you feel like an asshole?"

He frowns again. "I probably shouldn't have taken you out there with the waves so big."

"But I wanted . . . " I say. It's not his fault that I nearly got knocked out by my board. I forgot one vital piece of his advice: *cover your head when you come up.*

"She okay?"

I look over and see two other surfers hovering nearby, packing up their gear. The tall one is talking to Kai.

"I'm *okay*," I answer instead, pushing all the way up to sitting to emphasize my absolute okay-ness.

"I think she's good," Kai calls back. "Thanks for the help."

The help? Now I'm wondering just how many people out here witnessed my latest epic wipeout.

"We've all been there!" the surfer says to me. "Sucks to get pinned under. That was a sweet ride before you bit it, though."

"Uh, thanks," I say, still confused about how I made it back to the beach. I don't remember anything between being underwater and seeing people and pit bulls and places I don't recognize, and staring up into Kai's very pretty eyes, which are again studying me with caution.

"Are you sure you're okay?" he asks. "You were kind of out of it when I caught up to you. Those dudes said you were talking about a dog or something, and you said you were going to take a nap. You could have a concussion."

"I'm good. *Really.* I think I just got a little freaked out when I was held under, but I feel okay now." *Just shake it off,* I tell myself. *Shake it off.* I manage a smile despite the fact that my tongue is swelling up. "So when are we catching the next one?"

And unexpectedly, the serious look on his face is transformed by a truly genuine smile. "It was pretty awesome, huh?"

This is the first time I've seen Kai smile, aside from the time a small fish had brushed against my foot and I screamed and tumbled off my board in surprise. As I was trying, without much grace, to climb back on in the choppy water, I thought I saw the corners of his mouth turn up. Briefly. But not like this. When he smiles full-on, he has dimples.

"Yeah," I say. "It's like . . ."

"Flying."

"Yeah."

"I was six when I caught my first wave," he says. "Felt like a superhero."

"Which one?" I ask.

"Which what?"

"Which superhero?"

"Batman."

"Batman?" I laugh, imagining a pint-size Kai surfing in a full-body bat suit, black cape flying. "No Silver Surfer?"

He shakes his head. "C'mon. When you're six, superhero means either Batman or Spider-Man. Maybe the Hulk."

Batman. I've learned more about Kai in the last three minutes than I probably have in the last three weeks.

I make a move to stand. Too quickly, I realize, because I feel dizzy and sit back down in the sand. *It's fine. Shake it off. Take a deep breath.* I look at Kai. "Let's go back out."

And now I even get a laugh. With the dimples again. It's like he's a different person.

"Slow down there, boss," he says. "Maybe we should call it a day and give your head a rest."

Give my head a rest.

I wish. I want to tell him that my head feels infinitely better out there than it usually does at home, even after getting bonked by my board. Surfing allows me *not* to think. Only feel. The icy water. The wind on my cheeks. The movement of the waves beneath my body. In fact, the ocean is pretty much the only place I want to be right now. I refuse to let one weird moment ruin it.

Kai stands and offers his hand to help me up. I take it. And now, it's all I can think about. *What would that hand feel like in my hair? On my face?*

"Thanks," I say, rising to face him. He's eyeing me with an intensity that makes me panic slightly, afraid that he can somehow read my mind.

"Ouch. You should probably put some ice on that when you get home."

Touching my temple, I feel a bruise starting to bulge under the skin.

Ahh. Mystery of the intense look: solved.

"Yep. Ice," I say, nodding.

I look out toward the horizon, where the ocean meets the sky. The afternoon sun is breaking through spaces in the clouds. It's beautiful and looks like the kind of thing a person might post on Instagram, with an inspirational quote. But in my case, it just reminds me that I've lost track of the time and I'm *#late*.

"I have to go," I tell Kai.

Being late used to make my parents, at worst, slightly aggravated. Now, if I don't show up when I say I will, I know they're worrying about the heart. Is it still beating? Am I lying on the ground somewhere, grasping my chest? I realize I had better come up with a plausible explanation for the welt on my temple (Falling library book? A run-in with a swinging locker door?) and I still need to stop at my neighbor Mrs. Linney's house to feed her cat, water her roses, and safely stash my surfboard in her backyard shed. Her summer in Europe is convenient for a girl with secrets.

My phone is in my backpack in the truck of my car—a used Honda that my parents originally intended as a graduation gift until it became more of a we're-glad-you're-still-alive gift. I make a mental note to text my mom that I'm running behind. But as I pick up my board, something occurs to me: I hadn't noticed another car near the path on our section of the beach when I parked earlier.

I turn back toward Kai.

"Need a lift?"

"Nah," he says. "Thanks, though."

"Where do you live, anyway?" I ask, wanting to know just one thing more about this boy who minutes before was leaning over me, close enough to kiss.

"Nearby," he says. "See you next Wednesday."

≋ **WEIRD THINGS** ≋

I swivel my chair in front of the computer monitor in the school library and poise my fingers over the keyboard. I'm supposed to be working on a research paper for my AP Physics class—the one I didn't get to complete last December when I was busy getting my heart cut out—but instead I'm doing the thing my dad is always warning my mom and me that we should never do: Googling health advice. "The internet is a house of horrors for hypochondriacs," he loves to say. I wouldn't consider myself a hypochondriac, but where else am I supposed to track down answers without having to actually talk to someone? Like, for instance, my mom, who, due to her for-real hypochondriac tendencies, would probably rush me to the hospital the minute I tell her that I bashed my head—while surfing!—and then hallucinated a bunch of stuff that doesn't even make any sense. So, yeah, that's not going to happen.

But I can't stop thinking about yesterday. *Was* I hallucinating? Those images I saw when I was stuck under that wave are now burned in my brain, but why can't I remember what they mean? And why do I keep waking up to the same horrible nightmare, with my head feeling like it's been smashed by a brick? Something is definitely not right. Only this time, it's with my brain instead of my heart.

I type into the search bar: *Heart transplant. Neurologic complications.*

Okay.

It turns out that auditory and visual hallucinations are not uncommon for heart transplant patients. That's somewhat of a relief, I guess. At least I know it's not just me.

I keep reading. *Most commonly, transplant patients have reported hallucinations after surgery, while in intensive care on a ventilator.* Interesting. *Some people describe these hallucinations as "out-of-body" or "near-death" experiences, but these transient symptoms are likely due to the side effects of pain medications, e.g., opiates or benzodiazepines.* Hmm. It's been more than six months since my surgery. More than six months since I've been connected to a ventilator. And currently, I'm not on any pain meds. But I was. Could they have caused long-term effects? My eyes back up to the word *transient*. Temporary. Short-lived. Fleeting. Maybe the immunosuppressants that I'm taking now are triggering my recent symptoms. I'll have to double-check the side effects listed on my current crop of medications.

I try another search: *Heart transplant. Memory loss.*

As I scan through a list of medical journal articles and health reporting, something I've never heard of before catches my eye: *Organ Transplants and Cellular Memory.*

I click on the link and end up on what looks like a patient blog or forum of some kind. I start scanning the first entry. In it, Janet, a sixty-four-year-old office manager and soon-to-be new grandmother talks about how she feels like a "different person" following her heart transplant.

After I started getting back to regular activities following my transplant, on a whim I signed up for an art class at the community center near my house. I've never taken an art class in my adult life, and never considered myself a particularly good artist even when I was a child. But as soon as I saw the flyer for "Introduction to Still Life Painting" in the mail, I just knew it was something I really had to do. Once I started the class, my husband was floored by the paintings I was bringing home! He even joked that I'd been hiding my secret talent from him for years and wondered when we could get rich selling my work. When I eventually made contact with my donor's family, I found out that the woman whose heart I have had been a very successful artist. Some of her works are even sold through a gallery in New York! Now, I don't

*know if it's this cellular memory thing or God's will, but
somehow I think that I must have inherited her artis-
tic abilities, that my eyes and hands are channeling her
spirit.*

Wait, *what?*

"Hey, brainiac. Can you look at my trig assignment
again?"

I'm knocked out of my trance by the voice of Jane Kessler,
who pulls up a chair next to my workstation.

Jane, who I had never exchanged a single word with until
I got stuck in summer school, is my new friend here, mainly
because I help her with math. She scoots closer to me.

"*Well?* How about it?" She waves her assignment in front
of me. "I'll buy you lunch?"

I think she's trying to whisper, but Jane is not very good
at speaking in a library voice.

I don't even know why she's attempting to be quiet anyway. Nobody here cares—not the weird antisocial kid to my
left, who I've never seen without Beats headphones attached
to his skull, or the girl who talks to herself when she types,
and especially not Mr. Adams, who's hunched over his laptop at the librarian's station, most likely trying to watch the
Giants game on mute.

Summer school is definitely not like real school. Serious
school. The kind of school I used to attend. Until I learned
that this was the best option for completing my graduation

48

requirements, I had no idea that my high school even had a summer program. Most of the people here, I've never met before. Like Beats headphones boy, who, according to Jane, got suspended for throwing a chair in his history class and then missed a month of school because his parents sent him to one of those military-style boot camps. And Sydney and April, the two girls who had babies last semester.

But Jane, I know. Or at least know of. In school or out, she's the kind of person who is impossible not to notice. One, because she's loud. Jane is not shy about voicing her opinion, even when nobody has technically asked for it. And two, she always looks kind of fabulous. Like today, in her sleeveless black T-shirt, Doc Marten boots, retro-red lipstick, and very short shorts that I'd never be allowed to leave the house in.

Jane tells me that an F in trigonometry has foiled her graduation plans this year—a fact that she attributes to her trig teacher, Ms. Hines, "being a total bitch." I'm dubious about this. Unless Ms. Hines has had a lobotomy since I had her my junior year for the honors course, "total bitch" is not how I'd describe her. She used to give us multiple chances to make test corrections and kept candy on her desk for anyone willing to volunteer to work out a problem on the white-board. Mainly, I just think that Jane hates math. Or maybe school in general.

I turn my chair in her direction. "You're buying me lunch?"

She nods. "Your lunch wishes will be my command."

Another difference between summer school and real school is that previously, Jane would probably have had zero interest in hanging out with me. In real school, we did not swim in the same circles. Jane was not on the honors track. We didn't have any classes together. Nor did we ever encounter each other at any of the extracurricular activities that normally kept me and most of my friends busy until well after dinner most nights: sports, student government, music lessons, Math Club, Community Service Club, fill-in-the-blank-with-whatever-might-look-good-on-a-college-admissions-application Club. I don't think Jane does clubs. In fact, she probably didn't even know who I was before I became famous (at school anyway) for getting a new heart.

Jane, on the other hand, was kind of famous before I was. Or maybe *infamous* is more accurate. For telling Mr. Hoffman to "fuck off" in front of her entire history class when she got into an argument with him about the pros and cons of socialism. (I heard this from Mia Ryan, the most reliable conduit for school gossip.) For spray-painting a magnificent, albeit unauthorized, mural honoring Frida Kahlo on the school's football scoreboard. (It was homecoming weekend, so *everybody* saw that one.) For organizing a huge beach party that resulted in about forty kids missing school during the final day of STAR testing. (I was not invited but did hear about it for days after.) There are plenty more Jane-related rumors, but these I can't verify: That she is the reason why Dave Rubin broke up with Mindy Pierson, *and* why Lisa Tan broke up with Becca Strauss. That she's the one who stole and then sold the answer key to the tenth-grade geometry final. That she's the person to go to if you want to buy weed. Whether any of this is true or not, Jane doesn't seem to care what people think about her one way or the other. Nor does she seem to care about always having the right answer or getting straight As. In other words, she's everything I'm not. Or that I didn't used to be.

At the moment, however, she is at least attempting to pass trig.

"Let me see the math," I say.

She slides her chair next to mine and hands me her assignment. Intricately drawn Japanese anime characters run up and down the borders of the worksheet. They all have speech bubbles above their heads with the same words inside: "Trig blows!"

I look over her half-hearted attempts at working out the assignment and see immediately where she's screwing up.

"Okay, you can't get that answer because cosine has no meaning on its own. You always need to find the cosine of an angle."

She looks unsure. "Umm . . . okay."

"So if the cosine of x is equal to one, you need to find a value for x so that once you take the cosine of the value, you get one."

"You get one." Jane buries a hand in her platinum pixie haircut and nods in the way that people do when they don't want to admit they have no idea what you are talking about.

"Look at the graph of the cosine function . . . you *have* seen a graph like this before, right?" I glance at Jane. She's reading the results of my Google search.

"Jane. Are you even listening?" I ask, though it's clear that she's not. She seems to have issues with focus.

"What are you doing, some kind of report?" she asks.

"No, just research."

"About your heart?"

I still haven't told anybody about what happened at the beach on Wednesday or about any of the other stuff that's been freaking me out recently: The gaps in my memory. The nightmares. The feeling of not being able to reengage with my old life. But Jane is not my worrywart mom. And she's not Emma, who would probably just think that I'd lost it. Maybe it would be a bit of a relief to tell *somebody*. At least some of it.

"I'm looking for some background on transplant recipients. About side effects from surgery, that kind of thing," I tell her.

"Like what kind of side effects?" she asks.

"I'm not really sure what I'm looking for . . . I'm just curious about what other patients have experienced."

"Move over." Jane nudges me sideways and leans in closer to study my screen. After a few minutes, her eyes bug out.

"Holy shit, is this for real?" She nods toward the monitor. "This cellular memory thing? People can inherit their donor's abilities and memories and stuff?" She stares at me. "Oh my god, is that happening to you?"

"Jane, no," I say, already feeling like it may have been a mistake to invite her in to all this. Especially when I'm reading random, highly unscientific heart transplant theories on the internet. "It's not physiologically possible. Memory is a function of the brain. The heart is an organ that pumps blood. You can't acquire neurological processes through a heart. Just because some woman took a community center painting class does not mean she inherited anyone else's memories."

"But it says here that even cells in your heart include your entire genetic code. So wouldn't that mean that *maybe* a transplanted organ could transfer some of your donor's, like, *memory* cells to you and, then, voilà, you can paint?"

I shake my head. Where to even start? "First of all, there's no such thing as a 'memory cell.'"

Jane squints at me.

"So, since your transplant, have you picked up any new food preferences or hobbies? Anything that you didn't do before?"

Well, of course, I think. There are tons of things that are different since my transplant. They're different because I nearly *died* and had major, *life-altering* surgery. I did start eating meat again, but that was just for the protein, not because I have any new "food preferences." And, yes, I've taken up surfing. But for all I know, my donor could have been a vegetarian who didn't even know how to swim.

53

A tiny voice inside my head asks: *What about the other stuff that prompted this whole Google search in the first place? The memories that I can't place? The nightmares?*

But all I tell Jane is, "Nope. Nothing comes to mind. Honestly, Jane, I think this cellular memory theory is . . . not serious science." *It can't be.*

She crosses her arms.

"What about this lady who can paint now? How do you explain that?"

I gesture toward the computer screen. "Just because Janet here took an art class and thinks she painted a really good sunflower doesn't mean she inherited a lifetime of fine-arts experience. What's happening with her is probably more like the placebo effect."

"What do you mean?"

"Sometimes in drug trials, they give a control group a placebo, like sugar pills, so they can compare the results against the ones from the group that's taking the real thing. But the people in the control group don't *know* they're not getting the actual drug and, even though they're not, there are cases where some experience improvements in their symptoms anyway. It's the *belief* that they are taking something that could help them that seems to have an effect."

"So I don't get it," says Jane. "What does the placebo effect have to do with this heart transplant story?"

I'm in full-on class presentation mode now.

"Once this lady heard that her donor was a professional

artist, it made her *believe* that her own painting skills were *way better* than they probably are. Maybe she even painted with more confidence as a result, which meant her paintings really *were* better. Placebo effect. Get it?"

"Yeah, okay," Jane says. "But there are some other really wild stories here. Not just the painting one. You should totally read them!"

Maybe I will later, when I can focus and think. "How about we get back to your math?" I say.

"Ugh, do we have to?" Jane pretends that she's banging her head on the desk in front of her.

"Do you want to graduate, or what?"

She raises her head.

"Well, my mom says I can't use her car until I do, so yes."

I click out of the cellular memory forum. My dad is probably right: searching for health advice on the internet is a terrible idea.

It's late, and I'm staring up at the wood beams on my bedroom ceiling, unable to sleep. Unable to shake the thoughts that have been circling around and around in my mind. It all started before the beach, didn't it? Before the tunnel dream. Even before the memory gaps, or whatever they are. Because what I didn't tell Jane today is that the first weird thing to happen was right after the transplant, in the hospital. When I saw the crying man.

At first I thought he was one of the doctors or nurses

who kept flitting in and out of my room to change an IV bag, make a note on my chart, or adjust one of the many machines humming and beeping all around me. But he wasn't wearing scrubs, a white jacket, or anything that identified him as official hospital personnel. Plus, his demeanor stood out from that of the usual staff (detached and professional for most of the doctors—or trying-too-hard cheerful for most of the nurses). He was slumped in a chair next to my bed, his face resting in his hands.

He stayed there for a while, but since I was still on the ventilator, I couldn't speak. I couldn't ask him who he was. He didn't speak either—just wept quietly, and then slipped like a shadow out the door.

Once I was free of the ventilator and a bit less drugged up, I asked my parents who he was.

"Nobody but family is allowed in the ICU," my dad said. "Are you sure it wasn't one of the nurses?"

I told him I was sure.

"A dream, maybe?" suggested my mom. "Dr. Ahmadi said the anesthesia might make you feel kind of funky for a while."

"No," I insisted. "He was real. I know he was real."

I tried to sit up but was nearly knocked senseless by a heavyweight boxing punch of pain.

My dad jumped up from his chair, a look of panic on his face. My easygoing, goofball dad, terrified that I would come apart at the seams right before his eyes.

And admittedly, I did feel a bit stitched together in that moment, as the line of black sutures tightened across my chest. Maybe I *was* coming apart.

I lowered myself back against the pillows, hoping that would be enough to calm him down. "He was real," I repeated, no longer so sure myself.

My mom went out to check the visitor's log at the front desk.

Security was called.

And not long after, a tight-lipped hospital administrator, accompanied by a man in an official-looking uniform, showed up in my room. The administrator, her hair pulled back into a tidy bun, introduced me to Mr. Platt, the hospital's head of security, who proceeded to ask a bunch of questions.

"What did he look like?"

"He was tall, kind of muscular." My throat was raw from being intubated, so I had to whisper.

"Eyes?"

I realized as he was questioning me that I never got a good look at his face.

"I don't remember."

"Hair color?"

"Not sure. It was buzzed . . . close to his scalp."

I could tell this was starting to sound suspiciously vague to him.

"What was he wearing?"

Mr. Platt seemed bored, in fact, like this wasn't the first time he'd been called on to humor an ICU patient riding too high on pain pills.

"Jeans. And a black puffer jacket. I think."

Had there been a tattoo on his neck?

"Did he say anything?"

"No. He just cried." I added, "It was sort of like he was mourning my death."

"Okay." My dad stood up. "That's enough."

Mr. Platt excused himself to talk to the nurses who had been on that shift, both of whom I could see through the windows of my fishbowl room shaking their heads no.

The mystery man was never identified. My meds were adjusted, and my parents spent the night. But there's a feeling that I remember having about him for weeks afterward—one that I didn't tell my parents or Mr. Platt or anyone else. Even though I knew I'd never seen him before and wasn't even entirely sure if he was real or not, there was something about him that felt . . . familiar.

Now, as I lie here not sleeping, not able to stop thinking about tunnels and blood and crashing motorcycles and the crying man, all I can hear is the *thump, thump, thump, thump, thump* of this unfamiliar heart. It's like that creepy Edgar Allan Poe story, the one we all read in ninth-grade English, only this heart is not buried under the floorboards; it's buried in my own chest, and I can't get away from it no matter what I do or where I go.

I look at the clock on my nightstand. It's 2:15 a.m.

Answers. I like to have answers.

Tossing my duvet off, I get out of bed and retrieve my laptop from my desk. I climb back under my covers, power it up, and type two words into my browser's search bar: *Cellular memory.*

First, I find a few definitions and explanations via a variety of sources ranging from Wikipedia to publications that I've never heard of to one piece in *Scientific American* that cites some UCLA study on the neurons of sea slugs. Apparently, it suggested that long-term memories could be stored in neurons and then re-formed even when the synapses between neurons were destroyed. I'm not 100 percent sure how that might relate to a transplanted heart. But most of the stuff I'm finding goes like this:

Cellular memory is a hypothesis, yet to be scientifically proven, that memories can be stored in individual cells in all parts of the body, i.e., not only the brain.

Cellular memory is a pseudoscientific theory based on reported anecdotes from organ recipients who claim to have acquired the memories, habits, interests, and tastes of their donor.

This is what I thought. "Yet to be scientifically proven." "Pseudoscientific." "Based on claims and anecdotes." In other words, it's likely to be as real as Bigfoot or the Bermuda Triangle.

But still, I can't stop myself from clicking back on that blog I found in the library with Jane. I reread the story of our budding artist, Janet, and then scroll through a few other entries, including one from a man who swears he must have inherited his donor's personality because he now likes jalapeño peppers and it turns out that the previous owner of his heart loved jalapeños on everything. Jalapeños? I mean, *come on*. It seems ridiculous. Then I land on the story of Dave, a fifty-five-year-old sales executive, husband, and father of three:

> *About six or seven months after my transplant, I was at a coffee shop and saw a guy I was sure I knew. I meet a lot of people through my job, so I figured he had to have been someone I met through a previous sales call or at a trade conference. "Hey, Ryan, how's it going?" I said as he walked by, and I know I had his name right because he immediately looked my way. But as soon as we made eye contact, it was clear that he had no flipping idea who I was. I think he even came back at me with the universal I-can't-remember-your-name response: "Hey! I'm well, thanks." Then he went his way, I went mine, and I didn't think much of it. Later on, I really got interested in meeting my donor's family. I wanted to thank them and tell them how much this second chance meant to me and my*

wife and kids. The family agreed, and my wife arranged for them to come to our house one Saturday afternoon. She thought they'd be more comfortable at our house, not a public place. When the doorbell rang, I was pretty nervous. Turns out I had a good reason. I nearly had another heart attack right then and there when the guy from the coffee shop walked through the door—Ryan, the one whose name I knew and was sure I had met before. He was my donor's brother. His brother!

NOBODY
≋ CARES IF I'M LATE ≋

I'm caught in that weird space between sound asleep and awake again, and can't seem to pull myself out.

The tunnel dream is mutating.

I was, or am, somewhere else first, sitting beside the woman connected to all the tubes. A hospital room. *The ICU?* Her lips are dry and cracked. Her face is thin, her skin so pale, cheeks hollowed out. *I've seen her before . . . where?* But then I'm not in the hospital. The woman is gone. I'm on the beach, waxing my board. Something darts by to my left. It's the silver-gray pit bull—squat, barrel-chested—chasing a ball. The dog turns and gallops back toward me, dropping the ball at my feet, but before I can pick it up, I am speeding into the tunnel again, lights rushing by. The curve. The tree. Burning rubber. Squealing tires. Everything goes blank.

"Chloe . . . Chloe, wake up."

My alarm is blaring next to me and my mom is sitting on the edge of my bed, gently nudging my shoulder. She used to just flip on my super-bright ceiling light or yell from the kitchen "Chloe, get up!" when I overslept, but now I think she worries about startling me.

I look at my mom, at the glass of water she's set on the coaster on my nightstand, at the way the vibration from the alarm on my phone makes the water ripple.

"You're going to be late for school," she says.

"*Summer* school," I correct her, as I reach for my phone and turn off the alarm. "Nobody cares if I'm late."

She studies me carefully, and although I can tell she's trying to resist, she asks anyway, "Is everything all right?"

"I'm fine," I say. "Just lazy."

She stands and tries to pretend she's her *before*-Chloe-had-a-heart-transplant self. "No time to be lazy. It's seven thirty-five! C'mon, I'll make you a bagel for the road. And don't forget your medication."

"I won't," I answer, and decide not to sigh or roll my eyes.

When I come down to the kitchen, my mom holds out a warm brown bag, toasted poppy-seed bagel wrapped neatly inside. My favorite.

I take it and she moves in to give me a kiss on the head, just like she used to do at school drop-off when I was little. Her movements are quick and stealthy, as if she's trying to

63

catch a grasshopper before it jumps. She doesn't have to try too hard today. I lean in and wrap my arms around her, comforted by familiar sensations that I know are all mine: the soft, feathery feel of her favorite work-from-home wrap sweater. The coconut smell of her shampooed hair. I push the memory of the woman in the hospital room out of my mind.

"Oh, I almost forgot," she says. "Dad bumped into Emma's mom yesterday. She reminded him about Emma's graduation party this weekend."

The party is not just to celebrate the end of high school but also Emma's upcoming departure for Brown University.

I release my mom, breaking the warm fuzzy spell of our hug. "I know," I say.

Like Emma, everyone in our circle is heading off soon to various *U.S. News & World Report*–ranked schools: Alexis Stewart and Mia Ryan will be sharing a dorm room at UCLA; Jordan McGuire got into Penn; Craig Swanson is a legacy at Yale (lucky for him and his unremarkable GPA). Party season is in full swing, as our senior class gathers around pools and barbecues and beer kegs to finally let off some steam, take a million group selfies, and pair up with their no-strings-attached crushes before everyone goes their separate ways.

I could be participating in this fun-on-the-surface-but-competitive-underneath ritual of "Where'd you get in?" if I wanted to. I was mostly done with my college applications when everything happened with my heart, and my mom helped me finish and submit them. At the time, it was a welcome distraction from the wait for a donor. Later, when the acceptances started coming in, it felt as if they were meant for a different person. But I do need to make a decision soon. I can tell it's driving my mom to distraction, but she's trying her best to give me some space.

She wouldn't have before.

My mom picks up her half-full coffee mug from the counter and opens the microwave door.

"Did you and Emma have a falling-out or something?" she asks while waiting for her coffee to reheat. "You two haven't seen much of each other lately."

We haven't. But there was no official falling-out. It's been more of a quiet fade.

"No," I say. "She's just busy getting ready for school."

My mom turns to face me.

"I know you feel a little left out of all the graduation stuff. But it would not be kind to ditch her party, Chloe. You'll be there soon enough."

But that's the thing. Even though a top university is the destination I've been racing toward for the last six or seven years of my life, I don't know if "there" is where I really want to be anymore. But I can't tell my mom this. She's convinced she missed her own chance at the Ivy League because her New Agey '70s parents never pushed her hard enough.

The microwave beeps.

I pick up my backpack from a kitchen chair and fish for the car keys in the side pocket.

"Mom. Don't worry. I'll go."

Driving is a relief. Lately, I crave motion. Velocity. Speed. Movement chases the thoughts from my head and unleashes me, temporarily, from the past and the future. There is only wind rushing into open windows. The familiar Vicks VapoRub smell of the eucalyptus trees swishing past. Music cranked up as loud at it will go.

The traffic light at Mission Road breaks my momentum. I stop. I wait. I think.

When was the last time I saw Emma?

She visited me in the hospital when I was moved out of the ICU after the transplant and stopped by my house on occasion to watch TV on our family room sectional once I was discharged. I think she considered it her duty to keep me engaged with what was happening at school, so she always came prepared with a little gossip.

Example: "Wes Thomas and Jordan McGuire broke up."

This had been no big surprise. They were each applying to schools on opposite sides of the country.

"Saw that coming," I said, scooping more popcorn from the bowl and turning up the volume on *The Walking Dead*. A minor character was getting his guts ripped out.

Emma covered her face with a pillow.

"Ugh. What happened to *House Hunters International*?"

I shrugged. "You've seen one vacation villa in Ibiza, you've seen them all."

I could feel her shifting in her seat next to me, tightening her already-tight ponytail.

"Lily Kim was accepted early to Princeton."

"Wow," I said. "How's Addison taking that?"

Addison Watson, close friends with Lily and a contender for valedictorian, had wanted to go to Princeton since . . . possibly birth.

"They're not speaking."

"That seems like an overreaction."

"You think? Lily never said anything about applying to Princeton. I get why Addison's pissed."

"What, Lily can't try for the same school?"

"Chloe." Emma stared at me as if I had suddenly lost my mind. "It's pretty bad form to apply to a friend's top choice."

This got me wondering if any of the applications I submitted would prompt Emma to stop talking to me.

She did have one more piece of intel to share.

"Oh, and Justin Stein was suspended."

"Justin?"

Now this had surprised me—Justin was the last person I would have expected to be suspended from school.

"Got caught cheating on the AP chem exam." Emma was almost whispering, this was such scandalous news.

"Why was he cheating?"

Justin didn't need to cheat. He's super smart.

"He wanted a perfect score."

College application and acceptance season is a pretty tense time at high schools like mine. Everyone is exhausted. Everyone is trying to gain an edge. There are the kids who buy Adderall so they can stay up late and study after a full day of school and team sports. There are the parents who are constantly scheduling meetings with teachers, or better yet the principal, to protest "unfair" test scores. Weekends are fully booked with travel to soccer tournaments, SAT prep courses, and service projects. There are always a few kids who crack. Who decide to blow it all off and join the party-all-the-time crowd. Or end up in rehab. Or cheat. I guess that's what happened to Justin.

So although Emma was trying hard to be a good friend by keeping me company while I binge-watched zombies, I could tell it was making her twitchy. She had places to go and things to get done, and killing time with me was just that—killing time. There would be no extra credit for chilling out in my family room. Plus, our friendship was missing its usual competitive dynamic—and with it, a certain kind of energy—now that I had stepped, at least temporarily, out of the race.

Competition had always been a big part of our relationship. When we were little, we used to argue about who was faster, who was taller, who could eat the biggest serving of mashed potatoes. The day after my dad got me up on my first two-wheeled bike, Emma was out in the elementary school parking lot with her dad, intent on catching up. If she was reading Harry Potter in second grade, then I demanded that my mom get me the books too. But we shared as much as we compared. Favorite books. Silly dance moves. Our top-secret secrets. If we were always pushing each other to do our best, we also supported each other when our best fell short.

But in the last year, something had changed. The connection between us had become less supportive, more adversarial. All compare. No share.

I'm a math and science girl. Emma is the wordsmith. When we did homework together, I'd show her how to solve for x or explain the rules of probability. She'd help me edit my English papers. Until her parents invested a fortune on a specialized math tutor and Emma announced that she didn't need my help anymore.

"My mom thinks I should just follow Margaret's approach so I don't get confused," she explained one afternoon in late spring, last year. Margaret, an insanely smart graduate student at UC Berkeley, was helping Emma prep to get into AP Calculus our senior year.

Later, Emma started sighing when I'd ask if she could proof an essay on *King Lear* or give my history position paper on the Reconstruction Era a review. "Chloe, I'm not going to be able to help you with your college application statements, you know. You need to be able to do those yourself."

"Already done," I had replied. In reality, they were only partially done. But I wasn't going to tell her that.

The summer between junior and senior year, we didn't go away together to camp in Oregon, as we had the previous six summers. Emma was enrolled in an SAT-preparatory course that kept her busy for the better part of June and July. She'd already taken the test once, but her mom, a Stanford alum and COO of a San Francisco technology company called Novae, was encouraging her to try for a higher score. I'd already taken the SATs too and wasn't planning to again. "Why *wouldn't* you?" Emma had asked. "It's just another chance to do better." I couldn't tell if she was concerned about me wasting the opportunity or annoyed that I possibly didn't need it to begin with.

As senior year kicked off, Emma and I were back to meeting for lunch under the campus oak tree and after school to get our miles in for cross-country, but the weird undercurrent that had been there in the spring and summer remained. Emma's sympathy seemed less than genuine when I confessed that I hadn't made it into the AP History course taught by Mr. Britton, considered one of the school's best teachers. And I was maybe just a *little* bit satisfied when I noticed her struggling in AP Calculus, despite Margaret's best efforts.

Then came the party. And Liam Morales.

It was a warm night in late September. Craig Swanson's parents had departed for a wine country weekend, leaving their hilltop house and infinity pool under the care of their son—an opportunity too good for even the most die-hard overachievers to pass up. The books would get a break for a few hours.

We didn't really know Craig all that well, but Emma assured me that "everyone" was going. She wasn't wrong about that. The back patio at Craig's house was packed with people splashing in the pool, spilling drinks in the hot tub, and a few who were passing a vape pen around a huge out-door firepit. I remember immediately regretting my decision to go along. I've never been big on crowds.

Most of the night we spent standing with a cluster of girls who were, of course, discussing college application strategies. Aside from whatever was happening on Instagram and Snapchat, that's all anyone in my circle ever talked about.

Alexis Stewart had just announced that she'd applied to all nine University of California campuses.

"Even Riverside and Merced?" asked Emma.

"Well, only as an extra precaution," Alexis explained. "Don't want to end up like Jen Heatherton."

"Who's Jen Heatherton?" I asked.

"You didn't hear this story?" Mia asked me. "Jen is Sarah Wise's cousin. She was a year ahead of us. Anyway, Jen had a 3.9 GPA, was in honors courses, competitive sports, all that stuff. She only applied to Cal, UCLA, San Diego, and Davis. Davis was her safety school. Got rejected by *all four*. By then it was too late to apply to the rest without a deferral."

"You have to hedge your bets," said Alexis.

"Jen's the one who tried to kill herself last year," added Mia, next to me, more quietly.

"Well, a 3.9 is not competitive enough for those schools," said Emma. "What was her counselor thinking?"

"I know." Alexis shook her head. "But it was a 4.1 weighted . . ."

I wondered if Emma hadn't heard Mia's final comment and was about to ask if Jen Heatherton was okay now, but the conversation had already shifted to the fairness/unfairness of weighted versus unweighted GPAs.

People were applying to seven, eight, nine schools?

I too had applied to only four.

An annoying little gremlin perched itself on my shoulder and whispered in my ear:

Maybe you shouldn't have been so sure of yourself.

Skipping AP History is going to cost you!

Your essay was so boring. YAWN.

YOU are boring.

Your applications can't just be good—they need to be exceptional. ARE they exceptional? Are YOU?

Have you demonstrated knowledge? Passion? Integrity? Authenticity? Confidence? Initiative? A commitment to service? Special talents? Grit?

The gremlin would not shut the hell up.

"Does anyone know where the bathroom is?" I asked.

"Inside the sliding door and down the hall to the right," said Mia. "You can't miss it. It's huge."

I walked inside, found the enormous bathroom, and, as I washed my hands, reassured my well-lit reflection that everything was going to be fine. Everything was on track. I could always send out a few more applications if I wanted to. Even so, my heart—the one I used to have—was racing around in my chest like a hamster on a wheel. I took a deep breath.

Instead of heading back out to the pool and patio, I wandered farther into the house. Past the family room, where a bunch of kids were playing beer pong, as well as several rooms with closed doors. Bedrooms, I assumed, and likely occupied. At the end of the hallway, I peeked into a darkened room that looked like an office or a library, with shelves of books lining every wall except for the one that consisted entirely of a floor-to-ceiling glass door that opened onto a large deck sweeping out over the valley below.

I hesitated on the threshold of the room. It was empty, and it felt like I shouldn't be in there. But I was also curious.

I stepped inside and spent a little time studying the spines of the books on the shelves. It always fascinated me to see what other people read. Or at least what they wanted people to think that they read. Craig's parents were into Philip Roth, modern art, and mid-century architecture, apparently.

I pushed open the sliding door, made my way to a pristine white chaise lounge, and took a seat. Out there, the voices of the partygoers in the back blended into a pleasant hum, indistinguishable as individual conversations. I closed my eyes and concentrated on the light breeze tickling my face.

I remember feeling really tired. Tired of being at the party. Tired of talking about school.

Until Liam Morales dropped abruptly into the seat next to me, nearly scaring me out of my skin. My heartbeat surged so fast that it hurt.

"Hey, Russell."

He calls everyone by their last name. It's an annoying habit.

"Jesus, Liam. You shouldn't sneak up on people like that."

Liam had been Emma's crush since fifth grade. When we were in middle school, I spent many a sleepover night with her, studying his Instagram feed and devising plans to pass by his lunch table or "unexpectedly" bump into him on our way to the community pool near his house. Along with probably scores of other girls. Liam, with his impossibly long-lashed brown eyes and wavy hair, was the movie star of our class. And as we had made our way through high school, he had only grown more and more good-looking—a fact I was not unaware of as he sat mere inches away from me, shirtless and wrapped in a pool towel.

I also noticed that he was pretty drunk.

"I didn't mean to sneak up on you, Russell," he said. "Just curious who was out here drinking alone. Are you depressed or something?"

"No, just bored of talking about college applications."

Liam swayed his drink in my direction. "Cheers to that."

So we talked about something else. I don't remember

what. I actually didn't have a drink, so Liam shared the rest of his. It was soda mixed with a lot of gin and tasted terrible. Then he found a bottle of some kind of syrupy dessert liqueur in the office/library. We passed it back and forth.

Later, I do remember him telling me this: "You know, you're actually pretty cute. I'm kind of wanting to make out with you right now."

"Gee, thanks," I said, rolling my eyes.

He looked surprised that I wasn't immediately flattered. "No, I mean you're so serious all the time, it's sort of hard to notice."

"Am I?" I asked.

"I don't think I've ever heard you laugh."

"Really?"

"Really."

"Well, maybe you're just not that funny. You know how good-looking people don't have to work too hard to get people's attention?"

"So you think I'm good-looking."

"Liam, that means nothing. You know you are good-looking."

"But I'm not funny?"

"Only very lucky people can be both."

"Maybe you're just mean and have no sense of humor."

I kicked his chaise and he caught my foot in his hand. Then he ran his hand up my bare calf.

I'm not going to lie: Liam didn't have to work very hard

to get me to kiss him. My head was spinning from whatever it was we had been drinking, making me care less than I should have about Emma, who had been annoying me with her college admissions obsession that night. Plus, his hand on my calf was so warm. His face so perfect. His body so close. He pulled me toward him, onto his chaise.

I remember thinking that when it came to kissing, Liam knew *exactly* what to do with his lips. His hands. His tongue. Not that I had a ton of experiences to compare him to. I had kissed exactly three boys during my time in high school: Henry Shrader, once, in my sophomore year after the homecoming dance; Ajay Shah, on the orchestra trip to Disneyland, during the fireworks; and Matt Cohen, who I made out with for a couple of weeks, in my room, while we were working on a joint school project. He had always seemed a little unsure of his technique. But while Liam was the complete opposite of unsure, there was also something so methodical, so impersonal, about the way that he kissed me. I sensed that this was how he kissed every girl. Many girls.

As he started to untie the string on the back of my sundress, I pulled away, trying to catch my breath.

"Do you want me to stop?" he asked.

"Yes," I said, thinking, finally, of Emma. Thinking of how she'd never forgive me if she found out. And thinking that I wasn't entirely on board with where things were heading anyway.

A few weeks later, when my heart nearly exploded and I

got the news that I would probably die if I didn't get a new one, I almost wished we'd kept going. Not because I was pining for Liam. We didn't really have much in common. I simply didn't have time to wait for someone amazing. Or to worry about Emma's feelings. She would have plenty of chances to feel her heart race during first kisses. To go to parties, dance, flirt, hook up with hot college boys, maybe even fall in love.

And there was a pretty good chance that I was going to die a virgin. The end.

Anticipating another long, quiet day in the library, a place I used to happily spend hours at a time, I already feel like a caged cat. The summer syllabus for AP English Lit flies out the window, fluttering behind me like a bird with a broken wing.

≈≈≈ THE 360 ≈≈≈

The ocean has many moods. Today it seems kind of feisty, ready to toss some people around.

It's late morning, and instead of camping out in my usual study carrel in the school library, I've been sitting in the cool, damp sand for about thirty minutes now, watching Kai. A small group of surfers dotted the waves when I arrived, and although they were too far out for me to see their faces, I recognized Kai right away. I've become familiar with the way he moves. Athletic. Graceful. Fearless.

Beneath a misty bluish-gray sky, the waves are head height—big rolling swells that lift and curl over in an explosion of foam. As each one rises, the surfers paddle into the wave like a school of fish. Kai makes his pop-ups look effortless, quickly pivoting his board to skim sideways across the water, riding each wave as long and as far as it lasts.

It occurs to me now that I knew Kai before I met him. Well, not *knew* him, exactly. I'd seen him. He's one of the ones I couldn't take my eyes off of all those weeks ago when I drove on a whim to the beach. *The* one. Because when he's in the water, he's *beautiful* to behold. Like right now, when he propels his board right off the top of a swell, twisting around nearly 360 degrees in midair. It's a move that looks both exhilarating and impossible. A move, I decide, that I need to master. *He's been holding out on me,* I think, with a slight twinge of annoyance.

The next set is bigger and fiercer than the last. Kai launches like a rocket off a fast-rising wave, pivots, wobbles, and then drops straight down into the churning whiteness below. My stomach tenses, heart guns it to a hundred, and it's only after I see his head come up that I realize I've been holding my breath.

Minutes later, he's paddling back out and I scan the horizon behind him, trying to read the ocean for what's coming next. In the distance, another set rises up. A few surfers pick up the first wave as it sweeps toward the shore, but Kai paddles over it. Dives through the next.

Number three.

That's the one.

The wave barrels forward, gathering height and width. It's going to be a monster.

Kai plows right into it, and it seems to pull him up like a child's bath toy. But in one swift move he's standing. I track him as he pivots, then as he disappears into a swirling green tunnel.

As the wind slaps at my face, I almost feel like I'm speeding across the length of the wave with him, adrenaline coursing through my arteries and veins.

I wrap my arms around myself, realizing I'm shivering. It was sunny and in the seventies when I left my house this morning, but here I'm underdressed in a thin blue hoodie. I should probably go. Kai looks like he's getting ready to paddle in and I'm kind of embarrassed about him seeing me, sitting here like some beach bunny. It's not our usual lesson day.

Just as I'm about to stand up, I spot him walking out of the water with his board. He shakes his wet black hair, once, like a dog, and then swipes it back with his free hand. He scans the beach as if he's looking for something, until he makes eye contact with me. I feel my face flush. How long had he known I was watching?

I don't know whether to sit or stand as he makes his way toward me. Would getting up make it look like I was waiting for him?

This is so awkward.

"Hey," he says as he approaches. It looks like he has a slight limp today, and I wonder if he hurt himself when he dropped off that roiling wave.

"Hey," I answer, trying to sound normal.

"I . . . thought we were on for Wednesday?"

It occurs to me that he could be annoyed that I've barged in on his morning off, when he's free from helping beginners like me stay upright. In my head, I run through possible responses that don't make me sound like a stalker:

Oh, really? I thought you said Monday this week. My mistake!

Yep, Wednesday. I'm just meeting some friends. Who should be here any *minute . . .*

It's not Wednesday??

Ultimately, I settle on the truth.

I shrug. "I didn't feel like going to school today. Thought I might come out and practice, but it's kind of hard to do that without a wetsuit. Which I left at home."

I feel like a small child looking up at him like this. I should have stood.

"Yeah, a wetsuit is mandatory today," he says as he sits down next to me in the sand. Okay. This is *slightly* less awkward. "It's goddamn cold out there," he adds. I notice that his lips are blue. They are also nicely shaped. Full.

He's quiet for a few seconds, still catching his breath. His chest rises and falls. "You're supposed to be in school?"

"Yes," I say. "Summer school."

"Huh. You don't seem like the summer school type."

"What's the summer school type?" I ask.

He shrugs. "Sort of a fuckup?" Then quickly shakes his head. "Sorry. That was a stupid thing to say."

Nevertheless, I feel compelled to explain that I'm not in danger of becoming a high school dropout. "I missed the final semester of my senior year and I need to make up the credits," I say. "So . . . summer school."

"Got it."

He looks like he might be about to ask why I missed a semester of school, so I change the subject.

"So when are you going to teach me how to jump off a wave like that?" I nod toward the surf.

He laughs. "Patience, newbie. Took me a few years to work up to the three-sixty."

It's a nice-sounding laugh—warm, despite the cold weather. I think he should do it more often. He shivers.

"You're supposed to be in school and we both could use a parka," Kai says. "Doesn't seem much like summer, does it?"

I make a sweeping gesture across the shoreline. "I thought you were used to this. Haven't you been surfing out here since you were a kid?"

"Here? Nah. I learned to surf in Hawaii. Been here in the Bay Area for about four years. I don't think I'll ever get used to this water."

Hawaii. I've only been once, on a family vacation to a beachfront resort in Maui, when I was about seven. I swam in the pool the entire time because, back then, I was afraid of the waves.

Then something clicks in my mind. I say what I'm assuming aloud. "You're Hawaiian?"

He shakes his head no and grins. "And now you're about to ask me the question that every mixed-race person gets asked *all* the time."

"What question is that?"

"'What *are* you?'"

"Oh, so you're a mind reader, are you?"

"But you were thinking it."

"I was *thinking*, wrongly, that you're Hawaiian. But now that you're planting questions in my head . . ."

I can't help that I'm curious about him. I want to know more about his family and his life and why he was maybe limping a few minutes ago and where he lives and . . . just everything.

Kai continues. "Is he Hawaiian, Korean, Japanese . . . ?"

"*Kai.*"

"My dad is Japanese American," he says. "And my mom's side of the family are English and German, so, like, white."

I nod and then add, "Both sides of my family are white."

He smiles, and I'm relieved to see that he's not annoyed at how nosy I am today. "You don't say."

"Well, Irish and Polish, if you're looking for more specifics. Do you miss it? Living in Hawaii?" I ask.

"I was pretty little when we lived there, but I definitely miss not freezing my ass off when I surf. I miss warm nights. But this place is beautiful too, in a different way. It's wild, you know?"

"Yeah," I say. There was a time when I never would have

considered paddling out into the waves that are crashing in front of us. But now it's all I want to do. We sit in silence for a few minutes, staring out. My brain is desperately searching for something else, something *interesting*, to say.

Kai saves me from having to come up with anything. "How's your head?"

How's my head?

And just like that, I'm sucked back into all the anxieties that I've come to the beach to get away from. The headaches. The hallucinations. The nightmares. Forgetting stuff . . . or remembering stuff that I didn't even know I forgot. But I realize he's talking about when I got hit by my board last week.

"Oh, fine," I say, touching my temple.

"Good," he says. Then he squints at me. "You know, you kind of look like a Smurf right now."

I tug at the strings on my blue hoodie, which is pulled tightly around my ears. "Phew. That's exactly what I was going for."

He sort of laughs. Then there's another awkward silence. Kai stands up. "I'm freezing. I've got to get out of this suit."

And just to keep the awkwardness going a little longer, *Kai, getting out of his suit* is now scrolling like the Times Square news ticker across my brain, making my stupid face flush for like the third or fourth time today.

"Oh, don't let me keep you!" I say. Too loud. "I'm going to watch a little longer." I hope there are still surfers out there to watch. "See you Wednesday."

"See you Wednesday." He starts walking away, still with that hint of a limp, but then calls over his shoulder. "And don't forget your wetsuit!"

"I never forget my wetsuit!" I call back. "Well, I mean, except for today!" My voice is swept away by the wind.

"What?" He's already close to the path between the dunes that leads to the parking lot.

"Nothing! Never mind!" I gesture for him to keep walking.

He looks my way for another second and then disappears into the shadows cast by the dunes.

I'm freezing too, but there's no way I'm heading out to the parking lot until I'm sure he's gone.

I tuck my chin to my chest and pull my hands up into the sleeves of my hoodie.

Gah. I feel like an idiot.

≋ HOW ARE YOU? ≋

"Omigod, Chloe! How are you?"

If one more person asks, I'm seriously going to lose my shit.

It's Mia, launching questions at me in her rapid-fire, high-pitched voice: "We haven't seen you in forever! Are you feeling okay? What have you been *doing* this summer?"

This.

This is why I didn't want to go to Emma's graduation party. Everyone wants to know how I *feel*. Am I okay? Am I really back from the almost-dead? Do I need to sit down? Can they get me anything? It makes me feel like I'm no longer just Chloe. Now, I'm also A Story. One that gets told when my name comes up in conversation: *I saw her collapse that day on the track.* They are hungry for details. *What was it like? Do you feel different? How big is the scar?* And I hate being the center of attention. The target of all the concerned faces and the well-meaning questions.

"I'm fine," I say. "How's your summer going?" Asking Mia to talk about herself is usually a reliable way to shift the focus.

"Oh, you know . . . super busy. Alexis and I did this environmental service trip to Costa Rica in June and it was *so* amazing. Check out my Instagram—there are a ton of photos."

"Cool," I say.

"And now I'm interning at Airbnb. Emma's mom knows their chief marketing officer, so she was nice enough to help me line it up. Plus there's so much to do to get ready for school, and my mom is freaking out about what I need to get for the dorm, of course. But what about you? Did they let you graduate? What are you doing in the fall? Did you pick a school?" She stops to take a breath.

"I'm in summer school right now," I say. "I might defer a semester."

"Oh!" Mia frowns. "I'm so sorry, Chloe! That sucks— such bad timing."

"Don't be sorry. I could be, you know, *dead* instead."

"Right, of course! Well, we've all missed you."

I know she means this, but it's hard for me to return the sentiment, even if I'm not sure why. This entire event is the dictionary definition of the old me. My best friend's gradua-tion. Classmates that I've known since elementary school. A house where I've spent hours of my young life—playing *Just Dance* on the Wii, studying for the next day's science test, making plans for our Saturday sleepover. If I didn't feel at home here, how could I feel at home anywhere?

"I've missed you guys too," I respond, hoping I don't sound like a total liar.

I leave Mia with a promise to catch up after I say hello to Emma, and I wander into the crowd on the patio.

The party is perfect, as I expected it would be. There are fresh flowers. A food truck serving grass-fed organic-beef mini-burgers and your choice of regular or sweet potato fries. Emma's mom, as usual, has not missed a single detail. I spot her coming my way, clad in a chic summer shift dress. *Rachel Klein, COO, Novae, Inc.* might as well be spelled out in bold Arial font right above her head. Despite spending most of her time at the office, Emma's mom looks like she lives at a gym. She runs marathons. She manages the annual school auction fund-raiser. She "leans in." Like, *all the way*.

"Chloe, so glad you made it," she says, embracing me tightly. "Emma will be thrilled. How *are* you?"

"I'm good," I say, trying not to grit my teeth. I imagine it would be rude to lose it on Emma's mom.

"We've missed you. Where have you been this summer? I ran into your dad last week and he told me you were still completing a few credits for graduation."

"Yes. But I should be done in August."

"And you're all set on a school? Let me know if you need

88

a recommendation letter or a phone call—there are a few Berkeley alums on the board at Novae."

"I will, thank you," I say, scanning the patio. "I haven't had a chance to say hello to Emma yet."

"You haven't? Well, let's find her!"

Emma's mom takes my hand and pulls me through the party, stopping often to say hello to someone and offer an introduction. Most of them are her work colleagues—people who, as she would have reminded Emma before the party, are useful to know.

We pass Emma's dad, a lawyer, who gives his wife a quick peck on the cheek and my arm a squeeze, mouthing, "Hi, Chloe!"—all while continuing what looks to be an important phone call. We finally spot Emma standing near the olive trees that ring the backyard, talking to a tall woman wearing huge hipster glasses. Juno Barnett, the founder and CEO of Novae. She's twenty-eight years old and currently on the cover of *Fast Company*, since the big news is that Novae is on track to receive the highest stock valuation ever for a tech company founded by a woman. Emma seems tiny next to her.

Rachel presents me to Emma like a gift.

"I found Chloe. I'm sure you two have a lot to catch up on."

Emma seems both happy and relieved to see me. She trades places with her mom, and the two women are already deep in conversation as we depart. Novae people rarely take a day off.

"Your timing is perfect," Emma whispers in my ear. "Do

you know how hard it is to fake interest in a conversation about data science and machine learning?"

In truth, I do find machine learning kind of interesting, but I want to back Emma up here, *especially* since she hasn't asked me how I'm feeling.

"Yikes," I say. "Glad I could assist."

We walk together across the lawn, back in the direction of the house.

"Do you want to get some food?" she asks.

"Maybe later," I tell her. "But first, I brought you a going-away gift."

She narrows her eyes. "It's not another Apple Store gift card, is it?"

"No, of course not. But I will gladly accept any extras if you received too many, poor girl. C'mon, it's in the trunk of my car."

Emma follows me out to the street, where my car is parked next to an oleander hedge.

I open the trunk and present Emma with a dented and dirty Dutch oven. She stares at it for a second and then laughs.

"The Vampire Princess!"

When we were nine, we buried one of Emma's American Girl dolls, Julie, in my backyard, using a cracked Dutch oven that my mom was about to toss in the trash as the sarcophagus. Then we dug her up a few months later to see if she had "decomposed." We weren't expecting much but were pleasantly surprised to find that she had attracted a few spiders as well as a handful of dead bugs caught in their webs. After that, we called Julie the Vampire Princess.

Emma sets the Dutch oven down on the sidewalk. "I'm really hoping a rat does not jump out when I open this. I can't believe you still have her."

She pulls off the lid and Julie stares up at us, in all her undead glory. We had added our own touches in the weeks after we dug her up: red tempera paint around her mouth (now brown), ripped clothes, and dirt on her fused fingers.

"I think you should take her to Brown," I say, sitting down on the curb next to Emma. "If your roommate gives you any problems, just keep Julie on your bed and she'll think you are deeply disturbed and not to be messed with."

"I love it," says Emma. "Remember when we had her funeral?"

"We argued over who got to throw the first clump of dirt on her coffin."

"You wanted to try to embalm her."

"You wrote a very stirring eulogy."

Emma looks a little sad. "I loved being nine."

"Me too," I say. "We had so many good ideas back then."

"I know!" Emma laughs. "We were also planning to build a time machine in your garage."

"Don't forget our comic series about the vegetarian zombies," I say. "We were sure it was going to make us rich."

Emma looks confused for a second. "Did we do that? I don't remember that at all. Jesus, Chloe, I must be losing it. Too much to think about lately!"

We did make the comic, right? We sold a copy to my mom. Didn't we? Now I wasn't so sure. I don't even like to draw.

Maybe I'm the one who's losing it.

Emma brushes off the front of her skirt and stands up.

"I have to go meet one of my mom's work friends who went to Brown," she says. "She's supposed to give me a recommendation for the engineering program."

"What happened to English?"

Emma's face tightens for a fraction of a second. "My parents think an engineering degree might give me more options. You know how my mom's always talking about women being underrepresented in STEM professions."

"But is that what you want?" I lift the Vampire Princess from the curb and hand it to her.

"Of course."

She doesn't look as sure as she sounds.

Then again, I'm not so sure about anything anymore, so who am I to judge?

I follow Emma back into the house and we part at the threshold of her back patio. We promise to get together again, just us, before she leaves. Maybe we will. I hope we will.

As Emma disappears into the crowd, our friend Olivia catches me by the arm.

"Chloe! Where have you been all summer? How are you feeling?"

Ugh, not again.

I need to escape.

"Fine," I say, "but I'm starving, so I'm going to get at least three or possibly four mini-burgers."

"Wait," she says. "Aren't you vegetarian?"

"Not anymore. Not since . . ." I say, shrugging. We both know what I'm referring to.

"Well, it's hard to stick with it, isn't it?" She smiles. "Mia and Alexis and some of the guys from cross-country are at the table at the far end of the pool. Come join us after you get a plate. We have to catch up!"

"Will do," I answer, even though I've already decided to ghost.

The food truck is parked in the driveway, and instead of getting in line, where I'll surely run into yet another person who will ask me how I'm doing, I make my way to the street in front of Emma's house.

The chatter of the party recedes as I walk to my car. Once I shut myself inside, I exhale, realizing that all the muscles in the back of my neck have been squeezed tight. I'm glad to have escaped. But I don't want to go home. I reach for my phone and type "Jane" into the search bar of my contacts.

For a few seconds, I hesitate. Although Jane and I have been having lunch together almost every day at summer school and recently exchanged numbers, we don't text each other regularly. Definitely not on weekends.

Hi, I text, adding, *It's Chloe.*

Yeah, I can see that, Jane responds. *What's up, math nerd?*

What are you doing?

When?

Now.

Hanging at my dad's place in Pac Heights. Want to come over? He's gone tonight and there's a ton of weed here.

Technically, I'm not supposed to drive into the city without clearing it with my parents first. Especially now. *After.*

Also, I don't smoke. Or at least I didn't.

Don't.

Didn't.

I text back.

What's the address?

 INK

My parents are going to be pissed about the tattoo. Not because they are against tattoos per se—my mom actually has a tiny shamrock on her ankle—but because of the very remote chance that it could get infected and throw my whole recovery process out of whack. The thing with being constantly on immunosuppressants so that my body doesn't attack my heart is that it can't do such a great job fighting all the regular stuff it's supposed to fight off either: Colds. Flu. Strep throat. Blood infections. In fact, if someone so much as sneezes in my direction these days, my parents get really uptight about it, which is a pretty big departure from our life *before*.

Until recently, being an only child had meant getting treated more or less like an adult in my house. My parents weren't particularly concerned with rules. They didn't enforce a curfew. They didn't restrict my internet access or demand too many details if I was headed out somewhere with Emma. They would even pour me a glass of wine with dinner every now and then, especially when they were opening a good one and were feeling a little "European." Of course, this may have been because I'd never really given them much cause to worry. They knew I wasn't going to sneak out through my bedroom window in the middle of the night or have the number of the school's drug dealer on my phone. But now they're always checking on where I am and what I'm doing. They try to make it seem like they're not, that they're just touching base to ask if pizza is okay for dinner or if I have plans to go anywhere after school—but these are things they never really touched base about before.

In fact, my phone's recent history is primarily made up of missed calls from Mom and Dad:

3:00 p.m. and 5:45 p.m. on Monday.

5:14 p.m. on Wednesday.

Multiple times in the last six hours, including at 12:01 a.m., when Jane and I were at a shop on Haight Street, drunk, cementing our new BFF status by getting some ink.

It wasn't Jane's idea. It was mine.

We'd been hanging at her dad's Pacific Heights apartment, drinking an expensive-looking scotch whisky from his liquor cabinet. It smelled like leather and burned my throat but gave my lips a warm and tingly buzz. Jane's dad has a huge classic vinyl record collection, and we were playing albums one after the other, lying on a shaggy sheepskin rug among a pile of sleeves. Led Zeppelin. David Bowie. Radiohead. R.E.M.

Music was something that I didn't really pay close attention to before. In my pre-transplant life, it was mainly filler. Something that served as background during study sessions and sleepovers, that helped me keep up the pace when I trained for cross-country meets. Or that my mom and I could tease my dad about whenever he sang along to his cheesy '70s favorites. I mean, sure, there were plenty of songs I liked or that I could recite the lyrics to in an earworm kind of way, but I don't think I had ever once listened to a single album from beginning to end or devoted myself to a particular band or artist.

Now I couldn't get enough. Music was becoming an obsession. I cranked it up loud in the car. Lived with earbuds connected to my head. It opened my mind to another universe—one that I never knew existed. And it also made me feel less alone with my thoughts.

At Jane's dad's, I couldn't stop pulling records off the shelves, one after the other. I studied the jacket art and read the liner notes. It felt like I was discovering something . . . not new necessarily, but buried, like unearthing fossils. When I came across the Velvet Underground's *Loaded*, I carefully slid it from its sleeve and put it on the player. That subway station entrance on the cover—it looked so familiar to me, even though this night was, in fact, the first night in my life that I'd ever played any vinyl record, let alone this one. And when the trippy opening guitar chords of the second song started up, I turned to Jane: "*Shhh*. Listen. This is your song!"

She laughed at the chorus to "Sweet Jane." "My dad would love you. You know a lot about music."

"Not really," I answered.

Jane passed me the joint she'd been smoking, also from her dad's supply. "He's old-school about his pot," she'd told me. "Still likes to roll his own."

I held it between my fingers for a moment, watching it smolder.

I'm most definitely *not* supposed to smoke. Never. Ever. For heart transplant recipients, smoking is one of the things that is banned for life.

I took a hit of the joint anyway, trying not to look like a complete amateur in front of Jane.

"So your dad doesn't notice that you drink his whisky and smoke his pot?" This seemed like something my parents would be wise to, at least if I tried it more than once or twice. Not that my parents have pot in the house.

"My dad?" Jane snorted. "He doesn't notice anything. Honestly, he's usually not even here. His girlfriend, Grace, is, like, twenty-six, and she's always got something lined up on the weekend. And she *hates* it when I'm around, so they usually steer clear."

"Why's that?" I asked, stifling a cough.

"Because I'm a total bitch to her, why else?" Jane laughed. "Plus, I think she likes to pretend that my dad doesn't have a daughter that's basically old enough to be her sister. Her much hotter and more interesting sister."

The record wobbled ever so slightly as it turned on the player. I concentrated my focus on the soft, satisfying scratch that accompanied the music and imagined myself dissolving into the rug.

Then Jane asked, "Do you know who your heart donor was?"

Although the song was still playing, in my head the needle was yanked away from the turntable, bursting the bubble we'd been floating in thanks to the scotch, the pot, and Lou Reed.

"No," I told Jane. "Donor identities are confidential. If I want to try and find out, I can write a letter to the family. But it's up to them to write back."

Jane sat up on her elbows. "So are you going to? I mean, aren't you curious? Even a little bit?"

"I don't know. It just seems like it would be weird for them, and for me, so probably not."

What do you say, after all, to the loved ones of the person whose death was your ultimate lucky break? *Thanks so much! I'm sure I'll get a lot of use out of this heart!*

But I didn't tell Jane the real reason I wasn't going to write a letter. I already know that my donor's next of kin do *not* want to be found.

"I'm sorry, Chloe," Dr. Ahmadi had said a few days ago, returning my call from earlier that week. After what had happened at the beach and reading all those stories about cellular memory, I'd finally gotten up the nerve to ask about contacting my donor's family. Maybe if I knew more about the person who gave me their heart, I wouldn't feel so strange all the time. Maybe this heart wouldn't feel so foreign. Maybe once I knew for certain that I wasn't really inheriting anybody's memories or anything like that, I could stop questioning every impulse, every feeling, every desire, and every random thought that floats through my mixed-up head.

But Dr. Ahmadi put a quick end to my attempts at playing detective. "I checked with hospital records. Your donor's family has made it clear that they do not wish to be contacted. By law, I can't give you any more information than that. While I personally think it's therapeutic for the family to meet their loved one's transplant recipients, some just want to move on. They don't want to be reminded of their loss. You understand?"

"Of course," I said.

But I was also disappointed. The part of me that likes to ask questions and have answers wants to know more.

Before I could put the next record on the turntable, my phone buzzed with a call from my mom. I'd texted her after Emma's party to get permission to stay in the city with Jane, but I hadn't confirmed that I'd arrived safely. Instead of picking up, I texted back in all caps, *I AM ALIVE AND*

WELL. DON'T WORRY, then looked over at Jane and grinned.

"Let's go get a tattoo."

She laughed. "Now?"

"C'mon. It will be fun."

"It's illegal, math nerd. You have to be eighteen."

"Really?" I asked. "You have one." I've noticed the teal hummingbird on her shoulder when she wears a tank top.

"I know a guy. *And* my dad was okay with it. Are you sure your parents won't kill you?"

"They give me a lot of leeway on account of the heart," I lied. "You know, you only live once and all that. Or, in my case, I guess twice?"

Jane acted like she was considering whether or not to make the call, but I could tell I'd already won her over.

"Okay. But you *cannot* mention where, because my friend Chris could lose his license. And try to pretend you're sober." Jane made a call, then we stumbled out to wait for our Lyft.

At Chris's shop, Jane got a small infinity symbol between her shoulder blades. I got a heart on my right wrist.

Not a cute Valentine's Day one in a candy color, but a *real* one. It's anatomically correct, in red ink so dark it's almost black. A massive aorta arches between the branches of the pulmonary artery and superior vena cava. The coronary arteries twist across the ventricles like roots. It's in honor of the one that used to be mine. Only mine.

Jane says my tattoo is a little bit gross, but in a good way.

On the way back to her dad's apartment, Jane and I are quiet. It's late—early, really—and now I have a massive headache from all the scotch. My mouth is so dry that all I can think about is drinking a big glass of cold water. Like right now. Did I remember to take my medication earlier? That's probably why my mom was calling, back before we left. I have an image in my mind of the pill bottles lined up on the sink in my bathroom at home. Yes, I forgot. I pull my phone out of my jacket pocket. There are four additional missed calls from home. Crap. Well, I can't do much about it right now. I'll just have to tell my mom that my ringer was off or my phone battery ran out.

I look out the window and see a man walking up the sidewalk along Divisadero Street. Buzzed scalp. Muscular build. Black jacket. Tattoo snaking up the side of his neck.

Holy shit. A flash of recognition jolts me like an electric shock. *It's him.* The crying man who visited my hospital room on the night of my transplant. The one I've been trying to convince myself was just a medication-induced hallucination.

He's alone, his face shadowed by the string of Victorian town houses he's passing under, their bay windows jutting out over the ground-floor garage doors.

But it's him. Somehow, in some way, I *know* it's him.

"Stop the car!" I say to the driver.

"Chloe, it's, like, fifteen more blocks." Jane must think I'm confused. "Uphill."

"Stop the car!" I say again, opening the door as the driver pulls over.

As I jump out, I catch my foot on the curb and almost tumble to the ground.

Jane is still inside, trying to unbuckle herself.

I have to stop him. I have to see him.

And then what?

He's about a block and a half away and walking quickly. I start to run toward the intersection as the light turns to yellow, then red. Although it's past two a.m., there's still enough traffic on Divisadero to block my way.

Jane is catching up and cursing at me at the same time.

"Chloe, what the hell?"

The light goes green and I dash across the street just as he turns the corner up ahead. I keep running, as fast as my legs will carry me, wheel around the corner, and . . .

Nothing.

There is no one. Both sidewalks are empty. Fog swirls under the streetlights.

I sit down on the cold front steps of a darkened Victorian. I can feel my pulse pounding everywhere. In my wrist, still throbbing from the tattoo needle. In my chest, heartbeat *thump, thump, thump*ing against my rib cage. In my ears, as I hear the blood rushing in and out.

Jane is standing in front of me.

"What the hell, Chloe? What are you doing?"

Was I imagining him again? Seeing things that aren't there?

"That guy!" I look, in vain, down the quiet street. "Did you see him?"

"Did I see the guy in the black jacket?"

"Yes! Yes! You *saw* him?"

"*Of course* I saw him." Jane looks exasperated. "Why were you chasing him like a maniac?"

He's real. I'm not crazy. He's real.

"Chloe." Jane stares at me, impatient for an answer. "WHO IS HE AND WHY WERE YOU CHASING HIM?"

"I don't know, exactly," I say, realizing how weird I must sound.

I cross my arms over my knees, put my head down, and try to push back the tears that are welling up, but I can't.

I cry in frustration that the man has disappeared. In relief that he's actually real. In confusion. In fear. In gratitude that Jane has opted to just sit down next to me on the steps and let me have a meltdown. Cars sweep by in the darkness.

And then a sour spasm rolls through my empty stomach and I vomit all over my feet.

"Yeesh," says Jane, jumping up. "Guess it was a good thing we got out of that car."

She pulls me up to standing as a light goes on in the upper floor of the house behind us. "C'mon, we should probably go."

We slowly walk the rest of the way to Jane's dad's apartment. Jane makes me leave my shoes on the back stairwell and then drink a full glass of water, take two aspirin and a vitamin B12 tablet, wash my face, and brush my teeth. She calls this her "after-party routine." When I come out of the bathroom, I hardly have a chance to sit before she asks, "So are you going to tell me what that was all about or what?"

When I look over, there are two Janes, both sprawled on the rug with their heads propped against giant floor pillows. I look away and back again. Now there's only one. My still-queasy stomach desperately wants her to stay that way.

"That man," I say. "He came into my room the night of my transplant. At least I thought he did. Everyone else thought it was a dream, or some kind of hallucination from all the pain meds. I had even convinced myself that they were right, until I just saw him *walking down the street.*"

"So you *do* know him?" she asks.

"I don't *know* know him," I say. "But I remember him from the hospital. Like, I'm *telling* you, Jane, he was in my *room*, sitting next to my bed. And what's weird is that night . . . it sort of seemed like he was the one who knew *me.*"

Jane is thinking. I study her face, trying to find a focal point so that she'll stop uniting and dividing. Dividing and uniting.

She's wearing black jeans, an oversize white T-shirt, and boots that look like they'd take at least an hour to lace up. I compare my outfit to hers, which makes me feel both over- and underdressed. Overdressed because I'm still wearing the skirt and blouse that I had chosen for Emma's party. Minus my now-ruined shoes. Underdressed because my clothes seem hopelessly uncool in comparison to those boots.

"Chloe." She raises her eyebrows. "Maybe he knew your heart donor," she says. "Maybe he came to see you in the hospital because he knew the person who gave you their heart. Like, he wanted to see who got it."

My brain is slow to process, but as it does, I find myself nodding along. Even if nobody saw him come in or out of my room, he still could have done so without being noticed. The ICU is busy and chaotic. The nurses staffing the main station get distracted. If this man was my donor's next of kin, then it makes sense that he might have needed to see me, see where the heart went, in order to have closure. This even explains why he might not have wanted to be contacted. He'd already made his peace.

Then Jane sits up straight.

"Or—oh my god, oh my god—*maybe* it's like those cellular memory stories we were reading about the other day in the library. Maybe you recognized him on the street just now *because your donor knew him*. The memory of him has been, like, *transferred*, to you."

I shake my head. "Jane, Jane, Jane, Jane, *Jane*. I already told you, there is no scientific evidence that that's even possible. Zero." But even as I say this, I think of the woman who looks sick, of the silver-gray pit bull, of the vegetarian zombie

106

comic that I can remember but Emma can't. The man on the street. Where *is* all of it coming from? Could it be that none of these memories make sense to me because they're not mine?

Impossible. Jane is just messing with my head. And, like me, she's drunk.

"You know, there's no evidence that God exists either," she says. "Doesn't seem to stop people from going to church."

"I don't believe in God," I tell her. "I believe in science."

"Yeah, you seem like a science kind of gal." Jane nods at my chest. "Does it still hurt? Your heart?"

I think about this. "It doesn't hurt anymore, but I feel it. You know how you don't really notice your heart unless you're lying somewhere quiet or you get scared or something?"

"I guess," says Jane.

"Every time this one beats, I think about how it's not really mine."

Her blue eyes widen slightly and she nods.

We're both quiet for a minute, then Jane adds, "Well, there's only one way to know if this cellular memory thing is real or just bullshit. You need to find out who your donor was."

Before I can tell Jane that this is not going to be possible, she claps her hands together, making me jump. "My mom!" she says.

"Your mom *what*?" I ask. I wish she could turn down the volume on her voice. It's making my head hurt.

Jane grins at me. "She works in the maternity ward."

"And you are telling me this because . . . ?"

"At UCSF."

The hospital where I had my transplant.

"She has access to the medical records system. And she can't remember anything, so I'm sure she's got the login posted somewhere in her home office. Maybe we can find some information on your donor that way."

Hacking into hospital records. Sure.

But then I think, *Why not?* It couldn't hurt to just dig around a little bit, right? And even though I'm still skeptical about the whole cellular memory idea and probably wouldn't agree to break HIPAA laws when I'm sober, it would be such a relief to know something—anything—about my donor.

I dive over and hug Jane.

"*Thank you.* We should *definitely* do that. Also, I really, really love your boots. Can I borrow them sometime?"

Jane shakes her head and disentangles herself from my clumsy hug. "Remind me not to let you mix weed and whisky next time. Let's get you to sleep, Chloe."

But after I'm tucked into the bed in her dad's guest room, I can't sleep. I can't stop thinking about the man from my hospital room. About seeing him on the street. About the motorcycle crash. The dog. Emma. Jane. My parents. Kai. Images flash like lightning through my head. A female face: beautiful, breaking into a smile, dimples deepening. A blue house with a white porch swing. A twisted cypress tree. An EKG readout. Ocean. Tattoo. Traffic. Tunnel.

My brain is a pinball machine, each thought sending another ricocheting. It's all so loud and disorderly. So random and difficult to control.

I just want it to stop.

I'm tired of this game.

 **AFTER**

People often ask me what it was like, getting a new heart. Did I feel different after? Changed? Yes and yes—more than I ever bargained for, as it turns out.

But in the immediate aftermath of my transplant, here's what I noticed first: My feet weren't cold. A failing heart can't pump enough blood to your extremities. In the weeks before the transplant, my fingers and toes had turned blue. No matter how many blankets my mom had piled on the bed, I couldn't get warm. So as soon as I woke up, I noticed my feet. They felt like how feet are supposed to feel. There. My mom laid her hands on them and started crying, her shoulders relaxing in relief.

And the crushing, suffocating, all-consuming tiredness was gone. I was so, so tired before. Stairs had become Mount

Everest. Breathing was like trying to suck air through a tiny straw. Even thinking required effort. The head, it turns out, is hopeless without a well-functioning heart.

After the transplant, it was almost as if I could feel each one of the trillions of newly energized red blood cells, fat with hemoglobin, racing through my arteries and outermost capillaries, bumping up against one another in their rush to oxygenate muscle fibers, synapses, and neurons.

Oxygen is a beautiful thing. After living through the nightmare of not having enough, I'd never take breathing for granted again.

Dr. Ahmadi had come by my room once I was awake, giving us all a thumbs-up.

"Everything went great," he said. "Looks like you have a fully functioning, beautiful new heart."

He almost made it sound as if we had picked it out in a showroom, like a Toyota. But I couldn't stop, and I haven't stopped thinking about where it really came from. Who it came from.

When you consider it from a medical standpoint, the transplant of a living heart from one body to another is a pretty incredible achievement. Until recently in the course of human history, this mad scientist–level ambition was considered impossible. Before the heart-lung machine was invented to take over the oxygenation process during a procedure, there simply hadn't been enough time. A brain without oxygen couldn't survive more than a handful of minutes, nowhere near long enough for surgeons to do the painstaking work of removing a sick heart and replacing it with a healthy one.

And then there was the problem of rejection. Our immune response is programmed to make war on foreign invaders. And what could be more foreign than having your own heart replaced by one that used to belong to someone else? Early transplant patients often only lived a few days before their bodies attacked the new organ.

Immunosuppressant drugs changed everything. There are still plenty of risks, of course, but all things considered, I'm incredibly lucky, as everyone keeps telling me. Lucky to exist at a time when transplants are not just possible but successful. Lucky that a donor heart became available before my own ran out of gas. Lucky to be alive.

So, of course, my parents are, as I expected, furious about the tattoo. Well, my mom is furious, anyway. My dad is just bewildered. Anxious. Wondering what has happened to his level-headed, predictable Chloe.

I think they both suspected I was hungover when I arrived home yesterday morning. They wanted to know why I hadn't picked up my phone the night before. Why I was no longer hanging out with Emma and my other old friends. Why I had started acting like the sort of sullen, monosyllabic teenager that we used to make fun of. Why, why, why? I didn't have many answers for them.

"Chloe, what were you thinking?" my mom asked, her face tired from lack of sleep. Her faint worry line looked as though it had deepened to a full-on wrinkle overnight. "You left your medication here, and I know you know how irresponsible it was to get that tattoo. We are going to have to do a blood test now. Jesus! Do you even realize how lucky you were to get this heart? How could you put yourself at risk like this? I just don't understand what's going on with you lately!"

"I'm sorry—I just forgot!" I said, which, admittedly, was a weak answer.

"You forgot? You *can't* forget!"

"Everybody forgets stuff sometimes!"

"Well, you are not everybody!"

My dad interceded, as he usually does. It's the middle-school science teacher in him. He's used to defusing hormonally challenged students. "Chloe, we know you want to do the same things that every normal teenager can do. And you can, *mostly*. But you do have to remember that your heart is a little more special than others. Treat it that way, okay?"

I hate that word. *Special*. It's a cop-out word. Instead of saying the truth—that special really means *"Sorry about your shitty luck!"*—people try to make it sound like you're holding a winning lottery ticket. My heart is *special*? Yeah, right. One, it's not *my* heart. And two, *special* should refer to being able to do something really mind-blowing, like discovering a wormhole into another universe, and not something that requires a lifetime of medication, blood tests, biopsies, and the constant threat of rejection. And perhaps a shorter life span and complete mental breakdown in addition.

But I just wanted them to back off, so all I'd said was, "Okay. I'm sorry. I'll be more careful. I promise."

"Okay, good," my dad said, as if my promise ended the discussion. Problem solved. But Mom was not playing.

"That's it? 'Okay, good'? No, not 'Okay, good'! I don't think she's getting the seriousness of this. She can't just forget her medication! She could *die*!"

My dad does not like to hear the word *die*.

"Nobody is dying, Julia. Forgetting a couple of pills is not going to kill her. Don't overreact."

Even I know that telling an overreacting person not to overreact is kind of a bad idea. My mom had looked as if she was about to vaporize my dad with her radioactive eye beams.

"Are you serious? I hate how you get to be the calm good guy all the time! So you know what? *You* keep track. *You* get the prescriptions filled. *You* deal with the insurance approvals. *You* keep tabs on the pills that need to be taken, in what order, and at what time. And whether she's got all her appointments scheduled. And when she fails to take her life-saving medication, and is out doing God-knows what, God-knows *where*, *you* try to reach her cardiologist to find out whether she needs to double-up the next day or skip a dose. I'll just swoop in to let you know when you're overreacting and take her out to the movies after to give you some 'space.' Sound good? I'd really like that job so much better!"

"Julia, stop."

I think they'd completely forgotten that I was standing right there.

They hardly ever used to fight. But now they fight about me.

So today I am buckling down. Today I am making amends. I am at the library, staying late after classes to put the finishing touches on my AP Physics report. Now that I've finally turned in my *Grapes of Wrath* essay, it's the last big project that I need to complete in order to graduate. I read over what I've written so far:

Subject: *"Multiple Theories of the Multiverse"*
Thesis: *Physicists have developed a number of theories to explain the true nature of reality. Is our universe infinite? And, if so, is it the only one? In this paper, I will examine the multiple theories put forward to explain the possible structure of a multiverse and make a case for the existence of parallel worlds.*

I guess I could have stuck with the topic I'd originally proposed way back in October: "Exploring Newton's Laws of Motion in Our Everyday Lives." An object in motion stays in motion. Force equals mass times acceleration. For every action there is an equal and opposite reaction. Focusing on classical physics is a safe bet and would have earned me an easy A. But I've always been fascinated by quantum mechanics. Instead of dealing with the behavior of things we can see and measure with certainty, like the distance a ball travels after being hit with a bat or the speed of a car, quantum physics is concerned with the weird and chaotic world of subatomic particles, and what the behavior of these particles might tell us about how *reality* works. It's way more theoretical than classical physics and not even close to certain, but definitely not boring. And if I was going to be stuck in summer school working on this project, I figured that I might as well pick something I've been curious about ever since I watched my first episode of *Doctor Who*: Is our universe the only one?

My report begins with an analysis of the theory of inflation, which is the easiest one to explain: The big bang sent a huge explosion of particles hurtling through space—a massive cosmic dust cloud that to this day continues to expand. Reality, as we know it, took shape thanks to a very specific arrangement of these particles, a configuration that created our galaxy, our solar system, and the planet we call Earth. In a continually inflating and infinite universe, sooner or later this same exact pattern is destined to repeat, creating other worlds out there identical to our own. Warmed by an identical copy of our sun. Orbited by an identical copy of our moon. In this world, a duplicate me might even be writing these exact words, right now. Weird, right?

But not as weird as string theory, which posits that because quantum particles—the smallest units of matter and the building blocks of the universe—behave unpredictably, it's possible that other universes, and the galaxies, stars, and planets within them, have evolved according to completely different sets of physical laws. Universes where time moves backward instead of forward. Universes where there is no gravity. Universes where it's possible to breathe CO_2.

Jane, who I thought had already left for the day, is now reading over my shoulder. "You are a strange person," she says. "No wonder trigonometry makes perfect sense to you."

I turn around. "Jane, are you feeling all right? It's not like you to be here any later than necessary."

She laughs. "I know, right? But I'm only trying to save you from your nerd-girl ways. My friend Aliyah is having a party tonight. You should come." Jane seems to have a lot of friends who throw parties.

"I can't. I have to finish this." And now that I've fully immersed myself in the project, I'm kind of enjoying it too. More than I've enjoyed any school project in a long time.

"Suit yourself," she says. "But also, my mom and stepdad are taking my brothers to a baseball game later. If you change your mind, we can ransack her office for UCSF passwords before the party?"

After the scene yesterday with my parents, I'm not so

sure I want to add hacking into medical records to my list of offenses. I had to promise to check in with them to confirm every single time I take my medication to get out of being grounded over the tattoo. Plus, I already know they are not going to be very cool about me spending another night out with Jane. I never used to come home hungover (and without shoes) when I was with Emma.

"Maybe later this week? My parents are going to kill me if I don't turn this in by next Monday's deadline."

Jane sighs. "All right. But your parallel-universe self is probably going to have a lot more fun tonight than you are. Just saying."

"And you claim to understand nothing about physics," I tell her. "I'll see you tomorrow."

"Maybe," she says as she heads out. "It all depends on how much fun I have tonight."

Jane is on to something, even though she was making a joke. Another Chloe may, in fact, have just walked out the library door with her.

The many-worlds interpretation of quantum mechanics is the one I find the most brain-bending of all. It makes yet another assumption based on the unpredictability of quantum particles. If it's impossible to predict, with absolute certainty, whether a particle will zig, zag, or dance upside down on the ceiling, what if it does all three? This theory suggests that for every action with multiple *possible* outcomes, a parallel reality is created where each potential outcome *actually does happen.*

Multiple possibilities spawn many worlds. It's an incredible idea, almost the stuff of science fiction, but there are more than a few extraordinarily smart physicists who believe it could be possible.

I think back to all the Chloes I saw when I used to close myself inside the three-way mirror in the department-store dressing room with my mom. How I used to wonder "What if?" *What if the first Chloe exits to the right and the second exits left? What if the third forgets to study for tomorrow's math test? What if the fourth gets hit by a bus on her way out of the store?* What if all the "What ifs" happen? What if there are a multitude of universes that represent every choice, every chance, every conceivable possibility encountered by every single particle, every single cell, every single living thing? In an infinite multiverse where no outcome is 100 percent certain, anything that can happen *will* happen.

If the many-worlds theory is true, another universe exists where the genetic quirk that resulted in a defect in my right ventricle never appeared. In this reality, I was born with a perfect, normal heart. There was no collapse during cross-country practice, no desperate wait for a donor, no transplant, no pause in the progress of my life. Somewhere out in the cosmos, I'm carrying on as if nothing significant has changed. I'm preparing to start college in the fall like the rest of my friends—my mind preoccupied with dorm room storage strategies and the undergraduate course catalog. Emma and I spend hours analyzing the personalities of our soon-to-be roommates based on the twenty minutes we've spent talking with each of them on FaceTime. I finished my AP Physics project months ago, when it was originally due. I'm not even wondering "What if?" because nothing has happened to make me consider what my life would have been like now if I hadn't almost died. There's no medication to take every day. Or weird memories. Or dreams of burning tunnels. But also . . . no Jane. No heart tattoo. No learning to surf. No Kai.

And then it hits me. Despite everything that has happened, everything that is messed up and confusing and disorienting right now, everything that is making me doubt who I was and who I am, there's a question in my mind that I'm not sure how I would answer: If I could reroll the dice and have the chance to live in that alternate universe where everything carried on as normal, where there was no fork in the road, no before and after, no heart transplant, would I?

≋≋≋ WE MATCH ≋≋≋

Summer is the season when fog hangs over the coastline like
a wet blanket, often spoiling picnic plans for the tourists who
show up in nothing but T-shirts and shorts. The visitors will
get lucky today, though. This Wednesday is sunny and warm,
with a sky so clear and blue I can see all the way out to the
jagged peaks of the Farallon Islands, where white sharks are
known to glide through the kelp forests, hunting for elephant
seals.

Despite the warmth in the air, I zip up my wetsuit before
I head down the path between the dunes. I tell myself it's
only because the water will still be cold, not because I'm self-
conscious about my scar.

Kai is already on the beach waxing his board, the top
half of his wetsuit unzipped and dangling around his hips. I

hesitate before approaching, not sure how to act when faced with his naked torso, toned from paddling over ocean waves. *Get a grip*, I tell myself. *It's just Kai.* Yes, it *is* just Kai, but usually he's encased up to his neck in neoprene. And, okay, that is a *very* sexy tattoo encircling his left bicep. Which means that he must be at least eighteen. Or a lawbreaker like Jane. And now me too, I guess. He looks up just as I'm about to drop my backpack and board next to him on the sand.

"Hey, Batman," I say, randomly recalling our conversation about surfing and superheroes a few weeks back. It's the first thing—the only thing—that pops into my head. All the skin is scrambling my brain.

"Batman?" He half smiles and makes a what-the-hell-are-you-talking-about? face, clearly not remembering. "Are you supposed to be Robin?"

"No way," I say, slightly embarrassed that I brought up the Batman thing. "Robin sucks."

Kai nods toward the ocean as he pulls on the rest of his suit. "*Waves* suck today." The water is uncharacteristically calm, with only a light ripple of foam softly washing over the shore.

We head out anyway and practice pop-ups until my arms feel like wet noodles. Kai says it's good to work on muscle memory so that when I catch my next real wave, I'll be surer of myself, more centered, less likely to fall off. My balance *is* getting better, and I manage to ride a few baby swells toward the beach, each time feeling more and more at home on the board.

After a while, we give up on the waves and float side by side, straddling our boards as the sun warms our backs. I love the sounds that surround us out here. The water rolling into and away from the shore. The occasional call of a seabird. The soft rush of the briny ocean air in my ears, which has a texture and weight that distinguishes it from the air you breathe most of the time at school or home or walking down the street and never notice. No phones ringing, no chimes indicating incoming notifications and texts. I like that Kai never makes me feel like I have to make conversation about nothing. There are no questions here about how my final summer school projects are coming along or whether I've taken my medication. He doesn't ask about how I'm feeling today or if I've put any more thought into the college acceptance letters that sit, still untouched, on my desk. But then he really doesn't know to ask those questions anyway. To him, I'm the Chloe who knows how to read a surf report and who's able—just barely, but able—to catch a wave. I watch his hand trailing in the water, the tips of his fingers making small currents on the surface.

No surf means that no one else is nearby, aside from an old man doing the breaststroke about twenty yards away. He's wearing only a pair of swim trunks, and I wonder how he's not shivering. Despite the sunny skies, the water still feels pretty cold to me, even in a wetsuit. I look out at the beach, shading my eyes with my hand. A wet golden retriever runs along the shoreline, chasing gulls that circle and swoop around him, always just out of reach. Two blond kids are digging a hole in the sand. The late-afternoon sun sparkles on the surface of the water. Fingertips puckered and wrinkled, I'm just about to suggest heading in when Kai reaches out for my arm.

"Chloe. Look."

A large dark shape is spinning through the water very close to the left side of my board, and for a split second it seems like the world has been put on pause. The golden retriever, the digging kids, the man swimming in the water nearby are frozen in the frame. There is only me and Kai and the shadow spinning toward us. There is no time to move.

The shape flies out of the water, rocking my board back and forth, so close that I can smell it, so close that it showers me with a kaleidoscope of ocean spray.

A dolphin.

And then another. And another.

A whole pod of them keep coming, some leaping like the first one, some circling out of the water in twos and threes, another curious enough to swim around and then under our boards. I reach out and run my hand over a shiny wet back as it passes by. And just as soon as they arrived, they're gone.

Were they even there at all?

I look at Kai. His face confirms that I was not hallucinating.

"Holy shit." He laughs. "That was incredible. I've seen them out here before, but never this close. You touched one."

"I did," I say. "Its skin felt like rubber."

The water around us is still sloshing from the movement of the dolphins, and our boards have drifted a few feet apart. He reaches out for mine and pulls his closer. "I seriously thought you were about to get eaten by a shark."

I don't know what I thought. It all happened so fast, I hardly had time to imagine what kind of animal was moving toward me before it surfaced. But now that the moment has passed, I consider another outcome: an alien black eye, pink gums, and jagged white teeth, the water red with blood. In another universe, I could be dead, the subject of a dramatic reenactment on Shark Week: *Tragically, the young woman had undergone a lifesaving heart transplant less than a year before the fatal attack* . . .

I try to laugh off the idea of a shark encounter, even though in these cold, seal-friendly waters, it's possible. "Guess that would have been bad for your business, huh?"

"Well, I probably would have kept your tragic ending on the down low," he says. "I can't afford to lose any customers." I notice that he's still holding on to my board, his hand slightly behind my back.

The old swimmer man is treading water now and looking our way.

"Your girlfriend must be a mermaid!" he calls.

"I know!" Kai calls back, not bothering to correct the assumption that we are a couple. Our eyes meet and he shrugs.

I can feel a blush blooming on my face and am embarrassed about my body's indifference, yet again, to keeping what's going on in my brain under wraps.

"Think I'm going to head back," I say. "Getting cold!" I dive forward on my board and paddle quickly ahead, not at all cold.

The blond kids, a boy and a girl, are still digging on the shore when I walk out of the water, their sunscreened bodies dusted with a layer of sand like sugared donuts. They are 100 percent focused on their hole, now deep enough for the seawater to seep up and make a little pool at the bottom. Behind me, Kai stops and squats next to them to help them find a sand crab. And then he lets each of them stand on his board, so they can pretend they're surfing. I smile as I watch them. New recruits.

When Kai catches up to me, I sense that the frequency we've been operating on over the preceding weeks has changed. Although we walk together in silence back to where we left our stuff on the beach, the air crackles with electricity. It feels weird to hand Kai cash like I usually do, our business exchange complete. He seems uncomfortable taking it.

As I throw my bag over my shoulder, Kai gestures to my wrist. "You got a tattoo."

"Yes." I hold it out for inspection, my pulse quickening as

he moves close. He pushes up the sleeve of his wetsuit, takes my right hand in his left and holds his right forearm against it. On it is a small heart (traditional, Valentine's Day red) with wings. I hadn't noticed it earlier, when I was too busy trying not to stare at the larger one on his left arm—it's this beautiful geometric design that almost reminds me of a DNA helix.

"We match," he says. "Though yours is *a little* more realistic."

I am acutely aware of his skin touching mine. Can he feel my pulse pounding in my wrist? Is it giving me away? Do I want it to?

"Well, I'm all for accuracy," I say.

We both study the tattoos, the charge in the air giving me goose bumps.

"You'll have to tell me what it means sometime." His voice is quiet.

"You too," I answer.

But today I am not quite ready to share the story of my heart. And neither is he, I think, because a shadow of sadness has fallen across his face, one that I have seen before. His focus seems to have shifted to somewhere far away.

The sun is dropping lower toward the horizon, and people on the beach are packing up their bags and herding their kids toward the parking lot. It is later than I thought, which means I better get a move on if I don't want my parents to make good on their promise to ground me the next time I "forget" to tell them where I am, what I'm doing, and who I'm with.

I take a step back and lock eyes with Kai. There goes my face again. *God.*

"I have to go," I say. "Same time next week?"

Kai hesitates for a second before he answers, like he wants to ask me something. Or maybe I'm just reading *waaaay* too much into a pause.

"Sure," he says. "Same time next week."

 ICE

I can still feel the warmth of Kai's skin next to mine as I make my way up the path between the dunes. I'm anxious to be on the road, hoping I won't get caught up in rush-hour traffic. I've lost track of time again, something that I rarely did before. In fact, punctuality was one of my more reliable traits. But, in a larger sense, I think about "Time with a capital *T*" constantly, and about how our perception of it can seem so inconsistent. The days I spent in the hospital and at home after my transplant felt endless, made all the more excruciating when I considered what I was missing in the reality that existed for my healthy friends and classmates: holiday celebrations, prom, spring break. But today—sun-kissed, exhilarating, perfect—seemed to come and go in an instant. It's like the universe purposely screws with us. *You hate*

seventh-period PE? Well, time is going to slow to a crawl for that one! Ha ha ha!

My feet sink deep into the sand, and I stop to reposition my board and my bag, which are feeling heavy as I struggle up the path. I adjust the straps of the bag, shift the board, and then I notice it: a small but undeniable sensation of pain, like a trickle of ice-cold water seeping through my chest.

I lower my board and plant it vertically in the sand. I'm having trouble catching my breath. The world begins to spin like a too-fast merry-go-round and the images flash again— the dog, the tunnel, the dying woman, the man from my hospital room—making me feel light-headed and nauseous. I start to break out in a cold, clammy sweat and grab onto the board to ground myself. I need to stay calm. Breathe. So I can figure out what's happening. Is it my heart? *The* heart. This stranger's heart, finally rebelling against a body that doesn't belong to it?

No, I tell myself. No. No. No. It's nothing. I am being paranoid. This is in my head. Not my heart.

Kai is still on the beach. I imagine him finding me here, slumped over in the sand, face white, gasping for breath. I picture the look of surprise on his face when he says, "Chloe, are you okay?"

No. That is not going to happen. I am fine. *Fine.*

And just as quickly as the sensation arrived, it's gone. My heart rate returns to normal. The warm, perfect day envelops me in its beauty just as it had moments before. I hear the soft rush of the surf, watch a tern dip into the grasses between the dunes.

I pick up my board, loosen the collar of my wetsuit, and continue along the path to the parking lot.

It was nothing. Nothing at all.

The next day at school, I find Jane in the library, working—for a change—on her trig homework.

"Let's do it," I tell her.

"Do what?" she asks.

"Look up the medical records. Let's do it after school today."

Gather data. Collect evidence.

I'm going to get to the bottom of this . . . this *whatever* that's going on between my head and my heart, once and for all.

≋ HELLO, HEART ≋

You'd be surprised at how easy it is to hack into a hospital's medical records system. No special computer skills or coding genius are required. Consider all the doctors, nurses, and other staff who have access. And of that group, more than a few are lazy with their passwords—making them too easy to guess or writing them down somewhere so they don't forget. All you need to do is find one of those people. Just one.

Jane's mom.

Who is currently wending her way home from work in the northbound rush hour while Jane's stepdad, Paul, is with her brothers—the "terror twins," as she calls them—at their swim lesson. It takes us about five minutes to locate the password, which, as Jane suspected, was written in a small notebook that we found in the top drawer of her mom's desk.

"Social security number?" Jane is seated in front of an iMac, hands poised above the keyboard. We start with my records. Although my mom has copies of just about every biopsy, scan, EKG, and test result connected to my own case, I'm thinking the hospital's file on me might be linked to the record of my donor, or at least contain some identifying information. An address. A birth date. A name.

I tell her my social security number and she types it in.

"What was the date of your transplant again?" Jane asks.

"December eighteenth. Last year."

She types. Points. Clicks.

"Here it is." She reads a note from my record. "Patient, Chloe Russell, notified of available donor on December eighteenth at eight p.m. Admitted to the transplant center at nine twenty-five p.m."

That night. I remember it like a movie of someone else's life, one that I can replay scene for scene, but instead of *being* the main character, I'm only watching her.

I was so sick by then, I didn't even look like me. I had lost weight—too much for my small frame—and, aside from the dark circles under my eyes, my skin was so pale it was almost translucent. I looked like a vampire. Not the sexy kind. The skinny, scary, horror-movie kind. I see my parents helping me into the car and my dad throwing my bag—packed weeks before, when I was moved to the top of the recipient list— into the back. There's even a soundtrack. My dad had made a heart-themed playlist when we got the news that I was next in line on the list, which he put on to lighten the mood once we were on our way: Janis Joplin, "Piece of My Heart"; Stevie Nicks and Tom Petty, "Stop Draggin' My Heart Around"; Bonnie Tyler, "Total Eclipse of the Heart." It helped, a little. Dad's dated musical tastes at least gave us something to talk about, aside from the fact that we were all terrified. Hopeful and wired and excited too, but mainly terrified. I knew this was my last chance at staying alive. If the transplant didn't succeed, there would be no returns or exchanges on hearts. And, although they would never say it, I know my parents were thinking the same: should anything go wrong, and there were multiple things that could go wrong, this might be the last ride we would take together as a family.

"There better not be any Celine Dion on here," my mom said as we pulled onto the freeway.

"Of course not," my dad answered. "What kind of a monster do you think I am?"

I was pretty short of breath, even with the portable oxygen tank, but managed to add, "I guarantee you there's some Elton John, though."

By the time we reached the Golden Gate Bridge, a heavy fog had settled and we could barely see the taillights of the car ahead of us. Elton John and Kiki Dee's duet "Don't Go Breaking My Heart" (of course) was playing then, but we had stopped making jokes. My dad got quiet and concentrated on driving as swiftly as possible in the fog. My mom sat with me in the back and held my hand tight, going over the check-in details as if we were simply on our way to the airport for a family trip. I think she hoped that as long as we followed the instructions and stuck to the plan, it would all come out okay.

Jane starts paging through links and tabs, opening windows that display EKG readouts and X-ray images.

"Whoa, is that your heart?"

She points to an image of a chest X-ray, the contrast dye casting the arteries and veins of the heart in an eerie neon glow. I stare at the X-ray. Is it my former heart? Or the donor's heart? It's hard to tell without comparing them, side by side.

I do know that mine was abnormally enlarged, the myocardium having grown thick and scarred from the damage caused by ARVD. But I don't remember having any imaging done on the night of my transplant. The doctors already knew the condition of my heart by then:

F-.

"I think it's the X-ray they did on my donor," I say to Jane. This is the first time I've actually seen a picture of it.

Hello, heart.

I'm mesmerized by the image, so much so that I can almost see it beating right there on the screen in front of us, in time with the real-life twin in my chest.

"That. Is. *So*. Cool," Jane says. "It looks like your tattoo."

"Well, technically, my tattoo looks like the heart."

Jane rolls her eyes. "Whatever, nerd." She and I stare at the X-ray for a few more seconds before she clicks the image away and starts scrolling again. She scrolls and reads. Reads and scrolls. Until she whacks my arm, hard.

"Chloe! Here!"

Jane looks at me and grins like she just found the answer key for the trig final.

"I think this is a file on your donor." She clicks on a tab and starts scanning the information on the screen. But, as I slide my chair closer, her triumphant hacker face fades. "Wait . . . what? *Goddamnit!*"

"What? *What?*" I'm trying to read what she's reading, but her head is blocking my view. I gently nudge her aside so I can see.

"The name, birth date, and social are blacked out. Why would they do that?"

I know why.

"It's to keep the identity confidential," I say, reminding her of what I'd told her when I arrived at her house about an hour ago and almost chickened out about doing this. About my conversation with Dr. Ahmadi, when he confirmed that my donor's family did not want to be contacted.

"Shit. I can't look up your donor's full medical record without a name or number."

I guess this hacking thing is going to be a little trickier than we'd anticipated after all.

We continue reading through the file, just in case there's

anything useful. And, even though all the identifying information about my donor is blocked out, there are some other details.

Blood type, for example. My donor's was O positive, the same as my own.

This I already knew.

There are also EKG readings, echocardiogram results, enzyme tests, and even size measurements—all done on the night of the transplant to confirm that the organ I was about to receive was healthy and undamaged by whatever it was that had proved fatal to my donor's brain. Then, a single entry, near the bottom of the page. Cause of death: head trauma.

A loud, sickening crack.

"What do you think happened?" Jane asks.

I shrug, even though I'm pretty sure I know the answer.

Blood washes over my eyes.

"Probably an accident of some kind."

On a motorcycle. In a tunnel. The one I relive every night.

"That's really sad."

"Yeah," I say. "It is."

One second you are here, and the next . . . there's nothing. It's the "nothing" part that's the worst.

Maybe we shouldn't be doing this. It feels weird. Wrong.

Just as I am about to tell Jane that we should stop, she yells *"HA!"* and practically pushes me off my chair.

"Chloe! Look! Sloppy record keeping. They forgot to delete the address."

"What address?" I ask as I squint at the line she's pointing at.

52 Frances Street, Berkeley, California.

A home address. My *donor's* home address.

Jane grabs a Post-it pad and copies it down. She yanks the note off the pad and offers it to me.

I stare at it for a second. Do I really want to do this? Looking up information without anyone knowing about it is one thing, but showing up at someone's door?

"I don't know," I tell Jane. "What am I supposed to do with this? Ring their doorbell and say what? I have your daughter's, or your wife's, or your husband's heart? I think I may have inherited their memories? I tried to contact you but you didn't want to meet me so I hacked into UCSF's medical records system to track down your address like a creepy stalker?"

Jane sighs.

"*Obviously* you aren't going to do that, Chloe. Have you considered, perhaps, not telling them who you are? At least not right away."

"Lying."

"Selectively leaving out some details."

This too seems wrong. But something is compelling me to do it anyway.

"All right," I finally say to Jane. "A selective introduction. What are you doing tomorrow?"

School. We both have school.

"I think I'm coming down with a cold," I say. "That's contagious."

Jane needs little incentive to ditch.

She spins around in her mom's desk chair and yells, "Achoo!"

 **DIGGING**

I am digging in a patch of earth with my bare hands. The ground is thick with roots. I tear and pull at them as my nails break and bleed. I'm frantic to find something. Something I need.

The soil is warm. Moist. It smells of copper. Of compost. Dead leaves. I keep digging until my hands touch something rubbery, about the size of a baseball. I pull at it, hard, until it releases, trailing a dirt-encrusted and tangled knot of roots.

Only they aren't roots. They're blood vessels.

I'm wiping soil away from a human heart. And somehow I know, am *sure*, that it's *my* heart. The one that I was born with. The one that was taken from me. I hold it in my bleeding hands and I realize that it's moving. Pulsing. Alive.

Something wet and wriggling clings to my wrist.

A maggot.

It's stuck to my skin. Another squirms between my fingers. And then hundreds of them are falling from my heart, falling in clumps on top of each other in a writhing pile on the ground. I drop the heart, shake my hands in panic, scream—

I'm still screaming when my mom shakes me awake.

"Chloe! It's a dream. It's just a dream."

I stare at her, still imagining that I feel maggots crawling all over my hands. Crawling all over my heart.

"What, honey? What were you dreaming of?"

"I can't remember," I lie.

"You're as white as a ghost," my mom says. "Are you feeling all right?"

"I'm fine," I say.

"Are you short of breath?"

"No."

"Dizzy?"

"No."

"Chest pain?"

"Mom, no."

What have I done to her? I honestly think *she* might have PTSD from my heart transplant.

"Maybe I should stay home."

No, no, no. Jane and I are ditching today. She cannot stay home.

"Mom. It was just a dream. I'm fine. Really."

I make a goofy face to show her that it's all good.

My mom hesitates for a few more seconds.

"Okaaay," she says, with the worry line between her eyebrows fully deployed. "Call if you need me. I've got meetings, but just in San Francisco, so I'm not far."

"Will do," I answer, mentally willing her to get a move on.

Jane texts, *Here!* when she arrives; I find her outside on a black motorcycle, holding an extra helmet and looking like a badass.

"Birthday present from my dad," she says. "My mom is pissed, which was probably his main objective. The twins are *so* jealous."

"It's your birthday?" I ask.

"Last week," Jane responds.

I wonder why she didn't mention it. And I have to admit, I'm kind of floored by the extravagance of her present. My parents usually just take me out to dinner.

"Your dad must not worry much," I say, glad that my own dad is away at a conference and my mom is already en route to San Francisco. They would definitely not be cool with me riding a motorcycle, even if I was only going around the block, let alone across the San Francisco Bay.

Jane shrugs.

"Maybe we should take my car," I say. One week doesn't seem like a whole lot of time for her to practice her motorcycling skills.

Jane shakes her head. "Are you serious? There's no way

we're taking your Honda when I've got *this*." She tosses the extra helmet at me.

It *is* a beautiful bike. I'm already imagining what it will be like to streak across the bay on it, wind rushing, but . . .

I wave my phone at her. "How are you going to hear me navigating?"

She points to the bike. "It's got GPS."

"Oh." I hadn't realized motorcycles came with GPS, but this one—sleek and modern with a pristine matte-black finish—looks pretty high-tech. Like something a character in a dystopian sci-fi movie might ride. I pull up the address on my phone, which I had transferred from the Post-it. It takes her a little while to figure out how to get everything set up on the GPS, which makes me wonder for a few seconds how many times she's actually ridden this bike.

In the meantime, I strap my helmet on. It smells of new plastic and foam padding.

"Got it!" Jane looks up from the GPS screen. "Ready?"

I climb on the bike and circle my arms around Jane's leather-clad waist.

"Ready."

She starts it up.

"Happy belated birthday!" I yell over the growl of the engine as the bike lurches away from the driveway, wobbling as we pick up speed.

It's soon clear that "motorcycle operation" is an activity that Jane is unprepared to maneuver through with her usual, oversize confidence. At the fourth intersection, a car behind us blares its horn as the light turns green and she stalls out for the third time. I decide to intervene. "Oh my god, Jane, pull over! *Pull over!*" I yell as loud as I can in the direction of her ear. She swerves abruptly toward the sidewalk, bumping the curb hard.

"What?" Jane lifts up her face shield. Her brow and cheeks are slick with sweat.

"You're going to drop us." She looks at me blankly. "You know, tip the bike over? Did anyone teach you how to ride this?"

Jane looks embarrassed, which would make this the first time I've seen Jane embarrassed about anything. "It's not as easy as it looks."

A peculiar feeling comes over me, like some impulse, buried way back in my consciousness, is trying to break through.

"Let me try." I hop off and order her to slide back, which she does. It's funny how well people listen when you seem completely sure of yourself.

"You didn't tell me you knew how to ride," Jane says.

I don't. But what's weird is that the gears, the foot pedals, and many of the instruments on the bike feel familiar. "You didn't tell me you *don't*," I reply.

I climb back on, in front this time, grab hold of the handlebars, roll the bike away from the curb, and hammer the accelerator with my right hand. We take off into traffic, speed through a yellow light near the shopping center where I got my ears pierced when I was eight, and curve up the entrance ramp to the freeway. I hear Jane let out a whoop behind me. My entire body is tingling.

Holy shit.

The feeling that I have done this before is so powerful, so certain. But I know I haven't. I've never even sat on a motorcycle, forget having ridden one.

This can't be possible. It can't.

Memory is a function of the brain. The heart is an organ that pumps blood. You can't acquire neurological processes through a heart. Not. Possible.

And yet here I am, weaving a Ducati in and out of traffic like I've done it hundreds of times.

As we sweep across the Richmond-San Rafael Bridge, the speedometer ticks to fifty . . . sixty . . . sixty-five . . . seventy. A roaring wall of wind pastes my too-light jacket against the front of my chest and rattles the face shield of my helmet. But despite my nightly death-by-motorcycle dreams, I am curiously not afraid. I want to go faster.

Faster.

Faster.

Faster.

The rippling surface of the water streaks by beneath us, the Bay Bridge in sight to the right, the Berkeley Hills in view up ahead. We are almost across the bridge when images start to flash across my brain: A street sign. An Indian restaurant. A bookstore called the Cat's Corner.

A realization dawns on me: I already know the way. I don't have to look at the GPS. I haven't *been* looking at the GPS. I *know*. Exit 12 off of 580 at Gilman, turn left on Hopkins, right on Sacramento, and then left again at Frances, just past the restaurant and the bookstore.

Why—no, *how* do I know this? *Feel* this? Or maybe it's not *me* that knows. Could it be the heart? Like a distress beacon, finding its way home?

A shiver runs through the center of my chest as I steer the bike toward the Gilman Street exit. *Left on Hopkins, right on Sacramento, and then left again at Frances.* Even though I'm anxious about who or what I might find there—*will it be the man from the hospital?*—I have to follow through. I have to know.

Especially now.

Frances Street is a bit nicer than the busier streets nearby. It's lined with mature trees and small but charming Craftsman-style houses. I spot it right away: nicely kept and painted robin's-egg blue. As we pull up, I recognize the gravel drive, the purple hydrangeas, and white porch swing. In my mind's eye, I see an olive tree in the backyard, and a silver-gray dog—*the* silver-gray dog—lying on a redbrick patio, next to a neglected garden bed. My head is humming.

I stop the bike and sit for a minute, staring at the house.

"Is this the right address?" Jane asks as she climbs off.

"Yeah," I say, even before I see the number hanging above the doorbell. I pull off my helmet. But once I'm standing on the sidewalk, I feel frozen in place, not sure what to do next. "Jane," I whisper. "I *recognize* this place."

She looks at me with a curious expression. "You mean, like, you've been here before?"

"No," I say. "I haven't. And I've never ridden a motorcycle before today either."

She nods slowly, looking a little unnerved. "Well, that's interesting."

For once, she doesn't have much else to say.

I look at the house and then back at Jane. I'm afraid to knock on that front door. But I try to push back the fear and summon up my scientific side. The side that knows you have to collect data to learn anything. And that's why I'm here, isn't it? To get answers. About my donor. About my heart. About whatever the fuck is happening to me right now.

"I think I need to do this by myself," I tell her.

"Sure," Jane says. "I get it. I'll be here if you need me, especially since I can't go anywhere else without causing a major traffic incident."

I hesitate for a few more seconds.

"You can do it," she assures me.

"Okay, then." I hand her my helmet. "Here goes."

≈≈≈

A guy with a baby attached to his chest opens the door as I walk up the steps.

Not the man from the hospital. The one with the tattoo.

"Hi," he says. "Can I help you?" I'm not sure if he'd heard me coming up the walk or if they were already on their way out. The baby wears a sun hat and peers at me with big brown eyes.

A young dad. A baby.

I freeze again.

Oh, god.

Ten minutes ago, as I was racing across the bridge, I was so sure of myself. Sure that this is what I needed to do. And now, face-to-face with this man and this child, I start to wonder what the hell I was thinking. What if the heart belonged to his girlfriend or his wife? What if this man standing in front of me had *lost his wife*? What if this adorable baby chewing its drool-covered fist is now *motherless*? The two of them look like they're ready to go on a walk. It's a beautiful day. And here I am, about to drop a bomb on their front porch.

I recall Dr. Ahmadi's words again: *Your donor's family has made it clear that they do not wish to be contacted.*

My mind is reeling. What *was* I going to say, anyway? Now that I am standing here, I realize that I should have practiced. I should have come up with a plausible cover story. I don't even have a name to ask about. I decide that rather than simply being selective about the details, I'm just going to lie if I have to. Lie about how I got the address. Lie about why I'm here and what I'm looking for.

I smile at the baby and try to calm myself down. "I'm so sorry to bother you, but I'm looking for the family of someone who may have lived here back in December. Someone who . . ." My voice trails off. But while I'm thinking of what else to say, I get yet another strong, almost certain feeling: these two are not my donor's family. The house is so familiar, but this man and his child are not.

"Hmm," he shakes his head. "You're looking for someone who lived here in December? We moved in in February this year. I think it was vacant before then. Are you sure you've got the right address?"

I don't know whether to be disappointed that he's probably not going to be able to tell me anything useful or relieved that he's not grieving my heart donor. But this house . . . *I know this house.*

Prove it, I tell myself. Gather data. Collect evidence.

"Is there an olive tree and redbrick patio in your backyard?" I ask, and then hold my breath, not sure if I'm hoping to be right or wrong.

"Yeah, there is." He looks surprised that I know this. *Not as surprised as I am.*

No, more than surprised. *Stunned. Completely freaked out.*

There might not be a word in existence that describes how I'm feeling right now.

"I'm sure I have the right address," I say.

"Well, we just rent here. My wife started a fellowship at Berkeley in the spring. Don't know who was living here before us. Sorry."

I catch the scent of an overgrown rosemary shrub near the porch and a feeling of déjà vu overwhelms me so strongly that I can hardly breathe.

I remember.

I remember brushing my hand across the rosemary as I climbed the porch steps, stirring up its piney scent. I remember wheeling a motorcycle from the small garage in the back. Pulling a vinyl record from a collection stacked inside the dining room's built-in shelves. I remember the silver-gray dog sprawled on its back on the sofa. And I remember the woman—the one I think about, the one I dream about, the one whose image materializes in my brain like the ghost of someone I used to know—I remember her sitting at the kitchen table, coffee cup next to her and a book in her hand. Only this time, she's not wearing a cap and her light-gold hair is tucked behind her ears.

There are also things that I *know*. I know that the porch swing creaks when you push it back too far, that you need a lighter to start the white Wedgewood stove in the kitchen, and that the backyard patio is cracked in one spot, but cool and quiet and the perfect place to kick back and look up at the sky through olive branches when you need to clear your head and think. I *know*.

I feel unsteady, unmoored, as though I might fall.

"Are you okay? You look a little pale," says the man. "Sorry I can't help."

The baby squirms in the carrier, impatient for movement, new sights and sounds.

"I'm fine," I say, suddenly having the urge to flee. *You shouldn't be here*, I think. *This is not your home. These are not your memories. This is too weird, too disorienting, too impossible.* "Thanks anyway."

But as I head back down the familiar stepping-stone path that led me to the front door, the man calls me back.

"Hang on a sec."

The clock on the stove doesn't work.

He pulls his phone out of his back pocket and looks up a number.

The spare key is hidden under a clay pot in the backyard.

"Our landlord. He may know where the people who lived here before us went. Feel free to give him a call." He pulls up the number on his phone and holds it up so I can copy it down in mine.

"Thanks," I say.

"No problem. I hope you find your friend."

My friend. How funny that sounds. How strange. What *do* you call the person who gave you a heart?

I don't know how many seconds, or even minutes, go by before I can recover. It's Jane's voice that brings me back to the present.

"Well?" She's leaning on the bike, looking to anyone passing by like a person who knows exactly what she's doing. Before we became friends, I would have thought so too. But the more I get to know Jane, the more I realize that her bravado is sometimes just a mask, one she wears so that she feels strong and invincible, even when she's not. Not always, but sometimes. And it's not just her. I put on my science-nerd mask when I'm thrown by something that I can't explain. Emma puts on her "perfect daughter" one when she's too afraid to say what she really thinks. It's hard to live without them when you're still trying to figure out who you really are.

I stop on the sidewalk in front of her.

"The people who live here now didn't live here in December," I say, still trying to collect my thoughts. "The old tenants moved out. I got the landlord's number."

"And you're going to call, right?" she asks. "Today?"

"Yes," I promise.

"Cool." She hands me the helmet she's been holding. "All right, Daughter of Anarchy, take me home. Or to a biker bar."

I wait until later, when I'm home alone, to call. The landlord answers after four rings. This time, I do have a cover story. I tell him I'd sold an armoire to a person who lived in his rental house back in the fall and that I recently had found the key for it. I tell him that I lost the buyer's phone number.

"Sarah Harris?" he asks.

"Yes, that's right," I say, trying to keep my voice calm and normal, even as the heart in my chest starts to thump. "Sarah. Do you happen to know how I can reach her?"

The line goes silent for a second, and then he says, "I'm sorry, but you can't reach her. She didn't move. She died."

I pause, feeling like my entire circulatory system is pulsing in response.

She *died*.

"When?" I ask.

"December."

Oh. I almost feel like I'm about to laugh. Or do something similarly inappropriate, because I'm thrown, even though I shouldn't be. Sarah Harris is probably not going to be able to tell me more about my heart donor because in all likelihood she *was* my heart donor. I don't know why I wasn't expecting this as a possibility. I just assumed the tenant I was looking for would be a parent or a partner or spouse. Not the *one*. But of course this makes sense. The Frances Street house is, after all, the address that was in the file. My donor's address. Maybe she lived alone.

"Did she . . . I mean, is there anyone I should follow up with about this key?"

The landlord is quiet again.

"Not that I know of. Not now. A friend of hers moved everything out. The whole thing . . . very tragic."

"Do you happen to have her —?"

But he interrupts me before I can finish. "I'm sorry. I don't feel very good sharing personal information about a tenant.

153

You understand. I wouldn't worry about the key. The armoire is gone."

And before I can ask any more questions, he hangs up.

After the call, I can't turn off my spinning brain.

Sarah Harris.

Of course. She's the woman in my head. The one I remember. It's her. It *has* to be her. I remember her dying. I remember her living too. Smiling. Crying. Laughing. Sitting at the kitchen table. Standing on a beach. Driving in a car with the window down, hair flying. Lying in a hospital bed. How could I not have realized? The answer was right there in my head all along, waiting for me to connect the dots, waiting for me to solve for *x* to figure it out. These memories are Sarah Harris's memories. This *heart* was Sarah Harris's heart.

I call Jane and tell her that we have to go back to the records, because now I have a name.

"From the landlord?" she asks.

"Yeah," I say. "Sarah Harris. She was the previous tenant. And Jane . . . she's gone. She died."

"You think she's your heart donor?"

"Yeah," I say. "She must be, right? But I guess the only way to know for sure is to go back to the records. Now that we have her name, we can look her up."

"Ah, god*damnit*," Jane says. "I can't tomorrow. I'm at my dad's this weekend. And my mom is going to be around the house early in the week. We need her computer to get into the hospital's network. Maybe Thursday night? I'm supposed to be watching the twins, but as long as I let them on the Xbox, they won't bother us."

"Okay," I say, but I'm ready to jump out of my skin. Thursday is six days away, and even though I feel that Sarah Harris must be my donor, my head still needs confirmation—*proof*—of what I'm feeling in my heart.

 WAVES

What makes us who we are? Do we actually have souls that exist apart from our flesh, blood, and bones? Or are our personalities determined by the cells that surge through our bodies and the codes embedded in our DNA? Where do our thoughts and memories fit in?

I think of all the bits and pieces of my existence that I have stored up over seventeen years. The things I've learned. The names and faces of the people I love. The feel of sand sifting through my fingers. The smell of the warm, freshly laundered sheets my mom used to dump over my head when I was little. My dad cooking pancakes and bacon on Saturday mornings. Running. Laughing so hard while sitting at Emma's kitchen table that milk exploded out of my nose. The first time I saw snow. Where does all that go when we die? All of my memories, all the things I believe and know, all the colors that I've seen, all the voices and music and words that I've heard, the textures that I have touched, will they still exist somewhere out there in the cosmos? Will they continue to drift through time and space? Like waves?

I pull off the shirt I just put on five minutes ago and toss it on the floor. As I root through my closet for another, I decide that I hate every single item of clothing I own. I want something different. Something that will make me feel less . . . annoyed. Less unsettled. Less like this person caught in some weird limbo-land where nothing about me feels quite right. A new wardrobe. Maybe that will do the trick. I could get a cool haircut like Jane, put on a fabulous new outfit, and maybe everything will be better, like on one of those make-over shows on TV.

What would Sarah Harris wear? I say to the me who looks back from the closet door mirror.

Are her memories the ones that won't stop living in my head? The tunnel. The hospital. The dog. Did she ride a motor-cycle? Did she know the man who visited my room after my transplant? How old was she? I Googled her last night but didn't come up with much. All the Facebook and Instagram profiles I found for "Sarah Harris" were for people who are currently active. So, unless she's posting updates from the afterworld, they're not hers. I also tried a number of different spelling combinations, all of which yielded similar results. It's like she was a ghost, even when she was alive.

There is one more thing I can do on Monday: request a death certificate. Provided I'm spelling her name right, the Alameda County records department should have one on file, which would confirm the specific date and cause of her death. But, according to the county website, this will take at least a week.

In the meantime, I have five more days until I can get back into the medical records system with Jane. Five long days, which makes me wish that I could surf this weekend. I wish I could paddle out into the ocean and forget about my donor's heart, my donor's life, my donor's death. For a little while, at least. But my parents are around all weekend, and they still have no idea that I've been spending so much of my time this summer getting pummeled by ocean waves. And after the tattoo and forgetting to take my pills the night I stayed in the city with Jane, I don't think now is a good time to tell them. I have a movie date with Emma, anyway. This Saturday is her last in town before she drives across the country to move in to her dorm at Brown. We will go to dinner at the restaurant that's been our favorite since we were twelve — the one with a menu the size of a book. It's the place where we always used to celebrate our birthdays. Now it's just where we go, even if the food doesn't seem quite as fancy as it once did.

I pick Emma up in my car. She jumps quickly into the passenger seat and seems more relaxed than she did the last time

I saw her, at her graduation party. Maybe it's because she's about to put a few thousand miles between her and her mom.

"I can't believe it," she says, letting out a sigh of relief. "There's actually nothing left for me to do."

"Oh, come on," I say as I pull away from the curb. "Surely there's something you've forgotten to pick up at The Container Store."

"Oh my God, Mia won't stop talking about her drawer organizers."

"Well, life is hardly worth living without well-organized drawers. You don't want to waste any time searching for clean underwear."

She laughs. "God help Alexis."

"Are you excited for your trip?" I ask. "Where are you and Lily going to stop?"

Emma is going to spend a few weeks driving cross-country with Lily Kim, who is also going to a school on the East Coast, before freshman orientation starts.

"I don't even know yet!" says Emma. "We're just going to wing it."

"Whoa," I say. "I figured your mom would have required your daily itinerary."

"Ha ha," says Emma. "Well, I reminded her that adventurous travel is the perfect opportunity to build 'grit,' a trait essential to entrepreneurship."

"Good one," I tell her.

"Believe it or not, I've never seen the Grand Canyon," says Emma. "Or maybe we'll go to New Orleans."

"The perfect spot for the Vampire Princess!"

"Oh my God, that reminds me: my mom almost threw her out last week. She's into this purging our clutter kick right now, even though, well, you've seen my house. There's really no clutter. Can you believe it?"

"Yes." I laugh.

She grins. "I managed to rescue her from the curb, thankfully. She's in the trunk of my car."

"Excellent," I say. "Very bad luck to leave her behind."

"She'll be our mascot for the road trip," Emma says.

I feel a twinge of jealousy when Emma says this. *Our* means Emma and Lily. Not Emma and me. But hopefully the princess carries a little piece of our friendship with her.

The rest of the night is pretty mellow. We haven't seen much of each other this summer and don't have a lot to talk about. We both seem grateful for the movie so we don't have to.

I still feel really sad though. We've imagined going away to college for what seems like forever, and now it's really happening. For Emma. It's weird to think of her and all the kids that I've spent the last eight, ten, even twelve years of my life with heading off in separate directions. While I remain, the only one standing still.

Part of me knows that I would've felt sad even if I were going off to college too. Emma is my best childhood friend.

She is blanket forts and science experiments and baking projects and skating at Snoopy's Ice Rink at Christmas and first crushes and birthday sleepovers and summer camp. And in a few days, she'll be gone. At least the Emma that I know will be. She'll be different the next time I see her. So will I. I already am.

I want to ask Emma if she's sad too, but maybe she feels the opposite. Or, worse, maybe she feels sorry for me because I'm being left behind.

The lights in front of her house click on automatically when I pull up to drop her off.

"Good luck, and please don't forget to have some fun." I lean over and give her a hug, and she embraces me back tightly.

"Take care of yourself, Chloe," she says. When she pulls away, it looks like she's starting to cry.

"Are you okay, Em?" I ask.

"What if I made the wrong choice?" she asks.

"About Brown?"

"No, about engineering."

"You can change your mind."

"Yeah, I guess," she says. Then she laughs an embarrassed laugh. "Oh, I'm fine! It's just weird, you know? Moving away, saying goodbye, all of it."

"Well, you'll be back for breaks, right?"

"Thanksgiving."

"So I'll see you at Thanksgiving."

"Yes, see you then." She gives me one more quick hug, and then hops out of the car. But before she turns to the house, she leans back in. "I hope you figure everything out. I mean, you will. I know you will."

I wait till Emma is safely inside before I drive away. All this time, I thought she had no idea what was going on with me. That she was oblivious to my confusion, my doubts, my inability to reengage with my old life. I thought she was too focused on the road ahead to notice that I had drifted sideways. But I was wrong. And maybe I'm also wrong in being a bit envious that Emma seems to have her life all figured out. Like Jane, like me, like probably everybody else we know, maybe she's just been pretending that she's sure of herself. Maybe she's feeling just as weird as me, even without a new heart.

I wish her a road trip full of surprises.

YOU DON'T
〜〜〜 BELONG HERE 〜〜〜

The following Wednesday, Sarah Harris is still on my mind as I steer my Honda down the curving road to the beach. I dreamed about her last night. In my dream, she and the woman with the blue-green eyes I keep remembering in fragments were one and the same. She looked frail and gaunt and wore a hospital gown over her birdlike frame. A bandage was wound around her head. I sat next to her bed in a room that was otherwise bare and empty, like a prison cell. I asked her if she was my heart donor, and she just looked at me and laughed. But it wasn't a joyful laugh. It was a laugh that sounded angry and unhinged. It sounded all wrong. And later, as I raced through the nightmare tunnel to yet again meet my death, her laughter echoed in my head.

It's one more day until I meet up with Jane. One more day until we can at least confirm that Sarah was, in fact, my heart donor. And if she was, then I'll have to figure out a way to find somebody who knew her so that they can tell me more.

When I arrive at the beach, Kai is scanning the water, thinking, I assume, about the best path for our paddle out. The wind is strong this afternoon, and the waves look wild and chaotic.

"I don't know," he says, not turning to look at me. "Maybe we should bail."

"Why?"

"Surf's bigger than I was expecting. I'm not sure you're ready for this water."

This makes me bristle. It's not like he's the wave police.

"I want to try it."

It's not just that I want to. I *have* to. Surfing is the only thing that allows me not to think. Only feel. I need this today.

"See that riptide over to the right? Might be tough for you to paddle through it."

"I can do it," I say.

"You think, or you know?"

"I know. C'mon, the meter's running for your paying customer over here."

I see the muscle in his jaw tense ever so slightly.

"Let's go, then," he says.

I hurry to keep up with him as he heads toward the water.

He seems impatient today. Not in the mood to chat. Not the Kai from last week, who asked about my tattoo and touched his skin to mine.

We paddle out and watch the waves in silence, waiting for one that looks right. The sun is a pale white disk behind thick clouds, trying in vain to break through. Picking up ribbons of kelp as it races our way, the steely water gathers height ahead of us.

I hear Kai's voice to my right. "Go!"

I paddle fast toward the incoming wave, position myself for the pop-up, and remain upright for a few seconds before slipping off into the water as it sweeps me toward the beach. But I don't get pulled under, which is progress, I guess.

"You're hesitating too much," he says after riding in behind me. "Once you're up, you have to commit. Try it again." He reaches out a hand to help me up, but I ignore it and push myself out of the surf.

I try it again.

And again.

And again.

And again.

After an hour or so, I'm starting to feel rubbery-armed and tired, but I have at least managed a few respectable rides. I'm getting better at reading how a wave is going to break and at coordinating my body with the movement of the board. At falling without nearly killing myself.

Kai hasn't yet cracked a smile, but when we are done, he says, "Nice surfing today. You won't need me much longer."

I know he means this as a compliment, but I almost feel offended. Disappointed, for sure. Who am I going to surf with if I don't surf with Kai? I can't imagine paddling out there with anyone else.

"Well, you still have to show me how to do a three-sixty," I say, recalling how he'd launched himself off the waves a few weeks back.

He nods. "Yeah . . . the three-sixty. I don't know if I can really teach you that. You just have to feel it."

"I have to feel it," I say, rolling my eyes. "Is this some kind of surfer Buddha bullshit or something?"

"What? No." He runs a hand through his hair and looks out at the ocean. Why is he being so weird and evasive today? Maybe he's just pissed about the shitty weather.

The wind is picking up and the waves are getting wilder and more powerful, pounding hard against the shore. *Thump. Roar. Thump. Roar.* Most of the surfers who had been out there with us are starting to come in. *Thump. Roar.* And suddenly, I feel compelled to go back out. Alone. To prove that I don't need him to surf with me. That I *can* do it by myself. Because eventually I will have to.

I fasten the collar of my wetsuit. Pick up my board.

"I think I'm going to go back out," I say.

"Now?"

"It's okay, you don't need to come with me." I shoot Kai what I hope is a supremely confident look. "Our hour is done. I don't want to keep you."

"Chloe . . . don't. It's not safe."

"There are still people out there." I point to the few still bobbing in the water beyond the impact zone.

"Yeah, well, they are either really experienced with big waves or really stupid. We'll find out which soon enough."

But I barely hear what he's saying because I'm already stalking toward the surf. I can do this. I just need to get past the area where the breaking waves could break one of my bones. The wind whips across my face and nearly knocks me sideways when a gust catches on my board. I think I hear a fragment of Kai's voice, my name, but it's hard to tell. The roaring water and wind drown out every other sound. *Thump. Roar. Thump. Roar. Thump. Roar.*

I start paddling my way out into the surf, and within seconds a wave crashes right on top of me and slams me like a rag doll toward the ocean floor. But instead of getting scared, I get mad. *You think you can take me, Pacific? Not today!* And then I talk myself through it: *Don't panic. Stay calm. Hold your breath. Don't swallow any water.*

Another wave washes over while I'm still under. I open my eyes and see nothing but murk, kelp, and swirling sand. I don't see anything else. No people. No places that I do not recognize. Nothing that's not supposed to be here.

Which is comforting, despite the fact that I could very well drown.

When I finally surface, gasping, I see another wave barreling toward me, but this time I keep my head. I push my board back down into the water and duck-dive under before it hits me. I surface, breathe, dive again. And again.

And then I'm out of the impact zone, although still working hard to stay with my board even in the calmer waters beyond the chaos. Two other surfers are out here waiting for the next set. They both shoot me an annoyed look. Like I've broken some secret surfer code of conduct or something. The words "You don't belong here" might as well be written on their foreheads. I ignore them.

A huge wave steamrolls toward us and before either of them can tell me it's theirs, I propel myself in front of it, popping up when it rises and starts to break. And then I'm flying sideways across the wave as it curls overhead, encircling me in a whirling liquid tunnel.

Inside the barrel, it is strangely quiet. Otherworldly. And so fantastically beautiful, it's like nothing else I've ever seen. I am air and water. I am the emerald eye of a hurricane. I am spinning through the center of everything.

I make it halfway across the wave before losing my balance and dropping into the churning surf, where I am tumbled again like a sock on maximum spin. There is nothing to do about it but hold my breath and wait until I feel the water recede enough that I can surface and breathe. When I do, I bodysurf into the shoreline, and then—almost too tired to stand—I drag my board by its leash out of the water and collapse in the sand to catch my breath.

Mother Nature does not mess around. I feel like I just went a few rounds in a boxing ring with someone much bigger and heavier than me. But that ride in the barrel was worth it. Even though it was only seconds, it seemed like I'd traveled through time.

I'm still breathing hard when I make my way back to Kai, who is standing right where I left him. And he looks really, really pissed.

"Jesus, Chloe. That was so stupid. Stupid and dangerous. You could have broken your neck. I could have broken *my* neck if you'd needed help. People drown in water like that."

"But I didn't," I say. "I'm fine."

Though now I am embarrassed that he even had to consider paddling out to rescue me. That would have been humiliating.

"Only because you were lucky."

There's that word again. Lucky.

I sit and watch the other two surfers still wrestling with the waves. Kai remains standing for a minute or two, quiet. Then he sits next me.

"People think surfing is all about being fearless," he says. "But sometimes a little fear, or at least a little respect for what you're dealing with, is a good thing. *Especially* here, where conditions are less than ideal most of the time."

And that's what I'm considering as I study the pounding surf. Being out there should have been terrifying. But I wasn't afraid. At all. In fact, the more it seemed like I could possibly get killed, the more I liked it.

"You're right," I admit. "It *was* stupid. But . . . I wanted to keep going anyway. I don't know why, I just did."

I can tell from the look on Kai's face that he knows exactly what I'm talking about.

"I'm not going to lie. I've felt like that more than a few times, and not just surfing," he says. "And that's why I have a pin in my leg. *And* a pretty ugly scar on my back."

Bet I can beat you in the scar department, I think.

"What happened?" I ask.

"The leg . . . is a long story. I cut my back getting slammed into a coral reef. Thirty-six stitches."

"In Hawaii?" I ask.

"Australia," Kai answers.

"I thought you grew up in Hawaii."

"We traveled around a lot when I was a kid."

"How come?" I ask.

"My dad competed."

"He's a competitive surfer?"

"Yes. Was. Not really anymore."

"Wow," I say. "That's cool."

He shrugs. "It was cool for him. My mom and me, not so much. She kind of lost patience with the nomad life."

"Your parents are divorced?"

He shakes his head. "They were never married to begin with. But they split up when I was, like, eight? Or maybe I was ten. They were on and off for a while. It's funny, though. She used to be a kick-ass surfer too. That's how they met. Sometimes I wonder if she would have . . ." He trails off and points as something catches his eye out in the surf. "Check it out."

One of the guys I ran into has caught a big wave. I watch him drag his hand across the wall of water as he rides it, his board spraying a trail of white in its wake.

"He's good," Kai says. Then he turns his eyes to me, making me feel like I can't look directly at them and like I can't look away all at the same time. "You were looking pretty good out there too. Aside from almost breaking your neck, I mean."

The air is charged again. Electric.

"Thanks," I say.

We're both quiet for minute, but my heart is thumping so hard that I'm sure he's able to hear it.

"So what's your plan for the fall?" he asks at the exact same moment that I say, "So what happened with your leg?"

"It's a long story," he says again while I repeat his question, "My plan for the fall?"

"You go," I say.

"I was just asking what your plans are after the summer. That's when it actually gets more surfable out here. Better weather."

171

"Well," I start, wondering how much of my whole, complicated story I should get into. "I'm supposed to be going to college, but I'm probably deferring until the spring. Or maybe even next fall," I say.

He nods. "It's a lot of money."

"No, it's not the money. My parents have been saving since I was a baby. But that's the thing. I feel like heading off to college is just what I'm supposed to do. Like nobody ever thought that I'd even consider anything different."

"Your parents are going to pay your tuition and you're not sure if you're even going to go?" He shakes his head and laughs. "Spoiled much?"

I can feel my face heating up. "Wow, Kai. Tell me what you really think."

He doesn't even know the half of it. It's not just that my parents have been saving money to send me to college since I was in diapers. In a way, someone *died* so I could go. Someone who maybe even had kids of her own.

Wow. I hadn't even considered that until right now. My thoughts are pulling me in so many directions at once that it's making me seasick. Sarah Harris. College. Kai.

He looks at me again, bringing me back to the present moment.

"I didn't mean that. I'm just kind of jealous, I guess. I think I'm probably going to be paying off loans for the rest of my life after the next four years. Maybe your parents can adopt me."

I raise my eyebrows. So he's off to college too. Just like everyone else.

"Where are you going to school?" I ask.

"Cal, but also not till the spring. I'm trying to save a little more money first. Hence the surf lessons. I don't really want your parents to adopt me," he adds, smiling. "That would be weird."

Cal. As soon as I hear it, an acrobatic hummingbird takes flight inside my chest. One of the acceptances waiting on my desk is from the University of California, Berkeley.

"Oh, yeah? I've been accepted there too. Well, Cal and a few others. I'm also considering Columbia."

"New York, huh?" Is that a note of disappointment I detect? "I hear there are a few decent places to surf on Long Island."

"I guess," I say. "I honestly hadn't been thinking about the surfing."

"Me neither," he says. "Otherwise I'd be headed to Southern California. But Cal has the program that I want."

Interesting. Kai does have a life separate from surfing. I wonder what he was like in school. He must have had straight As if he's going to Cal. Was he popular? A loner? I wonder what he's like when he's not here, near the ocean. It's hard to picture. Does he have brothers and sisters? Is he a dog person or a cat person?

Before I can ask another question, he stands up. His eyes are on the two guys emerging from the water. The ones who were out in the waves with me earlier. He picks up his board.

"Maybe we should go before those two come up here to kick our asses. You definitely snaked their wave. I mean, I know you could probably take them and everything, but I'd rather not get mixed up in your living-life-on-the-edge shenanigans."

Kai, using the word *shenanigans*. I think this makes me like him even more.

I roll my eyes. "All right. Enough. Now you're just *trying* to make me feel stupid."

He smiles, with the dimples, and holds out his hand to help me up.

This time, I take it.

When I go to strip off my wetsuit in the parking lot bathroom, it feels like it's pinned to the back of my right shoulder. I turn around to look in the mirror, and see something sticking out of a small slit in the neoprene. I reach back to touch it. It's sharp, like a tooth.

There's no one in here to help, so I pinch the thing between my fingers and pull, hard, until it releases. It's a broken piece of shell that must have been hammered into my shoulder when I went down with that last wave. In my hand, I examine the bright red drops of blood clinging to the jagged edge. My blood. Or is it *our* blood? White cells. Red cells.

Cellular memory. Is this girl who is not afraid to get thumped by huge waves and stabbed by shells *really* me? Because the thing is, when I'm out there, it certainly feels like me. Maybe even more so than the person I was before.

Kai is already gone when I come out.

⋙ GOOD NEWS / BAD NEWS ⋙

On Thursday before lunch, Jane drops into the chair across from me in the library. She's wearing huge sunglasses even though we are inside. I think I've heard her refer to these as her "hangover shades." She's been wearing them a lot recently, I've noticed.

"I've got good news and bad news. Which do you want first?"

Is she serious? Who wants to wait for bad news?

"Bad."

"So everyone in my mom's department at the hospital had to change their passwords."

I sit up in my chair.

"Oh, no. Because of us? We're not about to get arrested, are we?"

She laughs. "That would be pretty wild, huh? My association with the class valedictorian ending up being the thing that lands me in jail."

"I wasn't valedictorian."

"Close enough. But don't worry. I don't think we're busted. It sounds like it was just some system security upgrade or something? I heard my mom talking to Paul about it—about how it was such a pain in the ass to set up and she had to call the weird tech-support guy at work who's always telling her she looks like Naomi Watts. He sounds creepy."

"*Okay*, but what about the password . . ."

"Right, the password. Anyhow, I tried to get into the system this morning after everyone left for work, but the log-in screen is different and the password in my mom's desk doesn't work anymore, so I think we are out of luck with the records. At least for the time being. Sorry."

Shit. Right when we were so close. I cross my arms and look at Jane.

"So what's the good news?"

"The good news is that there's going to be a huge party at my friend's place in the city this weekend and you should come with me."

"That's the good news? A huge party?"

"Yes." Jane nods. "I think it would be *good* for you to get out and have some fun. Forget about all this heart stuff for a little bit."

"This heart *stuff*?"

177

"You know what I mean."

"Jane. You were with me last week when I knew the way to that house. When I knew how to ride the bike. And now you're telling me to just forget about it?"

She hesitates for a minute, then she removes her sunglasses and looks at me carefully, as though she's debating whether to say something more. She takes a breath. "I've been thinking. Are you sure you knew the way there *exactly*? I mean, it could be that you've just been down that street before and that's why it looked familiar. Why you remembered it."

"You don't believe me."

"No, it's not that." Jane's face is serious, which is unusual for her. She also looks really tired. "I know that you're definitely going through *something* right now, which, under the circumstances, seems *totally normal*. It's just that . . . maybe this whole password thing is the universe telling you to, I don't know, let it go? Get on with your life? Because, the way I see it, you have this second chance and, instead of looking back, why not look forward? You know? Live your life for you without the burden of also living your life for someone else. Maybe it's better that you don't know that much about who your donor is. Was. Whatever."

Better that I don't know? I can't believe I'm hearing this right now.

"*You're* the one who told me that I should find out about my donor," I remind her.

Jane thinks about this for a second, and then she shrugs.

"You don't always have to do what people tell you to do, you know. It makes for a much more interesting time. Plus, it's not *such* a big deal now that we're pretty sure we know who your donor is anyway, right?"

But, for me, this is not just about knowing my donor's name. I wanted to find out more about her—so I could maybe make some sense of what's going on in my own head. Also, I just feel more comfortable with certainties. With proof.

At the same time, a little part of me wonders if Jane's right. Maybe I should just let it go. For now, at least. Although it's frustrating to get this close and hit a dead end, perhaps it would do me good to take a break.

We went to Sarah Harris's house, and she's gone.

The password for the hospital records system doesn't work.

Her family doesn't want to be found.

If I believed in signs, all signs at the moment seem to be saying: Stop obsessing. Take Jane's advice and live my life. Go to parties. Have fun. Act like I'm seventeen. Maybe if I do this, if I quit dwelling on everything that's different now that I have a new heart, my head will settle down and get back to normal. And I can stop driving myself crazy.

This heart is mine now. That's what matters.

I kick Jane's foot under the table.

"So what night is the party?"

 **EXORCISM**

Two nights later, I take Jane up on her party invitation in San Francisco. But first, we're supposed to have dinner with her dad. He's in town all weekend, and this is the *only* reason my mom let me come into the city for the night. She insisted on talking to him on the phone before Jane and I left my house earlier today, which was 100 percent mortifying, but he assured her that he would indeed be around and keep an eye on us.

Only now I think he must have completely forgotten what he told my mom, because it looks like he and his girlfriend, Grace, are on their way out as soon as we walk in the door. They are both dressed as if they are headed to a fancy party. He's in a shirt and tie and Grace wears a chic black dress. "Oh, hey, love," he says, giving Jane a quick peck on the cheek. He's got a trace of an accent that sounds vaguely British.

"Hey, Dad," says Jane. She gives Grace a cool stare. "Grace."

Grace looks like someone who hoped to have already been out the door. "Hello, Jane."

Jane's dad smiles big at all of us, seemingly oblivious, or at least acting oblivious, of the tension between his girlfriend and his daughter.

"Sooo . . . I forgot that Grace and I have this event at the de Young tonight. Do you and . . ." He looks at me, searching his brain for my name.

"Chloe," says Jane.

"Oh, yes. So sorry, Chloe. Jane is always scolding me, rightly, for not remembering people's names. Do you two mind if we take a rain check on dinner?"

"Fine by me," says Jane, even though she seems a little disappointed. I'm not sure if it's because she really did want to have dinner with her dad, or if she was relishing the opportunity to torture Grace. "How about you, Chloe?"

"Oh, yes, sure. No problem," I say.

"Thanks, love," he says to Jane as he lifts his suit jacket off the back of a chair and shrugs it on. Grace is already waiting by the door. "You two probably didn't want to hang out with us boring grown-ups anyway."

Jane looks pointedly at Grace. "Probably not."

"Okay, girls," Jane's dad says, "don't stay out too late.

Chloe . . ."—he says this with a flourish, proud of himself for remembering my name this time—"I promised your mum I'd keep you two out of trouble. So, no more tattoos on my watch, yes?" He takes his wallet out of his suit jacket and extracts a single bill for Jane. A hundred-dollar bill. "For dinner. And take an Uber, please."

A hundred dollars and an Uber. I guess this is his idea of keeping us out of trouble, though I'm pretty sure it's not at all what my mom had in mind.

Once they are out the door, I turn to Jane and give her my best wild-girl grin. "Let's take your bike."

Speed and rushing wind and city lights flying past are just what I need right now. Adrenaline. Movement. Moving forward, moving on.

She nods as if she's impressed. "Only if *you* drive," she says. "I do not feel like being responsible, in any way, for anything, tonight."

A few hours later, after spending half of our cash on dinner, we're climbing off Jane's birthday motorcycle in front of a small, box-shaped house in the Outer Sunset. As soon as I remove my helmet, I can hear the music thumping loud from inside. We climb the steps to the front door and ring the bell. A boy with curly brown hair and a red plastic cup opens it, spilling the sounds of the party out into the night.

"Jane! What's up?" He sets his cup down in a little alcove in the entranceway, wraps her in a hug, and adds, "Haven't seen *you* in a while, beautiful." He catches my eye over Jane's shoulder and holds his hand out. "I'm Nate, and this is not my house. My parents would kill me if I threw a party this big."

"I'm Chloe," I answer as we follow him into a packed living room, where the air is thick with body heat. Jane dives right into the crowd, and I notice that people right and left are greeting her with some variation of "Where have you been hiding?" and "How's it *going*?" and "What have you been up to this summer?"

Even though this is a very different party, with very different people, there's something about Jane's entrance here that mirrors my own experience at Emma's graduation a few weeks back. It's like she's been out of the loop for a while. Long enough for everyone to be curious about where she's been. And now I'm curious too, because Jane definitely seems to have been out partying *somewhere* recently, a lot.

Tonight is the first time I've hung out with any of Jane's friends, aside from the guy who gave me my heart tattoo. But he seemed more like an acquaintance. Immediately, I notice that she's different around them. Louder. Wilder. Determined to be the center of attention. Instead of Jane, she's JANE, in all caps, illuminated by stage lights. And I'm different too. As I make my way through the sea of people, unsure of where to go, my earlier motorcycle-riding, devil-may-care attitude begins to fade. Here, I'm more like the old me— uncomfortable in a crowd, too concerned about saying something stupid to say anything at all.

Jane appears to be looking for someone. I see her craning her neck and scanning the room. At first I think she's looking for me, that she's just realized she left me almost as soon as we walked in the door, but then she makes eye contact with a petite freckled girl whose honey-streaked hair is woven into two short braids. As soon as their eyes meet, Jane turns away and almost seems to pretend like she wasn't looking for her at all.

Jane disappears into the party and I find a place at the edges, where I get distracted by the view through the front picture window. There, I can just catch a glimpse of the ocean below. The Sunset district is home to Ocean Beach, the city of San Francisco's only surfable stretch of coast. Here, long rows of pastel-colored houses, like the one I'm standing in now, are strung across a hillside that ends in a long, wide beach edged by grassy dunes. I wonder if Kai ever comes out here. He probably does, just not with me. Notorious for its strong currents and big waves, Ocean Beach is no place for beginners.

It's too dark for surfers now. The cloud cover is patchy but the moon is waxing, giving off just enough light to illuminate a small sliver of water. A few bonfires burn on the beach. I close my eyes and imagine that I hear the sound of waves crashing on the shore, but a loud laugh breaks me out of my wallflower—or I guess I should say *windowflower*—bubble.

Jane. She and a tall, dark-haired guy in a flannel shirt are looking at something on her phone. I turn my attention to the party. Other than Nate at the front door, no one else has introduced themselves. Everyone here seems to know one another already.

Passively, I watch people talking and flirting, imagining what it would be like to be one of them: the Asian girl with pink hair and blunt bangs, for instance, wearing a tight pencil skirt and thick-framed glasses that make her look like a cool librarian. The girl with the braids, who Jane seemed to know. She moves with ease among all the partygoers, making intro-ductions and passing around cups. Right now, she's talking to a cute black guy in a plain white T-shirt who leans against the wall, and when she moves to the next group, I notice him noticing the librarian. *I ship it,* I think.

Next, my gaze lands on a white guy on the sofa in an oversize gray hoodie, his bleached-out hair twisted into a sloppy bun. Hold up. I *know* him. Where have I seen him before? I instantly recognize his face. But I don't know his name. Like the man with the tattoo. The dog. *Stop it,* I tell myself. *Stop it, stop it, stop it! You haven't seen him before. You are doing it again. Just stop. You are supposed to be forgetting about all of this. You are supposed to be moving on.*

But then his eyes meet mine and widen in recognition. He points. At me. "Hey! You're the girl who snaked my wave!"

Jane's head snaps up from whatever she and the flannel-shirt guy had been looking at on her phone. The guy in the gray hoodie is *loud.* Everyone in the room looks my way.

185

"Are you talking to me?" I ask. Maybe I just *think* he's pointing at me.

"At North Point Beach on Wednesday. You caught that huge barrel. That was you, wasn't it?"

Now it feels as if everyone is waiting for me to answer. But, despite my embarrassment at being singled out in a room full of strangers, I breathe a small sigh of relief. I didn't recognize him because he's some memory from another life—he's a memory from *my* life. This is just a regular, run-of-the-mill, "small world" coincidence. Nothing mystical or weird is going on.

"Umm, yeah, that was me," I say, hoping that Kai was exaggerating about what a faux pas it is to take someone's wave. "Sorry I cut the line," I add. "I'm still learning."

He looks surprised.

"Well, your surfing etiquette may suck, but you definitely have some balls, I'll give you that. What the hell are you doing out at the Point if you're still learning?"

I kind of just want him to shut up now because it's making me super self-conscious that everyone is listening, including Jane. I shrug. "Umm . . . am I not allowed there or something? I didn't realize it was experts-only."

"Well, you sure didn't look like a beginner to me. Nice ride, even if you did end up taking a thrashing for it."

"Thanks," I mumble, catching Jane's eye. She gives me a curious look.

I'm hoping to just blend back into the crowd, but now the

guy in the hoodie is coming over and handing me a beer that I don't really want. "I'm Tyler," he says. "Ever surfed down there, at Ocean Beach?" He gestures out the window.

"No," I say. But as soon as the answer leaves my lips, an image of a huge green swell, spider-webbed with foam, flashes through my head. I remember a spraying wave arching over me, blocking out the sky and the sun. I remember dragging my fingers across a racing wall of water.

Tough paddle out, I think. But tough paddle out *where?* As I'd just told Tyler, I've never surfed Ocean Beach.

"We'll start getting the grown-up waves in November and December. Gonna be wild and death-defying, as usual. You should come give it a try."

I shake my head, as much to clear it as to signal a polite decline to his invite. "Thanks, but I don't think I'm ready for Ocean Beach."

Except here's the thing. Just like riding the motorcycle and listening to the Velvet Underground on vinyl and dying in a tunnel every single night, I feel like I *have* surfed Ocean Beach. Many times. So much for forgetting about my heart donor. So much for moving on. I can't even get her—is it *her,* Sarah Harris?—out of my head for a few days.

Tyler is still talking, but I missed most of what he just said.

"I'm sorry, what?" I ask. "It's kind of loud in here."

"I said, did you meet Jenna? She's a hella good surfer. Kicks my ass every time." He yells across the room, "Jenna!"

187

"I'm right here, Tyler." The girl I saw Jane watching earlier, the one with the cute braids, joins us. She's petite but muscular. She almost looks like a gymnast. "Stop yelling."

"Oh, hey, Jenna," he says. "Sorry. I'm, like, really stoned. Anyway, this is Chloe. I've seen her surf and you should get her number, 'cause you're always complaining about how there's too many dicks and not enough chicks out in the lineup." He laughs and laughs at his not-that-funny joke.

"I only complain because you surf bros act like you own the waves." She turns to me. "I'll bet he gave you the what-do-you-think-you're-doing-here? look."

"Yeah, kind of," I say.

"Well, you'll get a lot more of that if you want to surf Ocean Beach, but don't let it stop you. Most of the guys out here are all right once you get to know them. Even Tyler." She gives him an affectionate shove.

"What? C'mon girl, you know I'm your number-one fan."

Standing with both of them, I start to feel a little more comfortable. Less out of place. It helps that we're talking about surfing. Still, I can't seem to shake that weird out-of-body feeling I've had since Tyler asked if I'd caught waves at Ocean Beach. That feeling of having lived another life—a life connected to, yet different from, the one I'm actually living right now. It's disorienting and familiar, electrifying and terrifying, all at the same time. But then the sound of glass shattering knocks me back into my current reality.

Jane, again, is the source of the sound. Although we

haven't been here that long, she's already unsteady on her feet and has bumped hard into a shelving unit, knocking several framed photographs to the ground.

Tyler looks at Jenna and shakes his head.

"Looks like your girl's trying to get your attention."

Jenna sighs. "Oh, *Jane.* I better go deal with that before someone ends up with stitches."

After she leaves us, Tyler explains.

"Ex-girlfriend drama."

"Jane and Jenna?"

Tyler nods. "All last year," he says. "But I think Jenna got tired of"—he nods in the direction of Jane and the broken glass —"*that.* She can be kind of a mess when she drinks."

"Oh." I'm starting to feel bad that I didn't know any of this. If I had, maybe I would have steered her away from coming here tonight.

"Jane's good people," Tyler adds. "She's just a little mixed up. She probably shouldn't party so much."

"I'm going to help Jenna clean up," I say, and make my way toward the broken glass.

When Jane finds me later, Tyler's words are still in my head. She drops down next to me on the sofa. "Hey, shark bait, I didn't know you surfed." She's slurring her words and her red lipstick is smudged. I'm not sure what happened to her flannel-wearing friend.

I shrug. "I've just been taking some lessons."

"Wellll, Tyler and Jenna are pretty good, so if you're

keeping up with them, you must have been taking lessons *a lot.*"

"Not really. And I've only run into Tyler once."

"And your doctor is cool with it?"

"I don't need permission," I tell Jane. "Transplant patients can go back to whatever physical activities they want to after, like, six months."

But is nearly getting myself killed in waves I have no business navigating really something my doctor would be cool with?

"It's fine," I add, trying to convince myself as much as her. "I'm always with someone."

"With who?" Jane asks.

"With who, what?"

Jane rolls her eyes.

"*Who* are you *always* with? I know all the surfers at school and you definitely don't hang out with them."

This is starting to feel less like a conversation and more like an interrogation.

"He's not someone from school. He's just a guy who gives lessons."

"Where?"

"At North Point Beach."

Jane leans in so close I can smell the alcohol on her breath.

"Are you sure . . ."

She starts laughing and laughs so hard she can't catch her breath. Oh. She's high too, I realize.

"Am I sure *what*, Jane?"

Jane puts her hand on my shoulder, making a face like she's concerned for me. "Are you sure you haven't made all this up? That this whole surfing thing is not one of those figments of your 'cellular imagination'?" She makes air quotes when she says this, which makes it even worse, somehow.

She's laughing even more hysterically now, doubled over against me on the sofa. I know she's wasted, but still. I feel like I'm eight years old again, and the mean girl from my class just said something so perfectly designed to make me cry that I'm afraid I'm going to crumple right then and there, in front of everybody.

"I'm going to the bathroom," I tell her.

Instead, I head straight for the back bedroom and start digging through the pile of jackets on the bed. Jane can ask someone else to take her motorcycle home. Or leave it here. I don't really care.

But what if she's right? I think. What if I really can't tell the difference anymore between what's real or in my head? What if I only think I knew the way to Sarah Harris's house? What if the tunnel dream is just that—a dream? What if the man I chased on the street in San Francisco only reminded me of the man I saw crying in my room after the transplant, who, in all likelihood, was an anesthesia-induced hallucination?

Maybe the only thing wrong with me is *me*. There's nothing mysterious or unexplainable going on. There are no cellular memories. Just me. Losing my shit. Lost heart, lost mind. Not much left to lose after that.

Jane catches up with me in the hallway and asks where I'm going.

"Home," I say. "I'm tired."

She lets out a drama-queen sigh.

"Oh, *come on,* Chloe, stay. I was just teasing. Don't be so serious."

"I should never have told you anything," I say as I squeeze past her.

"I don't know, it seems like you've been pretty secretive to me."

"What's that supposed to mean?" I turn around to face her.

"I didn't know you surfed. I didn't know you knew Tyler and Jenna."

"I don't know them," I say. "And they don't know me. You don't know me either."

Right now, it feels like nobody does. I'm not even sure *I* know me.

Out on the sidewalk, I take a deep breath of ocean air mingled with car exhaust. A line of red taillights trails down a series of descending intersections on Taraval Street, disappearing when the cars turn at the Great Highway, which marks the western end of the city and the beginning of beach. From here, it almost looks as if the cars are falling off the edge of the world.

As I start walking west, down Taraval, I hear the door of the house opening and closing behind me. It's Jane. She's trying to catch up, but I pick up my pace.

"What are you doing, Chloe?" she yells.

"The opposite of what you tell me to do!" I yell back.

She doesn't give up easily. I can hear her clomping down the street behind me in her heavy black boots.

"But, hello? You're my designated driver. How am I going to get the bike back to my dad's?"

I stop but don't turn around.

"You are being very un-friend-like," she says. "Un-fun. Unfair. Uncool." When I look back and see her with her khaki army coat buttoned unevenly, she seems like a sad little girl. Jane is pretty messed up. I noticed that she and the flannel-shirt guy had been doing shots earlier in the night. Who knows what else they got into later, when they'd disappeared into another room. What if she tries to ride the bike home without me?

"Okay," I say. "But I'm leaving *now*."

Although I've agreed to take Jane home, I'm still mad. Mad at her for being so mean. Mad at myself for being too wrapped up in my own issues to even realize that Jane is obviously going through some stuff too. Mad at my messed-up brain that won't stop making me question whether all the things that make me *me* are really mine. Mad at the world, for giving all of us this unbelievable gift—life—then spoiling it with a certain, yet unknowable, expiration date. Thanks to heart disease. Cancer. Gunshots. A motorcycle crash. As I maneuver the bike through the streets of San Francisco, I suddenly realize where I need to go.

The Broadway Tunnel. Because, somehow, I know that that's the one. The one from my dreams. The one where my heart donor died.

I'm going to have an exorcism.

Just like in the dream, air rushes through the seams of my face shield. I accelerate as I approach the entrance, and it feels as if the tunnel's mouth is opening wide, waiting to swallow me up. Bright yellow lights streak by, blurring into a single fluorescent line. The curve, treacherous at this speed, is coming.

This is where the tree should be. This is where the tree is, every single night.

This is where I die.

This is where I live.

Screeching tires.

Die. Live.

Broken glass. Burning rubber.

Live. Die.

Blood washing over my eyes.

I lean far into the curve, feeling its frictional force pushing against my balance. The tires of the bike squeal and echo inside the tunnel. I almost skid out but miraculously manage to maintain the barest minimum of control, the bike teetering briefly before accelerating out of the turn. Then I'm racing toward the exit, which opens wider and wider and wider and wider, the lights of Chinatown beyond filling up the night.

Jane is pounding my back with her fist. Has she been doing this for a while? I had forgotten she was even there. She's yelling something that's muffled by her helmet and by the sound of . . . a police siren. *Shit.* I see red and blue lights flashing in the sideview mirror, hear a robotic male voice directing me: "Pull over to the right. Pull over to your right."

I have never been pulled over by a police officer before. Do I even have my driver's license on me? Guess it's too late to worry about that now. I slow down and pull over to the curb in front of a dim sum restaurant, closed and dark. As soon as I stop, Jane jumps off the bike and whips the helmet off her head.

"Jesus, Chloe! You're going to get us both killed!"

"Jane . . ." I see the officer getting out of his car behind us, his eyes on Jane, who is evidently not inclined to help me finesse the situation at the present moment.

"I know I don't always make the most stellar decisions, but I *don't* want to die!" Jane may still be drunk, but I can also see that she's scared. Of me. I did almost get us killed. Without giving it a second thought.

"Jane . . ." I quickly flick my eyes toward the officer, now just steps away, in a silent plea for her to shut up.

"Everything okay here?" he asks Jane.

She glares at me. "Fine, officer."

"You're sure?" he asks.

"Yes."

He turns to me. "Step off the bike and remove your helmet."

I do as he says.

He gives me a hard stare. "Are you aware of how fast you were going?"

"I'm not sure, officer," I respond. Because I'm not. I wasn't watching the speedometer.

His stare is ice-cold. "Eighty. You were going eighty miles per hour in a forty-five-mile-per-hour zone. You're lucky you didn't cause an accident."

I'm always lucky, I think.

"I need to see your license," he says. *"Now."*

I fumble in my coat pocket and am relieved to find that I do have my license, at least. I hand it over to him.

"This is a driver's license."

Jane is looking down at the ground.

"Yes, is there a problem?" I ask.

He looks at me as if I'm the biggest idiot he's ever met. "You need a Class M1 motorcycle license to operate this vehicle, which you should know from the training course."

"Umm . . . there's a course?"

"A mandatory safety course." He prints a citation from the device he'd been entering details on and thrusts it at me.

"You're either going to have to call someone who is licensed to ride this vehicle to come pick it up or I'm going to have to impound it."

"She's licensed." I point to Jane. "I was just giving her a lift home."

He turns back to Jane. "You have a license?"

Jane shakes her head no. "I don't have a license, sir. This is my father's bike."

Not a gift, I think. *Liar.*

An hour and a half later, we sit in silence as the Uber that picked us up at the impoundment lot stops at a traffic light on Divisadero. Tattoos. Drunken parties. Hacking medical records. And now a $500 fine and summons to appear in traffic court. Jane and I are on quite a streak.

"I'm sorry," I say quietly.

Jane looks at me. "What are you doing, Chloe?"

"What do you mean?"

"I mean, what are you really doing with me?"

"We're friends."

"Are we? Or are you just using me to explore your wild side?"

"Jane, no."

"Do you think I'm glad that I flunked my senior year? That I didn't graduate? You have a good reason, but me, I just didn't go to class. Smoked way too much pot. Partied all the time. And nobody noticed. My dad certainly didn't.

He doesn't even notice when I steal his spanking-new Ducati right out of his garage. And my mom's too focused on her do-over family. But, believe it or not, I was *trying* to get my act together before you came along. I know what everyone says about me at school—that I'm wild and don't give a shit about anything, and I've done a pretty good job of proving them right. But tonight really scared me. I don't want any more run-ins with the cops, and I sure as hell don't want to get brain damage from crashing a motorcycle. So if that's what you're looking for, maybe you should find someone else to rebel with, okay?"

"Jane, come on, that's not how it is." I can feel a knot forming in the base of my throat. "Don't—"

"Save it," she says as the car pulls over in front of her dad's building. She opens the door and hops out, leaving me with one final thought: "Sort your shit out!"

But what she doesn't know is that in some weird, not-sure-I-can-really-explain-it way, that's exactly what I was trying to do. I only hope it worked.

≋≋ MOVING ON ≋≋

Jane and I haven't spoken since the night I nearly killed us in the Broadway Tunnel. She's not answering my texts. And she's avoiding me at school, which takes effort, since only four classrooms and the library are even open during the summer session. There aren't many places to hide.

I stop by the room where kids can get tutoring help. Jane is in the corner with a skinny, red-haired guy who I recognize from Math Club. He represented our school at the International Math Olympiad this year.

Jane ignores me and pretends to be riveted by the quadratic equations spread between them. Equations I could have easily helped her with, I notice.

Math Olympiad is the first to acknowledge me.

"Hi," he says. "Are you tutoring too?"

Could he be the one person at school who doesn't know about my heart transplant? Who doesn't know to make a concerned face and ask how I'm feeling? I feel, for a minute, like I've stepped into an alternate reality.

"Nope," I respond, "just working toward my GED." He laughs like I'm telling a joke. I ignore him and nudge Jane with my foot. She looks up and stares at me, her face blank.

"Do you want to get lunch?" I ask.

"Can't today," says Jane. "Me and my friend Dave here already have plans."

"Drew," he says, looking equal parts bewildered, thrilled, and terrified by this development.

"Drew," she says, her blue eyes locked on mine. "Drew's my lunch date."

Drew's pale face goes pink at the word *date*.

"Okay," I say. "Maybe later this week."

But she's already turned her attention back to the equations, focusing hard on freezing me out.

"Bye!" Drew calls behind me as I retreat, oblivious to my disappointment. Jane doesn't even look up.

Well, that confirms it, I think as I exit into the empty hallway, where my squeaky Vans echo on the polished floor. Jane's still mad at me. And I suspect it's not just because I put her life in danger. *What are you really doing with me?* she'd asked. I have been dragging her back to the life she's been trying to leave behind, I realize with a flush of guilt. Jane really does want to get her act together, pass trigonometry, and graduate.

And I'd been so wrapped in my own drama that I hadn't even noticed that she was struggling too.

But she's wrong if she thinks that I've only been hanging out with her because of her reputation as a party girl. Jane's smart, even if she doesn't believe it. She's funny. She'll happily binge-watch *The Walking Dead* with me and not once get grossed out. She's a talented artist. She doesn't post obnoxious selfies on Instagram; she posts beautiful, ultra-close-up photos of things most of us pass by every day and never notice—tree bark, a fern, a spider spinning a web. She let me borrow all her favorite manga comics, including the ones that are rare and hard to find. She *is* my friend. I want us to stay friends. But maybe that's not what she wants, or needs, anymore.

I head down the stairs that lead to the front lobby. On the "things I haven't totally screwed up" front, I did turn in my physics paper. Which means that, barring any further emergencies, I will finally graduate in a few weeks. Alone. There won't be a ceremony. I won't have a party. Even if I wanted one, nobody would be able to come anyway. Most of my old friends, Emma included, are already gone—attending freshman orientations, moving into their university dorms, moving on.

In the lobby, I hesitate in front of the glass case that houses a bulletin board, still pinned with announcements about graduation-week activities that are now past. Cap and gown pickup. Awards night. Senior picnic.

I think about that question I had asked myself when I was studying all those mind-bending theories about alternate universes a few weeks ago. Do I *really* want to go back to the life I had before I got a new heart?

All those months ago. Back when everything in my life was supposedly on track, when everything was going according to plan, back before I knew that anything was wrong with my heart: Sunday nights were always the worst. I recall that feeling I'd get in the pit of my stomach as I mentally prepared for the five overscheduled days ahead. *Cross-country practice every day after school, an English paper due, two tests.* I would lie awake in my bed, unable to relax, debating whether I should review chapter fourteen in my chemistry textbook just one more time, in case of a Monday morning pop quiz. I would stress about the essay question that had appeared on the previous Friday's history test, the one I hadn't anticipated, about how the Polish Solidarity movement impacted the trajectory of the Cold War. I would turn everything over and over and inside out in my mind. *What if?* I agonized. What if I blew it? What if all the studying, all the preparation, wasn't enough? Because when one test could mean the difference between an A in history and a B+, and that B+ the difference between a 4.1 and a 3.97 GPA, and a few tiny fractions of a percentage the difference between getting into a top school and one that was "lesser than," there was no room for error. You couldn't blow off studying to watch a movie with your parents, or get the flu, or even just go to bed early and catch up on some sleep. There was too much at stake.

Or at least it seemed so then. Things look different now. Now that I understand how little one history test or a chemistry pop quiz matters when the stakes truly are life or death. All that worry and preparation and anxiety. I wasted so much time and energy trying to be perfect, believing I *had* to be perfect. But it's so easy to see now—*after*: my life wouldn't have been over if I didn't get into a top school. Not even close.

I only have one other class to attend after lunch. I decide to blow it off. I'm already passing, which, I decide, is good enough.

I push through the double doors of the school lobby and into the sunlight, smiling at the irony of me skipping the final class of the day while Jane toils over quadratic equations with Drew. Maybe she'll come around. But for now, I may as well just go home. There's nothing else for me to do. Which is weird. And exhilarating.

 **TIDES**

I'm lying on the hammock in the backyard, moonbathing.

My dad and I used to do this on full-moon nights, back when the number-one item on my Christmas list was a telescope.

Tonight's moon, almost full but not quite, is enormous, and so bright it's making the yard glow in the dark.

Tomorrow, it will be a supermoon, in *perigee*, meaning the closest it can possibly be while orbiting the Earth, increasing its gravitational pull on the tides. Will this mean good surf?

I pull my phone from my pocket and look up the number I have for Kai. I hesitate for a minute. We don't really have a texting thing going. Or really anything going.

Do we?

I type, *Check out the moon* and hit send. And wait, staring expectantly at my lonely blue text bubble. There is no response.

Probably because we do not have anything going.

I imagine him out somewhere with his friends, wondering why I'm sending him dorky texts about the moon.

But then the ellipsis indicating an incoming message appears ● ● ●

I'm holding my breath. Those three little dots seem to hang there forever.

Looking at it.

Another ● ● ● appears and then, *Supermoon.*

I know, I type, my heart picking up speed.

My phone starts to vibrate in my hand and I nearly fall out of the hammock. He's *calling* me? I wasn't expecting that.

"Kai?"

I hear his voice but can't make out what he's saying. Our connection is filled with static.

"What? I can't hear you."

I sigh in exasperation as CALL FAILED appears on my screen.

Another text comes in. *Sorry. Shitty reception.*

And another.

I kind of hate texting.

You hate texting? I respond. *Are you a time traveler from some old-timey era?*

But actually, I think it's kind of nice. Texting is easy. Lazy.

You can ignore a text if you want. Calling seems more . . . intimate.

Another message arrives: *I like to hear a person's voice when I talk to them. Plus, it's weird to converse in abbreviations.*

It is kind of weird, I respond. *IMHO. LOL. J/K.*

You're messing with me.

Yes, I am.

What are you doing? he asks.

Listening to music, I type, and then add, wondering after I hit send if it sounds silly, *Moonbathing.*

WTF is that?

I thought you don't like to communicate in abbreviations.

I don't. But also hate typing on tiny keyboard. Explain.

Like sunbathing, but in moonlight.

There's nothing for a few seconds, then ●●● *I'm trying to picture it. Tell me more.*

I feel my face heat up. He didn't just, in a roundabout way, ask me what I was wearing, did he? I consider what I actually am wearing: sweatpants, a hoodie, and my fuzzy socks with Adidas slides. My brain cycles through possible responses that wouldn't make me sound like an idiot. I've got nothing.

Never mind. What were you listening to? he asks.

So chatty tonight, for someone who hates to text.

David Bowie. Life on Mars.

Great song.

I know, right? What are you doing?

Same as you.

Listening to music? All right, what song?

Hello My Old Heart.

I stare at his text. At the title of the song. It makes my breath catch. Logically, I know that this is just a coincidence. There are so many songs with the word *heart* in the title. Hundreds. Maybe thousands. And I haven't even told Kai about my transplant, so it's not like he could possibly have known. Still, it's weird.

You still there? he writes.

I don't know that one, I reply.

Search for the Oh Hellos.

With a shaking hand, I look it up on my phone's music app.

Got it.

Try it.

I'll listen with you, I type. *Let's play it at the same time.*

OK.

You ready?

Yep. 3, 2, 1 . . .

As soon as the music starts to stream from my earbuds, I melt. This *song*. It's so beautiful and sad and otherworldly. It's almost as if it's speaking directly to me. That the entire universe is speaking to me through the song. Telling me to let go of my old heart. To set it free.

I imagine Kai lying somewhere, one arm behind his head, looking at the same moon, listening, with me, to the same song. And I want to tell him everything. About my heart. About how glad I am to have met him. About how he'd picked the most perfect song for me to hear tonight— even though he didn't really know it—one that somehow completely captures everything that I've been thinking and feeling.

It makes me want to cry. But this is too complicated to say via text.

I love it, I write when the song is done.

Yeah?

Yes.

OK. Your turn. What have you got for me? he asks.

How do I top the perfect song? I can't, but it reminds me of another one I've been listening to a lot lately.

Perfect Day. Lou Reed.

We like the same music.

We do?

We do.

"We." This makes my heart go *BOOM.*

BOOM BOOM.

For the next hour, we go back and forth with other musicians and songs. His favorites. My favorites. Songs that make us sad. Songs that make us happy. Songs that make us want to crank up the volume in the car and roll all the windows down. Songs for rainy days. Songs for surfing. Until I get an alert on my phone warning that it's almost out of power.

My phone is about to die, I type. Somehow, I feel like

it wouldn't be the same to continue all this texting inside. Without the moon.

Chloe.

Yes?

Come surfing tomorrow, Kai writes.

Tomorrow is Friday, not Wednesday.

Does that mean this is different? Not a lesson?

And right then, my mom opens the sliding glass door.

"Chloe. It's past midnight. Give the phone a rest. It's going to scramble your brain."

"I'm coming in in five minutes," I tell her.

She looks up at the sky.

"Wow, look at the moon," she says. "I wonder if your dad is already in bed. He should come check it out. Maybe you guys should get out the telescope!"

Oh my god, no. We should not get out the telescope right now. I glance down at my phone, where Kai's last text awaits.

She ducks back inside and I hear her calling my dad, "Davis, are you still up?"

OK. I will, I text quickly back to Kai.

The usual spot. Same time?

The usual spot. Same time. See you tomorrow.

The phone feels warm in my hand.

Tomorrow.

# PERIGEE

The old man who swims without a wetsuit is back again today, doing his preparatory stretching in the sand. His hair is thin and white, but his body is wiry and strong. He must swim every day. I wonder about his age. Is he seventy? Seventy-five? Eighty? It's hard to tell because he looks both young and old at the same time. He turns my way and breaks into a brilliant smile.

"Hello, mermaid! How are you today?"

"Great!" I call back. "How about you?"

"Wonderful!" he says. "It's a beautiful day!"

"It is." I hope when—*if*—I ever make it to his age that I'm still able to greet a beautiful day with as much enthusiasm as he does.

Then he asks, "Did you know that mermaids hold the secret to eternal youth?"

"Uh . . . no?" I answer back.

"They do! Mermaids stay young forever."

"That's good to know," I say. He's kind of strange, but sweet.

But if that's the case, then I'm more of an anti-mermaid.

Ten years. Ten years is the average life span of a transplanted heart. Considering that I'm now seventeen, this means that it's quite possible that I may only make it to the ripe old age of twenty-seven. Not what most people would consider a full life. My parents may have only temporarily escaped having to bury their only child.

I remind myself that for younger recipients, recipients like me, donor hearts last even longer than the average. Fifteen years. Twenty. Thirty years is the current record. A woman from Pittsburgh who received a heart when she was a toddler is still doing fine at thirty-two. I imagine thousands of transplant patients quietly keeping tabs on her progress and doing the math for their own hearts. 17 + 30 = 47. That's just a few years older than my mom is now. Which still seems pretty young.

The old man finishes his stretching and attaches his swimming goggles.

"Enjoy your swim," I say with a wave as he heads toward the water.

"You too!" he replies. "You and your boyfriend should have the good waves today."

Hearing him call Kai my boyfriend makes my skin flame up again, even if it isn't true. He doesn't know, after all, that I'm paying Kai to teach me to surf. But what about last night? And today? When Kai asked me to meet him, it seemed as if he was not talking about a lesson. It seemed as if he just wanted to surf, with me, for fun. To hang out. At the very least as friends.

Friends is good, I say to myself.

No, it's not.

An image of Kai's tattooed skin flashes through my head. His eyes, which sometimes look green, sometimes gold, and sometimes brown, depending on the light. I think of the current sparked when his hand brushed against my hip last week when he'd reached out to steady my board. The connection I felt when we listened to music together last night. I don't want to be just his friend.

I wish I had a way to check the time, but my phone is in my car. It feels like Kai is late. Or maybe I'm just impatient for him to appear.

I wonder if time will always feel different for someone like me. Will my life constantly feel like a party that I know I'll have to leave earlier than everybody else? Or will I be satisfied that I had more hours and days than I was ever supposed to have? Even if more, in my case, is less than most.

Best not to think so far ahead. Today the heart in my

chest is beating normally, so normally, in fact, that it feels like my own. The waves are perfect, their peaks sweeping toward the beach in long, graceful formations. The old man is already diving into the surf, ready for his swim. Pelicans glide over the water, dropping down when they spot a fish. Kai is walking toward me, breaking into a smile when our eyes meet. Who knows what tomorrow will bring? But today, I'll live.

"You ready?" Kai says, dropping his stuff next to me on the sand. "Looks killer out there."

"I've been ready," I tell him. "Just waiting on you. I almost ditched you to go swimming with our friend instead. He thinks I'm a mermaid." I motion toward the old man out in the water, now just a small shape half hidden by the breaking waves.

"Are you sure you still want to surf?" Kai asks, squinting in the man's direction. "You can practice your backstroke instead."

"I'm sure." I laugh. "But try to keep up."

I give him a playful shove and make my way ahead of him to the water. We paddle out together and join the lineup. Wait, side by side, for our turn.

"You got this," he says, after the surfers in front of us have taken off and the next set comes our way.

I paddle ahead of the approaching wave, pop up, and balance myself on the board, feeling that I have indeed got it this time, just right. This one is longer than any I've ridden yet, but not as wild as the one that dumped me weeks ago when

I bashed my head into my board. Sea air whips across my face, and I inhale its sweet and salty perfume as I lean into the wave, synchronizing my body's movement with that of the ocean beneath my feet. Finally, I am skimming over the surface of the water effortlessly. Like a dolphin. Like a bird. Like Kai.

Every muscle fiber, every neuron, every cell of my body is 100 percent focused on the ride. And it's this feeling that makes me love surfing so much. When I surf, time stops. I don't think. I just am. Past and future fall away. There is only water and air and movement and sound. There is only now.

I stay upright all the way to the shore, and as I'm coming back to earth, Kai rides in right behind me.

"Nice!" he says, high-fiving me after he picks up his board. "You have graduated to full shredder."

There is a lightness to him today, pure joy apparent on his face. This is where he is meant to be. Where I am meant to be. I can't imagine a life now without the ocean, without the rush that I am feeling in this moment. Minutes later, we paddle out again. And again. We are like kids at an amusement park, giddy that the line for the fastest roller coaster is so short, and that we are able to get on, off, and back on again as much as we want.

It is almost dark when we stagger out of the water, drunk on adrenaline.

The beach is nearly empty. We drop our boards and collapse on the sand.

I'm glad I thought ahead and told my parents that I was
catching a movie tonight with Jane.

I look over at Kai. His eyes are closed. His chest rises
and falls. I hold my breath and listen, trying to hear his heart
beating.

"Chloe." He opens his eyes but doesn't look directly at me.

"Yeah?"

"Can you please not pay me anymore?"

He doesn't need to explain why. We do have a thing
going, it seems.

In answer, I reach over and slip my fingers through his,
and we lie like that for a while looking up at the indigo sky,
and at stars that first sent light streaming across the universe
billions of years ago. A universe so enormous that it takes
lifetimes upon lifetimes for their energy to reach the two of
us on this night, on this tiny stretch of planet Earth.

"So tell me about your heart," he says, running his thumb
over the tattoo on my wrist.

And I do. I tell him about the day at cross-country practice, the day that changed everything, when I fell to the
ground, gasping, like a freshly caught fish. About learning
that my heart couldn't be fixed. I tell him about the list—
my place on it dependent upon a succession of tragedies and
a cold calculation. Was I less or more sick than the patient

that applied last week? Or the one that would apply tomorrow? How many head injuries, traffic accidents, and gunshot wounds would it take to move me to the top? I tell him about the night we got the call to show up at the hospital, and the ride with my parents across the Golden Gate Bridge. About wondering what they were going to do with my old heart. Toss it out with the trash? Save it in a jar for science? Bury it? Wondering about the person whose death offered me a new life. Wondering what my parents would do if the transplant didn't work. I tell him about how weird it was to open my eyes after the surgery and feel so immediately different. How I would never take breathing for granted again. I tell him about the strange purgatory of recovery. Hours ticking away in my hospital room. Hours of school missed. Graduation missed. My former self missed. I tell him what I couldn't tell Dr. Ahmadi that day in his office: about how there have been times that I've wished I could rip it out, pulsing and dripping. And then there are other times when I feel it burning inside of me, stronger and more powerful than the one I had before.

"Well, I think you should keep it," he says softly. "It's a pretty awesome gift."

I turn to face him, the two of us nearly touching foreheads in the sand.

"What about you?" I ask, pointing to the spot on his arm, now covered in neoprene, where I had seen his own tattooed heart, weeks ago, when we had compared them on the beach.

"I got it after my mom died," he says. "I wasn't sure what else to do."

His mom. No wonder he sometimes seems so sad.

"I'm so sorry," I say.

"Yeah, well, she'd probably laugh if she knew. Or tell me I should have tattooed a more useful reminder, like 'Don't forget to floss.' My mom was big on flossing."

"Mine is too," I say. And then I want to take it back. My mom *is*. His *was*.

"I'm really sorry," I say again, not sure if I should ask him more about her. His loss seems recent, and still raw. "Do you live with your dad now?"

"Yeah, which is kind of . . . an adjustment. He wasn't very involved in my life until now."

He looks like he's just remembered something. "Shit. He's out tonight. I have to go home and let out my dog."

"Sure," I say, unable to hide the disappointment in my voice as I sit up. "I should probably go too."

He catches my hand. "Don't go. Come with me," he says. "You can give me a lift. It's too dark to take my bike."

"You have a motorcycle?" I ask.

"No," he says. "Bicycle. I can come get it in my dad's pickup tomorrow."

I grab my backpack from the car and hurry into the restroom in the parking lot to change. This is what I usually do after surfing: I peel off my clammy wetsuit, rinse off as fast as possible in the lukewarm shower, and throw on some sweatpants and a hoodie. However, since I was in a not-usual mood when I packed today, I have a light summer dress, which is not really warm enough now that it's getting dark and the breeze is picking up. The weather hadn't been my top consideration when I pulled it from my closet. As I put on lip gloss, I check my reflection in the scratched-up mirror. My cheeks are rosy from the ocean wind; my hair falls in barely tamed waves. The scar peeks out above the neckline of my dress, but I don't care anymore about hiding it. Tonight, I do not want to reach down and rip out my heart.

When I push open the rusted restroom door, Kai is waiting outside in jeans and a faded black T-shirt. It's the first time I've seen him in regular clothes and it sends a current through my entire body, head to toe. He doesn't say anything for a few long seconds, then: "You've got goose bumps."

"I'm kind of cold." I laugh.

He moves closer, hands me the jacket he'd been holding. "How come you don't have your Smurf hoodie? I really like that."

"You do, huh? It's in my car."

Now that we are no longer zipped into our wetsuits, it feels as if an energy that's been bottled up for weeks has been released, sending sparks into the air all around us.

I wrap myself in Kai's jacket and the two of us carry our boards to my Honda. The walk seems endless, like I've parked a mile away.

When we get to the car, he helps me secure the boards to the roof rack. I get into the driver's seat and pop the lock open for him on the passenger side. And once Kai finally pulls the door closed behind him, all I can think about is how little space there is between us. We look at each other.

"Hi," I say.

"Hi," he answers.

It takes me a second to remember what I'm even supposed to be doing. *Giving Kai a lift.*

But instead of asking where we are going, I do something else, something that "Before Chloe" would probably never do: I make the first move. Leaning across the gear shift, I reach my hand behind his neck and pull him close for a kiss. His lips—which are perfect in every possible way—taste like salt. And then he's leaning in to me and kissing me back, one hand cradling my face, the other buried in my hair. I brush up against the steering wheel and the unexpected blare of the horn makes us both jump, and then laugh, and for a moment there's an awkward, butterflies-in-your-stomach silence that I break by climbing toward Kai on the passenger side.

"Is this okay?" I ask.

His lips are already on mine again as he answers, "Yes. Absolutely. Okay."

I almost can't believe that after all this time thinking about what it would be like to kiss him, to touch him, that this is really happening. Some things are like I imagined, some not. Up close, he does smell like the ocean, a combination of sunscreen, seawater, and that nowhere-but-here essence I notice when I open my car windows on the way to the beach. Like wind, tinged with brine. I expected his black hair to be silky, but it is thick and coarse. I expected his lips to be rough, but they are soft. And Kai, always calm, always seemingly in control, is not his usual chilled-out self. I can feel his entire body vibrating with an energy that's *different* . . . more wired and uncontained.

Moonlight floods the parking lot and the inside of my car. I just want to freeze this moment, drop a pin to mark it on the map of my mind. But then I remember why we left the beach in the first place.

"Your dog," I whisper into his ear. "You need to let out your dog."

He rests his forehead against mine, catching his breath.

"Damn it. My dog."

Kai calls a neighbor, who has a key and can let out the dog. I silently give thanks for neighbors, for cell phones, for spare keys. His lips are on my earlobe, and my mouth again. I twine my arms around his neck. But then he leans back to look at me.

"Chloe."

"Kai."

His eyes, which appear almost gold tonight, seem to glow in the dark.

"What are you doing tomorrow?" he asks.

Tomorrow. I hadn't been thinking that far ahead.

"I have no plans," I say, smiling and lightly kissing his lips. I can't get enough of them.

"There's this band I've been wanting to see . . . maybe we can go together?"

I think he wants me to know that tonight is more than just tonight. It's the beginning of something.

"That sounds great," I say. "Let's do that." *Together.* I hesitate for a moment. "You know, I've been wanting to kiss you ever since you told me about the time you caught your first wave when you were six."

Kai laughs. "I've been wanting to kiss you since the day we met. I win."

"You win," I whisper. "Now, no more talking."

Kai moves one hand to my hip, and with the other he traces the pulse along the side of my neck. I slip my hands under his shirt, where heat radiates off his skin. Our kiss deepens, the air around us crackles, and, as he runs a finger over the scar that peeks out of the neckline of my dress, I slide my palm to the center of his chest. Our heartbeats, both hammering hard, so close, are almost indistinguishable.

And then, so suddenly that it takes my breath away, an icy stab of pain shoots through me. Like a cold, sharp knife, plunged straight into my heart.

I gasp, clutch the seat behind Kai to keep myself upright. My body breaks out in a clammy sweat. I feel like I'm going to throw up.

Something is terribly, terribly wrong.

Kai's hands are on either side of my face. He's talking to me, or yelling even, but I can barely hear him. Why can't I hear him?

I am underwater.

I am speeding toward a tunnel.

I am crashing into pavement.

I am drowning in the sea.

"Chloe! Chloe! What's wrong? What's wrong?" Kai's voice breaks through but then gets fainter, distorted. His features are falling in and out of focus. He is a shape in the fog, a shadow hovering above the water's surface. I reach out to grab his hand, but I feel him being pulled away.

I reach out again, but he is gone.

And then everything goes dark.

THE WORST
≋ PLACE ON EARTH ≋

I wake up in the worst place on earth. The hospital ICU.

Machines beep and hum all around me. A pulse oximeter is clipped to my finger. An arterial line is attached to my wrist. EKG electrodes are taped to my chest. My mom is curled in a chair in the corner, looking tense, even in sleep. An all-too-familiar scene that takes me back to the worst days. The days when I didn't know if I was ever going to get out. The days when I didn't know if I was going to live. The days before.

No. This is not happening. This *can't* be happening. It's a dream. It's not real. It's all in my head. Not my heart.

One of the things Emma used to say about dreaming rises to the surface of my mind. If you became aware that what you were experiencing was a dream, you could control it. You could change the outcome.

Maybe I can just leave. Switch the scene. Transport myself from the ICU to my bedroom. A park bench. The beach.

I sit up as quietly as I can and swing my legs to the floor. My plan is to just walk out, but I'm tethered. Wired up to various pieces of hospital equipment.

I pull off the oximeter and rip away the electrodes attached to my chest. Easy enough. But I'm temporarily stopped by the arterial line. This is more complicated to remove, since it's embedded into the radial artery at my wrist. I stare at it for a second, then quickly peel off the adhesive that holds the catheter in place, take a deep breath, and yank it out. Bright-red blood spurts across the white sheets, painting them like a grisly Jackson Pollock canvas. I clamp a hand over my wrist to try to stem the flow.

I'm so focused on stopping the blood that I haven't realized all hell is breaking loose around me. The machines are going ape-shit, sounding a multitude of warnings and alarms. My mom is up and leaping toward me, grasping me by the shoulders. She holds me steady even as I push against her in my attempts to break free. My dad walks into the room holding two cups of coffee, his face draining of color the moment that he takes in the scene. He reels around and disappears into the hallway, bashing one of the coffees against the door frame so that it spatters all over the walls and floor.

Maybe this is not a dream.

Maybe this is real.

I hear footsteps running in the hall outside my room. Two nurses enter, a man and a woman, followed by my dad, now empty-handed.

The male nurse, a big guy, takes over for my mom, gently locking me in his grip while the other nurse clamps my wrist with her hand just above the spot where the catheter had been inserted. She wraps the site of the wound in cotton and gauze. While she does this, she makes eye contact with me and smiles.

"Well, you sure know how to get everyone's attention, don't you?"

"I'm sorry," I whisper. "I thought I was dreaming."

"No worries at all. It happens more than you'd think."

The other nurse relaxes his grip, and together they steer me to a nearby chair.

The one who wrapped my wrist turns to my mom. "Mom, why don't you hang close to her while I grab a clean gown? Anton won't let her fall."

My mom is now by my side, smoothing the hair from my forehead. "My sweet girl," she says. "Welcome back."

How long have I been gone? I wonder.

I'm about to ask her, but then I notice my dad, still standing close to the doorway, looking like he might pass out.

The blood. It's everywhere. The bed looks like a crime scene. Deep-red splatters are all over the front of my gown. My dad is a huge chicken about needles and blood.

"Is Dad okay?"

"Davis?" The look on my mom's face is one that tends to pop up just when she's nearing the end of her rope: *Now what?*

In three swift steps, Anton reaches my dad and catches him by the arm. He gets him to another nearby chair. "Put your head between your knees, sir," he says. "Try to breathe normally." My dad complies. My mom stays with me.

"It happens all the time," the other nurse says when she comes back with a fresh gown. Her ID badge shows that her name is Kristen. "Especially with the men. They're such babies about blood."

Kristen gets me cleaned up. Then she and Anton change the bed. Once I'm tucked back in, Anton clips the oximeter on my finger again and reattaches the EKG electrodes, but doesn't reinsert the A-line. Kristen talks to my parents as if I'm not there. "The doctor is on her way. We could sedate her again, but I don't think it's really necessary. She was just a little disoriented when she woke up." And then she turns to me, her voice slower, louder, more cheerful. "All right, hon, I'm just going to put a couple pillows under your arm. We need to keep this wrist elevated for a little while. No more running away, okay?"

"Okay," I say. As soon as they depart, I take a good look at my mom and dad. They both appear tired and rumpled, as if they've been here overnight. At least.

I'm afraid to ask. But knowing is better than not knowing. "The heart," I say. "My body's rejecting it, isn't it?"

They glance at each other, then my mom speaks. "We don't know," she says. "They did a tissue biopsy last night, but we're still waiting on the results. The doctor on call was due about an hour ago, but she's running late."

The people who say "no news is good news" have no idea what they are talking about. When your life is in limbo, waiting to hear what's going on is excruciating. You need to *know*.

My dad tries to break the tension, even though he still looks a little like a reanimated corpse. "In the meantime, please don't go all *American Horror Story* on us again. I don't think I can take it."

We don't have to wait long. The doctor arrives, a bit breathless, a few minutes later. Guess she must have hustled up after getting the report that her patient was awake and ripping out arterial caths.

"Hello, Chloe. I'm Dr. Lee," she says. "I have your heart biopsy results."

We all freeze. Each, in our own way, steeling ourselves for bad news. Signs of rejection, at this stage in the game, are no joke. It could mean that heart failure, rather than just an immune response, is the cause. And if this heart is crapping out, what, really, are my chances of getting another? Technically speaking, a re-transplant can be done, but it involves going back on that awful list, more waiting, more days in the ICU. I don't know if I can do it. I don't know if I'd want to.

"You are a very lucky girl," she says.

I hear my mom exhale and watch the color return to my dad's face. Dr. Lee, on the other hand, seems a bit bewildered.

"The biopsy was negative," she says, and then gestures to the monitor next to my bed. "Your EKG readings are normal. The echocardiogram that we did is also normal. Which is unexpected, to put it mildly, because when you were admitted to the ER last night, you were clearly showing signs of a sudden cardiac arrest. We shocked your heart."

My mom takes another deep breath. Dr. Lee continues, "A cardiac incident of that nature always causes some tissue damage. Damage that we can see. Damage that we can read on an EKG. However, it not only appears that you've made a complete recovery in less than twenty-four hours, but our tests also show a heart as healthy as any seventeen-year-old's. It's like what happened last night never happened at all. Which, medically speaking, is nothing short of a miracle."

The doctor seems as if she still doesn't even understand the words coming out of her mouth. My mom starts to cry in relief. My dad puts his hand on her shoulder.

The room is spinning around me. My brain is reeling in my skull. Sudden cardiac arrest. Admitted to the ER. And then one thought interrupts all the others: *Where is Kai?* He must have brought me here. He wouldn't have just left. Would he?

"We are going to keep you one more day just to make

sure that everything is okay, but by tomorrow you should be free to go," says Dr. Lee. "Dr. Ahmadi will want you to come in to see him for a follow-up, of course. Maybe run a few more tests. But for now, let's focus on getting you out of here, okay?"

Always the optimist, my dad claps his hands. "Sounds good to me!"

After the doctor leaves, I question my parents.

"How did I get here? Did someone bring me?"

My mom looks perplexed. "You don't remember the ambulance?"

I do not remember an ambulance.

"Apparently someone called nine-one-one from the parking lot of North Point Beach. The paramedics found you in your car."

I remember nothing after those final seconds with Kai, when he was *with* me. We were practically glued to each other. He must have called for the ambulance. But then where did he go? Why wasn't he there when the paramedics arrived?

"Who called nine-one-one?" I ask.

"We don't know," my mom says. "They didn't leave a name."

"Did anyone come to the hospital? Has anyone been looking for me?"

My parents eye me suspiciously. "No, no one," my mom says.

"Were you expecting someone?" my dad asks.

"I just thought . . . maybe Jane . . ." Immediately, I feel guilty for using Jane as an alibi again. I probably shouldn't be bringing her into this.

"No, sweetie," my mom says more gently. "No one's been by."

And now it's my parents' turn for questions. A lot of them.

Why was I all the way out at the beach and not at the movies with Jane as I had told them? Why wasn't I picking up my phone when they called? Who *was* I with? And where did the surfboard on the car come from?

"Have you been *surfing*?" asks my mom, incredulous.

"Yes," I say, trying to sound as if I haven't been hiding this from them all summer. "I've been taking lessons."

And I'm damn good at it too, I think.

"Why didn't you just tell us that?" asks my mom. "Why were you lying about it?"

I shrug. "I didn't want you to worry." It's the truth, but only part of it.

Mostly, though, I wanted something that was just *mine*, that I didn't have to filter through any analysis of "What does this mean for someone recovering from a heart transplant?" I didn't want anyone to tell me that I couldn't or that I should be careful or that I should stop because it was too dangerous.

"Well, now that you mention it," my mom says, "it seems like something we should have cleared with Dr. Ahmadi, don't you think? I mean, I know he said you could exercise, but surfing seems a little extreme for someone whose sternum is still healing."

She looks to my dad for backup. "Davis?"

I look at my dad too, hoping he will back *me* up instead, as he usually does.

"With who?" my dad asks.

"With who, what?" I reply.

"Who were you surfing with?" It doesn't seem like he's going to be backing me up.

"Just this guy. He's . . . he teaches people to surf."

I feel my cheeks burning.

He was underneath me in the passenger seat of my car the last time I saw him . . .

"Well, how old is he?" my dad asks, starting to pace. "How did you meet him? Please don't tell me Tinder or *I* might have a goddamn heart attack."

One disadvantage of having a father who is a teacher: he knows about all the stuff that kids try to hide from their parents.

My hands were sliding under his shirt. He was tracing the line of my scar.

I force myself not to think of where I was and what I was doing with Kai. It's not that I don't *want* to think about it. In fact, under normal circumstances, I'd probably be replaying every kiss in my brain, on repeat. I just don't want to discuss it with my *dad.*

"Dad. *God.* No."

My mom puts a hand on his arm. "*Davis.* Ease up. We can talk about this later. "

This is interesting. Add a boy to the mix and it's like my parents have switched personalities. My mom is trying to stay calm while my dad freaks out. Despite my confusion about what happened to Kai, it almost makes me feel, for half a second, like a normal girl.

"All right," my dad says. "But this conversation is to be continued. When you didn't let us know where you were and you didn't pick up the phone, we didn't know what to think. Your mom was frantic. Especially when we got the call from the hospital."

Hearing their version of last night makes me feel even more terrible. Of course they were frantic. Why do I keep doing this to them? I don't *want* them to worry. I don't *want* to cause them any more stress than they've already been through over this last year. But there's something about being out in the ocean with Kai that makes me forget that I'm also this other girl who should check with her cardiologist before she takes surfing lessons. Who should make sure that somebody knows where she is at all times, just in case there's an emergency. Who needs to question every skipped beat of her heart.

"I'm so sorry," I say. "I should have told you where I was."

And then everything that's happened in the last twenty-four hours hits me: Kai. My heart. The hospital. My parents. I can feel the tears welling up like a wave about to explode on the shore. I shudder once, and then cry so hard that I start to hiccup, so hard that I can barely breathe, so hard that it makes my throat swell up and the blood vessels in my temples throb in pain.

My mom climbs into the bed and puts her arms around me.

"Chloe, Chloe, calm down, please calm down," she whispers into my hair. "It's okay."

And holding on to her like a life preserver, I pretend that I'm a little girl again and that everything *is* going to be okay.

Later, when my parents have gone to find more coffee and something other than hospital food to eat, I dig my phone out of the bag of clothes that one of the nurses left on the nightstand. I dial Kai's number. It rings. And rings. I wait for the voice mail to pick up, but it just keeps ringing.

I switch to text: *Kai?*

I text again. *Kai, where are you?*

And again and again and again. *I'm in the hospital. What happened? Where did you go? WHERE ARE YOU?*

My blue text bubbles wait, unanswered. My eyes start to burn, stinging with tears.

What is going on? Why is he not responding? He couldn't have just disappeared. People don't do that. *Kai* wouldn't do that.

I go over and over the previous day and night in my head. We surfed. We talked. We lay side by side on the beach under

233

a kaleidoscope of stars. My skin still smells of saltwater. Sand sticks to my scalp. I remember his hands in my hair. His lips on mine. I remember everything.

My parents return with coffee and sandwiches they picked up from a deli somewhere nearby. Kristen the nurse comes back in to check my vitals. Hours go by as I lie trapped, tended to, watched. Inside, I'm going crazy, but outside, I try to stay calm. I consider telling my mom then change my mind. I wonder whether, when I have a free minute, I should call the police. Maybe something happened to *him* too. After the ambulance came. Because otherwise, wouldn't he have waited? To be sure that I was okay?

I compose long, tortured, somewhat unhinged texts that I delete. I compose saner, more rational ones that I send. I lie awake that night listening, waiting for my phone to chime, to buzz, to do anything in response. But there's only silence.

The next morning, I am discharged from the hospital. My parents hover over me like eagles protecting their nest. One day goes by. Then another. And another. I keep texting. Calling. Checking messages. Staring at my phone. And then, on Tuesday night, it rings.

I'm in my room and dive across the bed to grab it, knocking over the lamp. *Please let it be Kai. Please let it be Kai. Please let it be Kai.*

But it isn't Kai. Or Jane. It's Emma.

I take a breath.

"Hi, Emma."

"Hi. Your mom left me a message about what happened. I just wanted to check in and make sure you're okay. Like not just physically okay, but okay okay."

"Thanks," I say. "I feel fine."

"Good."

We are both quiet for a minute, unsure of what else to say.

"I mean, no, I'm not fine."

"Tell me," she says.

And so I tell her everything. Everything that happened. Well, the abridged version, at least. I leave out a few things. Nearly crashing the motorcycle in the Broadway Tunnel. Getting drunk, and high, with Jane.

"So let me get this straight. You were with this guy, Kai, you almost had a heart attack *while you were making out with him*, and now he's not responding to any of your calls or texts? Are you sure he's not just being a regular, run-of-the-mill asshole?"

I force myself to seriously consider this possibility. Kai, who never once missed one of our meetings, who waited to be sure I was okay that day I recklessly went back out into the churning surf, who kept his head no matter what the Pacific Ocean threw our way—would that Kai have fled when I was in serious, possibly life-threatening, trouble?

"He didn't seem like the kind of person who would do that," I say. In fact, he seemed exactly the opposite of the kind of person who would do that. Which makes the whole thing more, not less, distressing. How could he just disappear?

"Well, don't be so quick to underestimate how thought-less some guys can be," says Emma. "Like, half the girls in my dorm have hooked up with someone who they've gushed about being *sooo nice* and then they never hear from them again."

At first, I wonder if she's enjoying being the voice of experience, which is funny because she's only been a college student officially for a few weeks. But maybe she's just being protective and doesn't want me to get hurt.

"How are things at Brown?" I ask, changing the subject.

"Good," she says. "I decided to switch back to English."

"Oh, Emma," I say. "I'm so happy to hear that."

She fills me in on her new life as a college freshman. Her classes are challenging, a bit intimidating even, but she likes the vibe there. The hot guy she met at a party last weekend happened to be sitting behind her in Introduction to Creative Nonfiction and now they're texting. Her roommate is from New York, and she is going home with her to visit the city next weekend. The Vampire Princess has been adopted by her entire dorm floor; on weekends she is moved from room to room as part of an elaborate party game known as "Pass the Princess."

"Nice," I say. "I'm glad she's being put to good use." And I'm glad that Emma seems to be loosening her ponytail a bit. But her college stories seem as relevant to me right now as the ones my grandma tells about the ladies in her retirement complex. Or maybe I just don't want to hear them because she has all these new friends and I have no one, since Jane doesn't want to talk to me and Kai is MIA.

Kai.

I know what I have to do as soon as my parents relax enough to let me out of their sight. It's the only thing I can do. Go to the beach. Surely someone there knows him. Might know what happened to him. But what if nothing happened to him? What if I find him there, coming in from the surf? That would be so devastating. Enough to break my heart.

No. It won't. I've already survived a real broken heart. I can take it. And knowing is better than not knowing, no matter what.

I pretend I hear my mom summoning me for dinner. "I have to go," I say. I'm too distracted to be much of a conversationalist at the moment, and I don't want to make Emma feel bad.

"Your surfer guy still might call," Emma reassures me. "Maybe he just lost his phone."

"Maybe." And as I say this, a little spark of hope flares up. He *could* have lost his phone. "Thanks for calling, Em. I'll talk to you soon."

I hold the phone for a while after Emma hangs up. *Maybe he lost his phone.* Okay. But that still doesn't explain why he didn't wait for the ambulance or show up at the hospital or try to reach me some other way to make sure I was all right.

I reread the text conversation that I had with Kai when we listened to music as the moon lit up my backyard. Five days ago. Is there a clue here that I'm missing? Something, anything, that might help me understand what's going on? "Come surfing tomorrow," he'd said.

There has got to be an explanation.

I dial his number again. It rings three times and then a loud tone blares in my ear, followed by a message: *We're sorry; you have reached a number that has been disconnected or is no longer in service. If you feel you have reached this recording in error, please check the number and try your call again.*

No longer in service.

What. The. Fuck.

LOOKING

Luckily, my parents have jobs. And in a few days, their work commitments present the opportunity that I've been waiting for. Real school is now back in session, so my dad is occupied until at least four, and Mom has a meeting in San Jose, which means she'll be gone most of the day. I wait until I see her car disappear at the end of our block, then grab my keys and jacket.

Around noon, I arrive at the beach. As soon as my feet touch the sand, I scan the horizon for Kai's familiar profile sweeping gracefully across the arc of a wave. There's no sign of him in the water. So I sit and wait. It's sunny but windy, so I pull on my jacket. Part of me hopes that he emerges from the dunes any minute now, board under his arm. Part of me hopes he doesn't. The first option means he's a huge jerk. But at least I'll have an explanation. The second option is worse. Because then I'll have to keep wondering what happened.

As the sun moves across the sky, I watch surfers come and go, in singles and groups of two or three. They wax their boards, fasten the collars of their suits, paddle out through the waves. Kai does not appear. I ask around. Has anyone seen him? Does anyone even know him? But I am met with only shrugs in return. One guy thinks he may remember someone like Kai, who offered private lessons, but says he hasn't seen him recently. "I've been in Costa Rica for the last couple months," he explains. "Maybe he has a website. Or, like, an Instagram?"

Maybe he does, but I have no way of knowing—a fact that is making me shake my head in frustration and disbelief. Because after all these weeks, all the hours we've spent out in the ocean together, the night in my car, here's the thing that is killing me: I don't know his last name. How is that possible? I recall the scrap of paper I found pinned to the bulletin board in the surf shop:

WANT TO LEARN TO SURF? I SPECIALIZE IN BEGINNERS. CALL KAI.

But in the beginning, I hadn't even thought to ask. And he was so quiet at first. Maybe because he was sad about his mom, maybe because he was just feeling shy. Until these last weeks of summer, when it felt like our orbits had aligned. When I sensed him moving closer and closer. Something was pulling us together. Something powerful. I'm sure of it.

But I'm not sure what to do next.

And then I think: the shop. The place where he posted his name and number. Maybe someone there will know him.

The bell on the door rings when I step inside, and immediately I am reminded of the first day I came in, after all those hours I had spent watching the surfers from the beach.

Watching one in particular. He was drawing me in before we even met.

My plan was to buy a board. The guy working at the shop looked as if he'd just woken up from a nap and smelled a little like weed, but he seemed to know his stuff.

"You've surfed before?"

"No," I told him.

"You're going to want a longboard then," he said. "Something that's stable and wide."

He pulled out a bright-yellow one from a rack at the back of the store. It looked enormous. I didn't even know how I would carry it.

"That seems kind of big," I remember saying. I had thought, mistakenly, that small people got small boards, and taller people got long ones.

"Trust me, you'll be happy you have this. Until you get comfortable standing, at least. We've got a bunch of used ones. You probably don't want to spend much until you're ready for a better board."

He had been right about not spending much. About

a month later, at Kai's suggestion, I was back for a trade-in. Shorter boards are harder to balance on but easier to turn and maneuver. By that time, I was getting frustrated about not being able to pivot smoothly.

The same guy was working that day, and he had seemed impressed.

"Ready for a trade-in already, huh? You must be picking it up quick."

"I'm working on it," I said. *Was I really picking it up quick?* Sometimes, I thought Kai was just trying to be polite when he told me I was doing great.

But that first day, the guy in the shop had seemed dubious that I knew what I was doing. After outfitting me with a wetsuit, a leash, and the board, he'd asked, "Where are you planning to take that?"

"Across the street?" I really hadn't thought the whole surfing plan all the way through yet. Impulsive decisions had become another one of my "after-transplant" traits.

He had laughed at me.

"I would highly recommend surf school if you've never done it before. Or private lessons."

"Okay, where do I do that?"

"Surf schools are two beaches down. That's where you can catch some baby waves. For private lessons, check the board."

Did he say baby waves? I was looking for something more exciting than that.

I'd decided to try my luck with the bulletin board. A

bunch of flyers advertising lessons were pinned there, some professionally done and printed on glossy paper, others just handwritten notes. I zeroed in on Kai's right away. Somehow, I had a feeling that he was the best choice, even if his no-frills advertisement, which included a fringe of numbers that you could rip off at the bottom, looked like it had been there for a while. *He must be familiar with this spot,* I'd thought as I put his number in my back pocket.

Now, I almost feel like I conjured him out of thin air.

The guy who sold me my first surfboard is perhaps the only person who works in this shop because he's kicked back on a chair behind the counter again today, reading a magazine.

"Oh, hey," he says, standing up as I approach. "Don't tell me you're ready to trade in your board again?"

He still smells like weed.

"No, not today," I say. "I'm looking for someone who gives lessons. I found his number on your bulletin board? His name is Kai."

"Kai? The guy who looks like he's maybe Asian? Black hair?"

My heart starts to drum faster.

Finally. I feel like I'm about to start crying from relief. He's not a figment of my imagination, at least.

"Yes. That's him. You know him?"

"A little. He used to come in here and I'm pretty sure I've run into him out in the lineup a few times. Awesome surfer, if

243

he is the guy I'm thinking of. But I don't think he gives lessons anymore because I haven't seen the dude in a while."

He's wrong about Kai no longer giving lessons, but that's not what I'm looking for. Not anymore.

"You wouldn't happen to know how to get in touch with him, or his last name? Or maybe where he lives?" I ask. *Nearby.* Kai had told me he lived nearby.

He makes a face like he's thinking hard and then says, "Nah. He might have mentioned it, but I don't remember. I didn't *know* him, know him. He just used to come in here occasionally. But, like I said, I haven't seen him in months. Sorry if he blew you off. Dudes can be dicks."

The backs of my eyes hurt. *Sorry if he blew you off.* Is that what happened? If Kai's a dick then what does that make *me,* the girl trying to find him?

Pathetic.

"Okay, thanks," I say as I turn to go. But just as I push open the door, the guy calls me back.

"Oh, hey, wait up!"

I turn around. He looks like how I feel when my brain finally connects with the answer to a math problem I've been struggling over.

"Harris. I *think* his last name was Harris. He used to buy stuff here and I'm pretty sure that was the name on his credit card."

Harris.

I stare at him for a second, trying to make sure that he's

244

actually talking to me. Maybe he is in on some joke I'm not aware of. Maybe I'm hallucinating. Maybe I'm unconsciously conflating this conversation about Kai with other conversations I've had about other people in the last few months— conversations that are careening around and getting mixed up in my mind. Maybe I didn't hear him right.

"I'm sorry, what was his name?" I need him to say it again.

"Harris. At least I think so."

I feel dizzy again, like the day at the beach when that strange iciness had trickled through my chest.

"Are you okay?" he asks. "You look like you saw a ghost or something."

I shake my head.

"I'm fine," I say. "Sorry. Thank you."

It's a coincidence, I tell myself as I walk back to the beach parking lot. Harris is such a common name. I know this because I already searched for it when I was trying to find information about Sarah. There were thousands of people named Harris. *It has to be a coincidence.*

The ocean wind sweeps across the lot as I approach my car, stirring up tiny swirls of stray sand. And soon enough, my senses, momentarily overtaken by the brine in the air and the roar of the surf, transport me back to the night of the full moon. The two of us looking up at the sky with our fingers entwined. Him handing me his jacket because I was cold.

Kai Harris.

Sarah Harris.

He told me his mom died.

He told me that's why he got the tattoo on his arm, with the heart.

What if it's not a coincidence? What if . . .

What else did he tell me?

I think back to every conversation we had.

He told me she used to surf.

He told me he had a dog.

So many details from the memories that have been haunting me about my heart donor and memories about my time with Kai are overlapping and merging into this messed-up whirlpool in my brain, and I can't tease them apart. Until one detail in particular jumps out. The woman I see in my memories . . . the one who I've assumed must be Sarah Harris. Even though her hair is light and his is dark, her skin is fair and his is not, even though at first glance you might not notice: when they smile, they look alike.

But it still doesn't make sense.

Because I also told him.

I *told* him about my heart.

And he didn't react the way someone who knew his parent was a heart donor would react when learning that the person he was with had received one, did he? If Kai's mom is Sarah Harris, and Sarah Harris is my heart donor, wouldn't he have had some response when I told him about my transplant? Wouldn't he, in fact, have been really, really freaked

246

out? Even if he didn't believe that she was *my* donor, just the fact of meeting someone who had received a heart around the same time that his mom ended up being a donor would have had to have been strange for him, right? Of course it would.

I take a deep breath, filling my lungs with ocean air. It's just a coincidence. It has to be. There's no way he wouldn't have said something or had some reaction to learning about my heart transplant that night.

Unless. The thought hits me like a punch. *The night of the full moon.* Maybe, when we talked about it that night, he didn't know about his mom being a heart donor. Maybe some other family member had signed off on it when she died. Maybe he hadn't been told.

But he knows now.

Kai had to have been the one who called 9-1-1. And then, I think, he would have needed someone to pick him up at the beach lot. It was too dark to take his bike. Did he call his dad? Would he have explained what had just happened? Would he have told him about my heart?

Maybe he did. Maybe this prompted his dad to tell him about Sarah being a donor, and he figured out the rest. And maybe Kai—like me, right now—didn't know how to feel about this news or how to react.

And that's why he ghosted.

# FINDING

Instead of heading east back over the hills, I decide to take
the long way home and drive south, down the coast. I need
to clear my head. I need motion. Speed.

I put some music on—The Drums, "Days"—and open
all the windows. Maybe I shouldn't even try to find him. Not
now. He changed his phone number. He obviously doesn't
want to see me. And why would he? If he is Sarah's son, I'm
nothing but a living, breathing reminder of what was probably the worst day of his life.

The coastal scenery flashes past. Gnarled oak trees.
Hillsides covered in golden, rippling grass. Clusters of impossibly tall sequoias, the ground beneath their trunks thick with
ferns. A gust of air blows across my face and, mingled with it,
the scent of wild lavender.

And that's when I see it—or rather, remember it.

A house, overlooking the Pacific. A wind-weathered red-wood fence. A gate with a rusted latch.

The memory, so vivid, nearly makes me veer across the dividing line of the narrow, two-lane road. Heart thumping, hands shaking, I pull off onto a crumbling patch of pavement near the shoulder and turn off the ignition.

Great. Now this.

It's shaded and peaceful where I've stopped, underneath a stand of pines. But I'm still gripping the steering wheel, my knuckles white. It feels as if everything that has happened over the last weeks and months is coming to a head, whether I want it to or not.

Breathe, Chloe, breathe.

I need to calm down. To think like a scientist. Maybe that will help me figure things out. The lavender . . . Thanks to my fifth-grade science project on the five senses, I know that your sense of smell is the one most likely to trigger a really vivid scene from your past. It's because your olfactory bulb is directly wired to your amygdala and hippocampus, the brain regions responsible for emotion and memory. And right now? My amygdala and hippocampus are lighting up like an exploding supernova.

I lean my head back. Close my eyes.

Maybe I can control this.

For so long, I've been trying to push these flashes of memory away when they appear. But what if I embraced them instead? Maybe they are trying to tell me something that I need to hear. Maybe there's a message written in them, if I would only look.

I try to stay calm. Open my mind and my heart. *Look.*

I know where this house is. And I'm really, really close.

The seaside town of Bolinas sits on the western side of the San Andreas Fault, just a few miles off the Pacific Coast Highway. But you'd pass right by it if you didn't know where to look. There's no sign marking its existence. The story is that anytime the state of California posts one on the highway, the locals tear it down. People who live here pride themselves on being off the grid—a feat increasingly impossible in today's always-Instagrammed, shared, Tweeted, GPS-mapped world. But I find it without much trouble. I've been here before, a few times. On a school field trip, where we searched for sea stars, anemones, and deep-purple urchins in the rocky tide pools. And once, my parents and I stopped at a restaurant in town for barbecued oysters on the way home from a hike in Point Reyes. I turn off the highway and onto a road lined by swaying eucalyptus trees. To my left, a line of brown pelicans dives and swoops over a shallow lagoon.

The town at the end of the road consists of one main street and a small collection of buildings, including a bar, the oyster restaurant, a used bookstore, and a corner market with a farm stand in front. Above it, a collection of houses is sprinkled across the top of a windswept mesa. I pause at the only stop sign in town, and a strange, unsettling feeling washes over me. It's the same feeling that I had weeks ago on the Richmond Bridge, the day that Jane and I went to Berkeley. The feeling that I already know the way.

I continue along the main street and turn onto a steep, curving road that takes me to the top of the mesa. As the road flattens, I slow down, rolling past one house, and then another, and then another, each worn and weathered like old fishermen by salt and wind, until I come to the one with a redwood fence, faded gray.

There's a gate with a rusted latch.

The air is infused with the scent of lavender.

This is the place.

I park along the fence and get out for a better look. The house is kind of a funky shape, with different types of siding in some places, as if it's been added on to and modified several times.

The little bedroom on the third floor has a window in the back that looks like the porthole of a ship.

Next to the gate, there are thick hedges and an old-fashioned detached garage that looks too small to fit a regular car.

Old painting canvases are stacked up in the corner inside.

Although the garage and the hedges are blocking my view, I know without looking that there's a twisted cypress tree in the yard beyond, overlooking the ocean.

251

Below the yard is a path that switchbacks through thickets of wild lavender down to the beach.

My heart is drumming fast and I'm feeling dizzy, but maybe it's because I've been holding my breath. I exhale.

"Nearby," he told me. "I live nearby."

It still could be a coincidence. It could be that I'm mixing it all up in my head. But there's no way to know unless I unglue myself from this spot.

I lift the latch and walk through the gate, following a series of stepping-stones that lead me beyond the hedges and garage. There's a small lawn. And, yes, the cypress tree. A breathtaking view of the ocean beyond. From here, the waves look like the folds of an unmade bed on the water's surface. I inhale lavender, sea salt, and juniper. And then *wham*, like a punch to the chest, a memory hits me so hard that I'm nearly knocked off my feet:

I'm walking down the switchback trail that ends at the beach. In my hand, I'm holding a . . . tree branch? No, a stick. I fling it ahead of me. A flash of silver streaks by, a curling tail, diving into the lavender, chasing. I pause, look toward the jetty that juts out into the ocean below, and watch as a group of surfers paddle into the incoming swells.

This place is triggering my amygdala so much, I almost feel like it's going to short-circuit my brain.

I walk up the wooden steps to the front door, take a deep breath, and knock. And wait, half terrified that someone—that *Kai*—will answer. But no one appears to be home.

Before I can decide what to do next, a car door slams on the other side of the fence, making me jump. I whip around, bracing myself to face him, hoping that just seeing him will ground me, will help me find the right words. *I had no idea we were connected in this way. If I did . . .* What? What would I have done if I'd known? I can't really say.

But the person striding toward me is not Kai. He's much older. A man. And ahead of him, bounding across the yard, is a dog. Not just any dog. *The* dog. The silver-gray pit bull that keeps appearing in my thoughts and in my dreams. The one disappearing into the lavender after that stick. Scar above her right eye. Bright-orange collar. Huge head. *Very* happy to see me, although we've never actually met. Her curled tail whips back and forth as she weaves in and out of my legs, almost knocking me off my feet.

I lean down to scratch her ears. "Hey, girl."

My hands confirm that she is real. Her fur is warm. Her ears are soft. She rubs her head against me. Like she knows me. Like she loves me more than anyone else on earth.

"Can I help you?" the man asks. There are a bunch of things I notice all at once. He's Asian. Handsome. Fit. And also: he has a buzzed scalp and a tattoo snaking up the side of his neck.

It's him. The man from the hospital the night of my transplant. The man I'd chased down Divisadero Street with Jane. Standing here, in front of me, also undeniably real. Undeniably alive. Although I'd never gotten a good look at his face until now, it's familiar in the same way that every-thing else here is.

But what is he doing here?

I think of what Kai told me, that night on the beach: that he used to live with his mom, but not anymore.

Is this . . . Kai's dad? He told me his dad was Japanese American, as this man appears to be. It's all coming together, like some implausible, impossible puzzle. The dog, this man, Sarah Harris, Kai.

"I hope so," I manage to say, and then my throat freezes up and I'm unable to speak another word.

The man's eyes travel to the dog, who is still nuzzling me and licking my hand. "Ruby, *off.*" He shakes his head. "Obviously she's a terrible watchdog. So who are you? What do you want?"

His stare is flustering me, making me question why I ever thought it would be a good idea to just show up here. But it's too late to turn around now. "I'm Chloe," I blurt. "My name is Chloe Russell."

And as soon as I say my name, all the color drains from his face. He studies me for a long minute, as unreadable as a statue.

"Chloe Russell," he says finally. "I know who you are."

My pulse is racing. *He knows who I am?*

I watch the muscle in his jaw clench in a very specific way that triggers something in me—a feeling? a memory?—but I can't quite put my finger on why. There's a long, uncomfortable silence. Then his stone face morphs into a grimace and he runs his hand across the top of his scalp.

"I'm the one who filled out the paperwork," he begins. "I'm the one who gave the okay for the transplant to proceed. I'm the one who got the request from you, through your doctor, about your interest in making contact." He shakes his head. "Chloe Russell. Your name has been seared in my brain since I got that letter. I wasn't expecting to meet you."

It seems like a million years ago that I talked to Dr. Ahmadi about reaching out to my donor's next of kin. And *he's* the one. The one who didn't want to be found.

Dr. Ahmadi's words echo in my head: *Your donor's family has made it clear that they do not wish to be contacted.*

Is he angry that I've come here? *Is* he Kai's dad? If he is, Kai could come walking through that gate at any minute. What would he think if he saw me talking to his dad?

"I'm sorry. I don't know what I was thinking," I say, suddenly having the urge to flee. "I shouldn't have barged in on you like this."

I take a step forward, toward the front gate, toward the refuge of my parked car, but he holds up a hand.

"It's okay. Stay. Please." Then he motions me to the set of chairs near the edge of the yard that faces the ocean. We both sit, and Ruby settles at my feet. I can't stop staring at her, and at him, as I try to process the absolute strangeness of this moment. The feeling of knowing them in some way and yet not knowing them. Of recognizing them but not

255

understanding exactly why or how. It's like trying to recall a name or a word that you sense is *right there*, on the tip of your tongue, but not being able to grasp it. For a few minutes, there's only the sound of waves crashing on the beach below, seabirds calling, wind sweeping up the bluffs. I wait until he's ready.

And then, in a voice barely louder than a whisper, he tells me, "He was my son. Your donor was my son."

His son?

What is he saying? *Not* Sarah Harris? Not the person who lived at that address in my records, who *died* in December, who I feel so strongly is somehow, in some way, connected to my heart? Am I wrong, then? Maybe I haven't heard him correctly . . .

"It's not Sarah? Sarah Harris?"

"Sarah? No." Tears well in his eyes. He looks out at the Pacific, shakes his head, then turns to face me. "Sarah is . . . *was* . . . his mom. You didn't know . . . ? How, exactly, did you find me?"

My thoughts are flying in a million different directions at once. My head spins. My chest aches.

I can't explain how I found him. He'll never believe me if I tell him about the memories. About how I remember *him*, Ruby, the way to this house. He'll think I'm crazy. But I can tell him part of the truth: "Her address was in my medical record. I tracked down her landlord in Berkeley. He told me that she'd died in December, but maybe I misunderstood? My transplant was on December eighteenth, so I thought . . . But I must have gotten everything all mixed up. I'm sorry." It all comes out in a rush.

He leans forward, puts his head in his hands. It is so exactly the pose from my memory of him in my hospital room that I have to swallow a gasp.

I hear him mutter a curse, and then he starts to talk. "No. I'm the one who's sorry. I should have responded to you when your doctor reached out. But I wasn't ready to meet you. Not then. Sarah did die on December eighteenth. But she wasn't your heart donor. She was sick. She'd been sick for a long time. And later that night, my son, our son, was in a motorcycle accident. In the Broadway Tunnel. A tree . . . a Christmas tree fell from a car into his lane, and when he swerved to miss it, he skidded out and was hit by another car. He was thrown from the bike and . . ."

I'm feeling sick, because I already know the rest. Pavement rushing up. Blood.

He lets out a long breath. "He was pronounced brain-dead as soon as he was brought in to the ER. But his heart . . . his heart was perfect, untouched. I could still feel it beating."

I'm speechless. Stunned. They died on the same day? How unbelievably awful. No wonder he hadn't wanted me to contact him.

And then he keeps talking, almost as much to himself as to me. "I hadn't seen him in a while before that night. He lived with his mom." He looks at me. "I wasn't a good father.

Wasn't around when he needed me. But that night, I was the only one who could give permission for the transplant."

He bows his head, and his shoulders start to shake. He cries without making a sound. Just like he did the night of my transplant. The night he had to give the okay for a surgeon to cut out his son's still beating heart. And give it to me.

The night of my transplant . . . That memory of him crying in my room—was he in *my* room? The nurses seemed so sure that no one other than my parents and hospital staff had been in or out. I think about all the memories that led me here in the first place. About what Jane said the night we saw this man on the street in San Francisco. Could his son's last living moments in this world have been, in some elemental way, transferred to me? Through our heart? It all seems so impossible, but here we are.

I want to ask him. I want to be sure, but all I can say is, "I'm so sorry . . . I'm *so* sorry."

His son.

His son . . . I'm still trying to make sense of what I learned earlier, at the surf shop. Kai's last name is Harris. I was assuming, *believing*, that Sarah Harris was his mother. But *is* Kai related to any of this? Could my donor be . . . a cousin? Or—it has to be that the name has simply given me the wrong idea. He has no connection to any of this at all. Yet he led me here all the same. I wouldn't have found this man, I wouldn't have found out about my heart, if I hadn't gone looking for Kai.

The man stands, interrupting my thoughts. I almost expect him to ask me to leave, my presence here a horrible reminder of everything he's lost.

"Wait here," he says.

He crosses the yard and goes into the house, the screen door banging behind him.

I have so many questions. How old was my donor? What was his name? What had he wanted to do with his life? Who did he want to be? Suddenly I am ashamed at how ambivalent I've been about the future. What would this grief-stricken man think if he knew that I had almost crashed a motorcycle in the same tunnel where his son had died? That I had been skipping doses of my anti-rejection medication? That I had been smoking? I've been unforgivably careless with his son's precious heart. The weight of carrying *his* hopes and dreams, in addition to my own, is almost too much to bear.

But do I wish I hadn't come here? Do I wish I hadn't told him who I am? *No,* I think, *no.* It's still a relief. Knowing is better than not knowing.

After a few minutes, he comes out with a laptop. He boots it up and types something into the search bar.

"Here." He turns the laptop toward me. "These are the most recent photos his mother sent me. From last fall, around his seventeenth birthday."

For a long, bewildering moment I stare at the screen, the images refusing to sink in.

And then I nearly drop the laptop onto the ground.

My ears start to ring. The horizon beyond the edge of the yard tips on its axis and turns upside down. My heart, *his heart*, beats so hard that I feel as though it's going to explode from my chest and land in a bloody heap in front of me on the ground.

The photos of the boy who gave me his heart are not possible.

These photos don't make any sense.

These photos are of Kai.

≋ DEAD IS DEAD ≋

Wake up! I tell myself. Because I know I must be dreaming. I must have dreamed I was sitting in a yard overlooking the ocean. At the house that has the gate with the rusted latch. I must have dreamed of a visit to Bolinas. Dreamed up an encounter with the man who claims he is Kai's dad. Dreamed the dog. Because what just happened can't be real. What just happened can't have *actually happened.*

Wake up! I tell myself. *Wake up!*

I don't believe in ghosts. Never have. Never will.

Dead is dead is dead is dead.

I open my eyes, not sure where I am, not sure who I am, not sure if the ground beneath my feet is going to hold steady, not sure of anything.

I am lying on a cracked leather sofa, a throw pillow

behind my head. I look around and try to find something to anchor me to reality. The inside of this house is stuck in another decade, not modern and uncluttered like my own. Yet there is so much that is familiar: the ancient television with a VHS player on top; the oil painting of the twisted cypress tree outside; and the '70s swag lamp hanging from a golden chain over the dining room table. Across from me, a huge window looks out at the yard and at the sea beyond, where waves endlessly sweep, crest, and crash on the shore. I'm definitely not home in my bed. I'm definitely not just waking up from a dream. I'm still in Bolinas. And I must have passed out.

Kai's father appears from the kitchen and hands me a glass of water. He seems uncomfortable. Anxious. It's clear that he's unsure about what to do. Call my parents? Drive me home? Dial 9-1-1? I sit up and try to pull myself together. I take a sip of the water, then set it on the coffee table. Stuffing my shaking hands into my jacket pockets, I focus on breathing normally.

"I'm okay," I say, anticipating his question. "It's just kind of emotional to meet you. To see the photos of . . . your son."

I don't believe in ghosts.

I note that there are moving boxes stacked near the right side of the room, some still open, some sealed with packing tape. And, near the door, several surfboards are propped against the wall. Seeing the orange one with black trim sends the world tilting again. It's his. The one he carried with him every time I met him at the beach.

It's Kai's.

Dead is dead is dead is dead.

I need to get out of here. *Now.*

"Are you sure you're okay?" Kai's father asks. "I mean . . . should we call someone? I'm concerned about you being all right to drive home."

More drama for my parents. Another trip to the hospital. "Calling someone" is the last thing I need.

"I'm fine. Really," I say. "I should go." I stand up and try to look like I'm in control, when all I want to do is fall apart.

The next ten minutes are a blur. His name is Michael, he tells me. Michael Yamada. He gives me his number and asks for mine. He makes me promise to text as soon as I walk in my front door. I tell him again that I am fine.

I'm not fine, of course. But I can't tell him the whole story. I can't tell him why. He would never believe me. No one would believe me.

I don't believe me.

I drive home in a daze, thinking about every impossible thing I just learned. Michael is Kai's father. The same man I remember from the night of my transplant. The man I spotted on Divisadero Street. Ruby is Kai's dog. The one I remember chasing balls in the sand. The one I remember diving into lavender on a hill above the ocean. Sarah Harris was Kai's mother. She is the woman who dies in my dreams, the woman who lived at the address that Jane and I visited in

Berkeley. Kai had her smile. And I know all this because, as unlikely as it might seem, some of his memories must have merged with mine.

This I can almost accept. This I can almost wrap my head around. This I have been already half believing for months. Every cell in your body contains your complete genetic code. Your DNA. The blueprint for what makes you *you*. Maybe habits, personality traits, even memories really can live on through a transplanted organ. It would explain why I remember Kai's parents, why I inspire such a ridiculously joyful reaction in his dog, why I know the way to the places he has lived. Why I relive his death almost every single night. It doesn't seem completely out of the realm of possibility that I have inherited some of Kai's life along with his heart.

It's the rest of the story that I can't accept. That I can't believe. If Kai is my donor, then how can I explain this entire summer? The surf lessons. All those times we met on the beach. How can I explain the living, breathing, flesh-and-blood Kai whose skin I touched, whose lips I kissed?

It's not possible for someone to be alive and dead at the same time. Not possible at all.

Which means that ever since I met him, I have either been out of my mind, or everything I thought I knew—about life and death, about objective reality, about the nature of time and space and the agreed-upon, scientifically accepted laws of the physical universe—is completely, totally, and incredibly wrong.

 **FALLING**

I am never going to get out of bed again.

My bed is the only place that makes sense. The only place that is safe. If I try to get out, if I even try to dip a toe over the edge I will fall, fall, fall into a deep, bottomless black hole. Into nothing. Into oblivion. I will keep falling forever. But if I stay here, if I never leave, maybe things that make no sense at all will stop happening.

My mom has come into my room three times.

Four times.

Five.

Chloe, are you all right?

Chloe, what is wrong?

Chloe, answer me, damnit!

She called my dad at work. And the last time she was in here, she threatened to call 9-1-1. I knew that would mean having to go to the hospital. Having to get out of this bed. So I opened my eyes and told her the truth. That my heart was fine. My head was not. I wanted to be alone. I wanted to sleep. I would do whatever she wanted later if she just left me alone and let me sleep.

The blinds are twisted tight. I burrow under my blankets. I try to think as little as possible. So that I see nothing. Hear nothing. Feel nothing.

But my mind has other ideas. It won't stop. Can't stop. *Waves. Tunnels. Heartbeats. Kai.*

He was real.

He was not a ghost.

I don't believe in ghosts.

I hear my mom moving around in the house, feel the light vibration of her footsteps. She's on the phone, speaking in a voice so low and muffled that I can't make out the words. I don't need to. She is most certainly talking about me. Stressing out about me. Worrying. Unable to do her work.

I dig around in my nightstand drawer for the bottle of anti-anxiety pills that the doctor had prescribed when I came home from the hospital a few weeks ago—after whatever the fuck it was that happened with my heart. And with Kai.

His heart.

Our heart.

There are fifteen pills. Briefly, impulsively, I wonder what would happen if I swallowed them all. Would I fall asleep and never wake up? That seems kind of relaxing. I'm so exhausted. . . .

But even after everything that has happened, everything that's making me question my own sanity, I don't actually want to die. I just want to sleep. To give my thoughts a rest. So I swallow two of the pills and lie there, looking up at the ceiling until my eyelids get heavy, so heavy that I can't possibly hold them up for even a millisecond longer, and then I am floating in a deep and dreamless sleep.

When I awake, my mom is sitting on the edge of my bed.

"Hey, sweetie," she says. "You feeling better?"

"A little," I say.

"Good."

She climbs in bed just like she did at the hospital and puts her head on my extra pillow. We both lie like that for a bit, staring at the ceiling.

"Are you going to tell me what's going on?"

I don't *know* what's going on. But I hate that I'm making my parents worry. Again. Maybe I can share at least a half-truth.

"I went to see my heart donor's father."

I can tell that she's surprised by this and not sure how to respond. She doesn't even know that I had reached out to

Dr. Ahmadi about contacting my donor's family in the first place, all those months ago.

"I see," she says. "That must have been . . . Was it hard? I wish you'd told us, Chloe. Dad or I would have gone with you. You didn't have to do it all alone."

"I know. I'm sorry I didn't tell you. Anyway, it was hard. Really, really hard. And not at all what I expected." Even this small confession makes me feel a little better. A little less like I'm about to explode from keeping everything bottled up.

My mom is quiet for a while, and I wonder what she's thinking.

"I'll never forget the first time I saw your heart," she says finally. "We were doing an ultrasound a few weeks after I had a positive pregnancy test, and I was holding my breath. I don't know if you know this, but we had a number of false alarms before we had you. Your dad and I had been trying for a long time."

I didn't know this.

"So this was pretty exciting stuff—getting to see you for the first time. But it wasn't exactly what I expected. Ultrasounds are really fuzzy, and all we could see is what looked like a little bean beating there on the screen." My mom smiles at the memory. "I laughed out loud, thinking how weird it was that this—I don't know *what* because you didn't even look like anything resembling a baby yet—that this tiny beating pinto bean was my future child. That's how we got your nickname, you know."

"Little Bean" is what my parents used to call me, until one night at dinner when I told them that I was too old for them to call me that anymore. "It's embarrassing," I'd said.

My dad had protested: "Aw, c'mon, Little Bean, it's a great nickname!"

But my mom got it. "You might have to remind me when I forget, but I'll try," she'd said. I didn't have to remind her. She understood that just about *everything* embarrassed me when I was twelve. My dad, not so much.

She looks at me and pushes a coil of hair away from my forehead.

"When we found out about your heart defect and how sick you were last year, it seemed, somehow, like I had failed you. *Was it my fault?* I wondered. Like maybe I had eaten too much canned tuna when I was pregnant or was too forgetful about the prenatal vitamins. I couldn't stop thinking about the half glass of Chardonnay I drank in my third trimester on your dad's birthday."

"Mom, what? That's crazy."

"I know it sounds ridiculous now, but that's what I thought."

Her eyes get that look like she's about to cry.

"We were so relieved after the transplant—we *are* so relieved that you are still here with us—that I haven't thought as much as I should about how strange it must be for you. How strange it must be that some other mother once waited to see the heart that's now beating inside your chest. That

269

your life is now connected to this person who you've never met, will never meet, but must wonder about all the time. Every day."

Never met. Will never meet. I wish I could tell her the whole story. I want to tell her. But I know that if I try to talk to her about Kai, about everything that's been going on since my transplant, it will only make her worry even more. About my head *and* my heart. So instead I just listen.

"I know you are trying to find your way back after this," she continues. "And I know this whole experience has changed you. How could it not? It's changed me too. I'm still finding my way back too. So is Dad. But things are going to be all right because we all have each other. Okay?"

"Okay," I say.

But I feel a *but* coming on.

"We are going to find somebody for you to talk to, and I need you to agree to go."

This is not a terrible idea. "I will," I promise.

"And we also need to talk about the surfing."

"Don't make me quit," I beg. *Don't make me quit. Don't make me quit.*

"It's dangerous," she says. "We have to run it by Dr. Ahmadi. Does this boy you are taking lessons from know about your heart?"

And just like that, the momentary release of telling my mom about meeting Michael Yamada is overtaken by my inability to make sense of anything else.

Very good question, Mom, I think. *Probably not. Because he's dead and his heart is my heart, which is not possible and why I am likely having a mental breakdown and haven't been in the mood to get out of bed.*

I hear the doorbell ring.

"We'll talk more about this later," my mom says, slipping out from under my covers. The bell rings again, longer this time. The ringer, whoever it is, must be holding it down.

"I hope you don't mind," she says as she heads to the door, "but I borrowed your phone to track down your friend Jane. It seemed like you've been missing her lately."

Although I'm kind of embarrassed that my mom has called Jane, I'm also glad that Jane has actually showed up.

I get out of bed to find a sweatshirt. My feet sink into the shaggy purple rug. I do not fall into oblivion.

"Your mom is a total pain in the ass," Jane says as she sweeps into my room. She flops onto my bed, acting like she hasn't been ignoring me for weeks now. "She called me like six times. My parents can't even remember my friends' names."

Maybe that's true of her dad, but Jane's mom, who I met over the summer, does, in fact, know my name.

I pull my sweatshirt on and sit at my desk.

"It's good to see you too, Jane."

"Oh, stop being so dramatic," she says. "If I didn't want to come, I wouldn't have. What's going on? Your mom said you are acting super weird and won't come out of your room.

271

I think she's worried that you may be on drugs." She squints at me. "Are you?"

"You mean aside from the pile of pills I have to take every day for basically the rest of my life? No."

"Well, on the bright side, swallowing a few pills for the 'rest of your life' means that you'll *have* one."

"Jane," I tell her. "Everything is messed up. *I'm* messed up."

She sighs. "*Everybody* is messed up, Chloe. I don't know why you think you're so special."

"Not ordinary messed up. Like seriously, maybe *neurologically*, messed up." I take a deep breath. I have to tell somebody. I *want* to tell somebody. "I don't think I have a firm grip on reality at the moment. I'm scared."

"What are you talking about? What happened yesterday? Your mom said you seemed fine before she left in the morning and that you weren't fine when she came home."

So I tell her everything. About visiting Michael Yamada in Bolinas. About learning that his son's heart is the one beating inside my chest. About finding out that Sarah Harris was my donor's mom. About confirming that my donor died in a motorcycle crash. And about Michael showing me the photos of Kai.

Jane jolts up in my bed. "Wait a second, *what*? That can't be possible. That's *not* possible."

"This is what I'm telling you!" I say. "I have been taking surf lessons from someone who doesn't exist. From my *dead*

272

heart donor. Or not taking surf lessons. Maybe I'm halluci-nating, a schizophrenic, I don't know what."

Jane stares at me.

"Please don't look at me like that," I tell her. Now I'm thinking that I shouldn't be saying anything about this to anyone, even Jane.

"No," Jane says. "No. It's a different guy. Maybe they look a little alike or something."

"Jane, no, it was him. I know it was him."

She's quiet for a second, thinking, and then, "Can you ask his dad for a photo? Do you think he'd send you one?"

"I already have one. I asked him for it yesterday."

After I'd confirmed with Michael that I got home safe, I had to ask him for proof. To be sure, again, that I hadn't dreamed the whole thing up. *Would you mind sending me a photo of your son?* I asked.

He texted me back right away. Maybe it was his way of confirming I wasn't a figment of his imagination either.

"Send it to me," Jane says.

"Why?" I ask. "You never met him, right? Nobody I know has met him! You even thought I had made him up, remember?"

To me, the scariest thing possible is to have something wrong with your mind. With your ability to tell fact from fiction. Real from unreal.

"Chloe, just do it." She leans over, picks up my phone from my nightstand and hands it to me. "You say nobody you know has met him, but what about Tyler? I can send it to him and ask if he knows him."

Tyler. From the party in San Francisco. The one who called me out for taking his wave. Jane is now talking to me like an adult talks to a child, in a slow, careful voice. "Let's just ask him. I'm telling you, they probably just look alike and you're only thinking it's the same guy because you are going through some shit right now. Which is totally understandable, all things considered. Okay?"

I want this to be true, so I unlock my phone and find the text from Michael Yamada. In the photo he sent, Kai is at a restaurant, next to his mom, looking a little embarrassed to have to pose behind a cupcake with a birthday candle on top, but smiling anyway. Their dimples match. Looking at it again, at his smile, at the tattoo peeking out below the sleeve of his T-shirt, I'm more certain than ever that the Kai I met at the beach every Wednesday and the Kai in this photo are one and the same, but I move aside to show Jane anyway.

She stares at the photo for a minute. "You're sure you're not just getting faces mixed up in your head? I mean, maybe there really is something going on with your brain. Cognitively speaking. Like, I once heard about this thing called face blindness?"

"Maybe . . ." I answer weakly. I know she's trying to help, but all of her attempts to apply logic to the situation are making me feel worse. Even though, if the tables were turned, this is exactly what I would do too. Jane and I are more alike than she thinks.

"Jane, I'm sorry about everything. About almost killing us on the bike, and I should have been looking out for you at that party, and all this time you've been dealing with all my . . . shit. I'm just . . . I'm sorry."

Jane's face softens.

"Thank you for saying that. Now send me that picture."

I do as she says, and then she types out a message to Tyler: *Do you know this guy?*

A few minutes—to me, an eternity—later, her phone chirps. She holds up her screen so we both can see.

I don't know him . . .

My stomach lurches. So it's true that I can't tell real from unreal. Fact from fiction. What is wrong with me?

But then something else appears on Jane's screen.

• • •

Tyler is sending another text.

I've seen him, though. Serious shredder.

Where? Jane types.

At the Point. With your friend . . .

Chloe?

Yep. Chloe.

Jane's face freezes, while my heart, Kai's heart, our heart, begins to race. The blood vessels in my temples pulse so hard that I can barely put together a complete thought.

Now Jane is calling Tyler. She puts him on speaker.

"Hey, Jane . . ."

"Hey. So you've definitely seen the guy in that photo? Recently? You're *sure* it's him?"

"Jane, are you, like, tripping, or something? I told you yes. Definitely. Same tattoo. And . . . I don't know how close you are with Chloe or anything, but if you are, maybe back off? I think she and that dude are together. At least they seemed to be the last time I saw them."

"That's not why I'm asking!" Jane snaps.

Now she seems even more rattled than I am. "When's the last time you saw them?" she asks Tyler.

"I don't know . . . maybe a few weeks ago? They were paddling out when I was coming in."

The date of the full moon. The last time I saw him alive. Or not alive.

Alive. Had to be. Otherwise, Tyler is hallucinating too.

Jane and I have forgotten that we still have him on the line. His voice makes both of us jump.

"Yo, do you have me on speaker?"

≋ **THEORIES** ≋

As a person who believes only in science, my knowing Kai—surfing with Kai, kissing Kai, maybe even falling in love with Kai—is something that I can't explain. At least not in terms of any established, agreed-upon theory about how the universe works. This is what I turn over and over in my head as I sit in the sand and watch the waves.

It's Wednesday afternoon. The onshore wind hits me square in the face. I should have checked the weather before I left the house. There are a couple of surfers in the water, but the waves are no good. Crumbling into foam before they rise high enough to carry a board. "Nothing but closeouts," Kai would say. For a minute, I forget that he is not coming. That he's not about to emerge out of the dunes any second now, his board under his arm.

The guys out there now must be beginners. They don't yet know how to read the wind and the waves. They bob up and down in the choppy water, like buoys, not realizing that they probably aren't going to catch anything today.

Studying them, I think about how I've spent so much time this summer on the surface of the water without really knowing much about what's underneath. An entire world beneath me, one that is almost as foreign as another planet. Sea lions weaving their way through kelp forests. Fish darting in and out of coral reefs. What must it be like to live down in the deep, in the spaces where the light hardly reaches, where weird, alien-like sea creatures glow like carnival rides in the dark? If I miss so much of my own planet, perhaps my under-standing of the universe is much smaller than I thought.

The wind blows sand sideways and I zip up my jacket. Pull my hood over my head.

"Not going to play in the waves today, mermaid?"

I'm jolted from my brooding by the old swimmer man. He stands next to me holding his goggles, a towel around his neck. It's almost as if he appeared out of nowhere.

"No, not today," I say. "They're no good."

"The waves do what they do," he says. "There's no good or bad."

I almost want to say, *Thanks, Yoda*, but I know he's just being kind, in his way. I nod toward the water. "Looks pretty cold for a swim."

"Oh, I don't mind the cold," he says. "Gets the blood flowing."

"Actually," I say, "hypothermia does the opposite. Just a word of warning."

He chuckles. "Such a smart one. Don't you worry. I've been swimming here since before you were born."

"Well, be careful anyway," I say. "I'm not *that* confident in my CPR skills."

He laughs. "Let's hope it doesn't come to that."

He pulls his swim goggles down over his eyes and holds on to the ends of the towel with both hands.

"I'll leave you to wait for your boy."

My chest squeezes tight.

"He's not coming," I say, clawing my fingers through the damp sand.

"Not coming!" he says. "Hmm. That's a shame."

I nod in agreement. "It is."

He smiles. "Ah, to be young and in love again . . . I bet he'll change his mind. You two had the look."

I stare up at his weathered face. "The look?"

"The look of people who belong together. Even if he doesn't show up today, he will eventually."

Then he continues on toward the water, dropping his towel in the sand just behind the high-tide line. I watch him dive into the surf, my eyes filling with tears.

The look of people who belong together.

Somewhere deep down, there's a part of me that still hopes, despite all recent evidence to the contrary, that the old man is right. That Kai *will* show up eventually. Because that's why I'm sitting on this beach, if I'm honest with myself. Maybe if I wait here long enough, he'll appear.

But that's not possible, right? People can't be dead and then alive. They don't exist and not exist at the same time. Time moves forward. It can't move back. Not possible, yet it *was*. He *was* alive. Here, on this very beach, he existed, even when he didn't. Tyler saw him. The old man saw him too. But how? It still makes no sense.

Unless . . . I think.

What if?

What if time splits?

Multiple probabilities.

Multiple universes.

Multiple realities.

I recall that poem from freshman English: *Two roads diverged in a yellow wood* . . . In one universe, you take the road less traveled, and in the other you get eaten by a bear. Or rescue Little Red Riding Hood. Or find a magic ring.

Suppose we *do* live in a multiverse, where multiple probabilities spawn multiple realities.

If this is possible, maybe there's one, or two, or twenty universes where Kai never did die in that tunnel.

Where he reconciled with his dad.

Where he still paddles out into the ocean most afternoons and launches himself off racing waves.

Where he teaches beginners to surf.

Could one of those universes somehow, in some way, have intersected with mine?

≈ KAI, DECEMBER 18TH ≈

Like for most significant events in my life, he doesn't show. So why am I surprised? This is how it's always been. Birthdays. Parent-teacher conferences. The time I broke my arm falling out of a banyan tree. But this? This sort of takes the selfish, irresponsible, deadbeat-dad shit to a whole new level.

Because I could use just a little help burying my mom.

The one who raised his only child.

Mom must have known he wouldn't step up and do the responsible thing. That's why, as I found out in these last few weeks, she basically planned her own funeral. She made all the arrangements. She wrote me instructions. There's a list with numbers for me to call, including one for the eco-friendly burial provider, which is something I wouldn't have thought of, but is completely her. Also, the life insurance agent and the caterer "*who will make sure that everyone is fed after the service.*"

"*You are going to be okay,*" she'd whispered, pressing the list into my hands. "*You are thoughtful and kind and brave. Stay that way, for me. I love you always, sweet boy.*"

She was hardly recognizable at the end. Dying does some pretty messed-up things to a person's body. There were more than a few times in the ICU when I wanted to run out, to run away, because I could hardly deal with how horrible it was, and it took all the strength I had to not let it show on my face.

Instead, I cracked jokes about our Berkeley-on-steroids neighbor, who gave tarot card readings to half-drunk college students in her velvet-draped garage and was always adopting stray cats. I played Mom's favorite music. Velvet Underground. David Bowie. Radiohead. I read a bunch of books aloud, even if I wasn't sure that she was still able to follow along.

After she was gone, I had to call my grandma to tell her the news. She lives in an assisted care place in Southern California and hadn't been able to come here to say goodbye. When I told her that Mom had passed, she sobbed so uncontrollably it was hard to understand a word she said. And then I called my dad. No answer. Left voice mails. No response.

There are other people I have to call. So many. Mom's work colleagues. Jake and Tom, our friends from across the street who are dog-sitting Ruby. Our landlord. I did reach Jill, Mom's closest friend, who was on her way to the hospital but got stuck in evening rush-hour traffic when it happened. She'd been coming by on and off all week, bringing me more food than a whole houseful of people could eat. I could tell she felt terrible about not being with me today, but it wasn't her fault. It's hard to know when . . . to predict the timing of it. I told her she should turn around. There wasn't anything left for her to do at the hospital.

"Stay with us tonight, Kai," Jill said. "She wouldn't want you to be home alone. And tomorrow, we'll stop by your place and pick up some clothes and things. You are staying with us as long as you need."

"Thank you," I said. "There are a few things I need to do here first, and then I'll come by."

"I'll come help," she said.

"No, it won't take long. I promise I'll come over after."

I felt bad lying, but I knew she wouldn't take no for an answer. I just can't sit around tonight in someone else's house. Right now, I need motion. Velocity. Speed. Enough movement to shake off the weight of the last few days. The last weeks. And to shake off the guilt that I am also relieved that I don't have to spend another day in that hospital room. That it's over.

I check my phone one more time before I start up the bike. There are no messages from my dad.

I feel like an idiot for reaching out to him in the first place. Maybe I was temporarily deluded. I'd been thinking back on the times when I was really young and he and Mom were still together. When he sometimes took me out in the ocean in the mornings. When he taught me how to navigate the impact zone

284

and how to hold my own in bigger and bigger surf. When he sometimes, for a little while, acted like a real dad.

But in the end, competing always came first. More often than not, he was far more interested in doing his own thing, leaving it to Mom to cover the rent and juggle work, parenting, and all the other stuff that keeps a family going. Eventually, she got tired of moving from place to place—Hawaii, Australia, South Africa—tired of him being gone for days without calling, tired of playing the disapproving grown-up, constantly ruining his endless summer. She wanted to finish her degree. To settle down in one place. To plan more than just a few weeks or months ahead. So we left. And he was free of responsibility. Free of us. I don't know why she stayed as long as she did. Love doesn't always make sense, I guess.

I pull out of the parking garage and head north. I need to get out of the city. I need to get away from the traffic and the stoplights and the noise. I ride across the bridge and race up 101, thinking that I'll switch to Highway 1 in Mill Valley and follow it along the coast.

Motion is good. You have to focus on what you are doing. Can't think of anything else.

But tonight it's not working.

I can't stop thinking.

Thinking about Mom.

And my dad.

It occurs to me that he could be traveling. Maybe I just assumed he hasn't been picking up when he's actually

somewhere remote, out of reach. With him, this is always pos-
sible. I know he's been staying temporarily at the rental house
that used to belong to my grandparents in Bolinas. I could go
there right now. To be sure.

I keep riding north. I pass through Stinson Beach, sweep
around the lagoon, and make the left into Bolinas. Ride by the
farm stand, through town, and up onto the mesa. I slow, but
don't stop, when I get to the house.

The lights are on.

His truck is parked out front.

He's there.

I guess my dad decided, again, that we didn't need him.

So fuck him. From now on, I won't need him. Not ever. And
if karma exists, someday he, unlike my mom, will die alone.

I make a U-turn at the end of the road and head back
toward San Francisco.

The fog is pouring through the Golden Gate in great billowing
heaps as I descend toward the bridge. Only the upper cables are
visible, and the tops of the towers, each studded with a bright
red light. It looks and feels like a ghost bridge, suspended over
nothing, unmoored to land. The amber streetlamps barely pen-
etrate the thick fog. Headlights appear out of nowhere. The San
Francisco skyline is hidden. It's almost as if the city itself has
disappeared.

Visibility improves once I drop into the underpass at the
base of the bridge and loop around onto Lombard Street. Traffic

is busy. It's holiday rush, with taillights blinking all the way up to Van Ness. I slowly navigate between the cars until the traffic lets up. It feels good to move again.

The Broadway Tunnel is up ahead. I have always loved speeding through it. Dark and tubelike, it gives me the sense that I'm slipping through a wormhole into another universe. Another life. I am a space warrior. A Time Lord.

The entrance sucks me in like a great black hole and I drop down into its vortex, lights blurring together to form a single bright line. December air mixed with car exhaust seeps through the seams of my face shield.

I lean into the curve and just as I'm pulling out of it, I see something in the middle of the lane, directly ahead of me. A Christmas tree . . .

Fuuuck.

I swerve, barely missing the tree, but feel the bike sliding under me. It seems like it simultaneously takes an instant and forever for me to skid into the guardrail.

The impact is hard. Around me, car tires shriek as they lock up on the pavement, the sound echoing off the tunnel walls.

I smell burning rubber. My head is ringing. My leg feels like it's on fire.

And then . . . nothing.

I open my eyes. There is a woman leaning over me, frantically yelling into my face.

Mom?

Brown eyes. Reddish hair. She is not Mom. This woman is younger and, I note dimly, dressed up for a party.

It takes me a moment to register that I am lying on the floor of the tunnel. I am under my bike. There are cars stopped at odd angles everywhere. I hear the sound of sirens in the distance.

"Don't move!" the woman is yelling. "Don't move! The ambulance is almost here!"

She seems pretty upset.

My leg is pinned. I try to free it and pain rises from it like a rocket, setting off fireworks in my brain. The woman has a hand on my shoulder. She's trying to keep me from sitting up.

Horns are blaring. Red lights are flashing. I see paramedics running toward me with a stretcher. I shift my weight just a bit and another explosion of pain shoots through my leg.

I pass out again.

When I wake up, I'm in a hospital bed. Is this the same hospital I left just hours before? My head hurts. My leg hurts. It's in a cast. And there, over in the chair in the corner, looking terrible and desperate: my dad.

I stare at him. He looks like he hasn't slept in a hundred years.

"Kai," he says, his voice a mix of relief and sorrow. "Kai." He puts his head in his hands. In a whisper, he says, "I'm sorry. I couldn't. I couldn't see her. Forgive me."

"She's gone," I tell him, even though he already knows.

And then I do the thing I've been trying not to do for months, that I especially didn't want to do in front of him. I start to cry. Not a holding-back cry. Not a trying-to-be-brave one, but a real one. Like a kid who's more lost than he's ever been.

My bike is totaled. My leg is broken. I have a concussion. But I am not permanently damaged. I will live. The driver behind me—the one on her way to a Christmas party—acted fast. She stopped in time.

My dad is still there in the morning, when the doctor comes in with an update. "Your CT scan looks good," she says. "No swelling in the brain. We can discharge you in a few days once we're sure you can move around with the leg. It's going to require some rehab."

She hesitates for a second, gives my dad a pointed look, then continues. "Maybe think about getting a car. You were lucky. Know what we usually call motorcycle riders here in the ER?"

"What?" I ask.

"Organ donors."

A MULTITUDE
≋≋ OF UNIVERSES ≋≋

What happens in the universe where Kai gets to live?

Maybe I die because I don't get a heart in time. It's a scene that's all too easy to conjure up: Hospital room. Oxygen mask. Nurses rushing toward me with a crash cart. My soul aching for everyone and everything I'm leaving behind. And for everything I'll miss. Trips I'll never take. Books I'll never read. Crushes I'll never kiss. The last thing I see are the shock paddles poised above me, and then there's nothing. *A nothing so complete and empty, I know without a doubt that I am dead.*

Or maybe I live but don't even know he exists. I never do walk into that surf shop, never find his number pinned to the wall in there, never know the thrill of racing across a wave like a sea goddess and feeling, for a few brief moments, like I'm invincible.

Maybe I never have a heart defect to begin with. I don't collapse on my high school's track and miss the final semester of my senior year. I graduate on time. There's no summer school, no helping Jane with her trigonometry homework or getting a heart tattoo. Instead I end up on some other path, in some other story, with its own mysteries, twists, and turns.

Maybe we all still come together somehow, and in some way that I don't even imagine yet. There are so many possibilities, so many forks in so many roads. Enough to fill up a multitude of universes.

≋≋≋ WHAT IF? ≋≋≋

How far away is a parallel universe? Light-years? An eternity? What if other realities aren't far away at all, but instead so close to our own that if we only knew they were there, we could reach out and touch them? Some physicists believe that parallel universes are all around us—reality upon reality stacked up against one another like pages in a book.

If this is indeed true, is it possible for two separate realities to merge? A couple of pebbles are tossed into a pond, sending ripples outward. If the ripples extending from each pebble reach each other, their trajectory is changed, and the pattern on the water morphs into something else. Something less recognizable, less predictable. Kai and Chloe. Chloe and Kai. Could something that mixed up our matter, our cells—something like a heart transplant—have shifted our trajectories? Caused our separate realities to overlap?

The day that Kai and I first met was a Wednesday, of course. Partly sunny with a light offshore wind, the waves waist-high. I felt awkward in the wetsuit, unsure of what I was even supposed to wear underneath (*Swimsuit? Nothing? I decided on swimsuit.*). I was also starting to second-guess the surf-shop guy's advice about the board I bought: maybe it *was* too large. As I sat on a log that had washed up on the beach and watched the waves, wondering what I had gotten myself into, a voice materialized behind me:

"Chloe?"

I turned toward it.

"Kai?"

Did the universes spinning around us give any indication, in that moment, that we were at the center of some kind of impossible cosmic crash?

If they did, we didn't notice. I was thinking *nice hair*, maybe he was thinking *cute freckles*, or whatever you think when you lock eyes with someone for the first time and there's something there, an attractive force you may not even be fully conscious of yet.

I remember him explaining the basics: board waxing, how to read the water to find the best path for the paddle out, how to spot riptides. First, we just practiced pop-ups for a while on the sand. I felt like an idiot doing this, especially once I started to sweat in my wetsuit. I didn't want to sweat in front of this guy.

"How well can you swim?" he'd asked.

"I'm a great swimmer," I lied.

We bodysurfed first, so I could get a feel for how to read and ride a wave.

Despite the water being so cold that it made me gasp at first, I found that I was a stronger swimmer than I had thought. I loved letting the waves sweep me to shore. Hearing the roar of the surf in my ears. For the first time since my transplant, I was having fun. Losing myself. I wasn't thinking about hearts. Or summer school. Or hospitals. Or scars.

We made plans to meet again the next week.

As the summer progressed, Kai and I found each other every Wednesday on the same beach. Maybe, I think now, it was the only place we *could* meet. The only space in the cosmos where our realities had extraordinarily, miraculously intertwined. Sometimes he was there before me, waxing his board. Sometimes I would arrive early and sit in the cool sand, watching for him to walk out of the dunes. Every Wednesday, we paddled out together and floated on the surface of the water—sometimes so close we could almost touch, sometimes farther away, but always within sight of each other. A universe of two, of Chloe and Kai, took shape.

But it couldn't last, could it? By crossing the boundaries that kept our realities apart, we were breaking the rules. Rebelling against the laws of physics. Even if we didn't know it. I think back to that night when we'd texted in the moonlight, and how garbled the connection was when he'd tried to call. Maybe our texts found a way to cross universes when our voices couldn't. Maybe I'll never understand how it all happened.

Perhaps multiple universes *can* occupy the same physical space, but science insists that we should only be able to perceive one reality at a time. Otherwise, our existence would fall into chaos, wouldn't it? There would be nothing certain to hang on to if every *or* turned into an *and*: right *and* left, up *and* down, live *and* die. How can you shape your own destiny if choices don't have consequences? Because even in a multiverse where every probability is possible, in individual realities, some probabilities must cancel out others. And in this particular universe, if I live, Kai dies.

Ultimately, you can't share the same heart.

 GOODBYE

Kai doesn't have a grave that I can visit. There is no headstone inscribed with his date of birth and date of death. No place to lay flowers. After he died, his dad scattered his ashes in the waves.

A few weeks have passed since Tyler confirmed that he'd seen Kai and me, together, on the beach. Since I found out that the impossible was, somehow, possible. In that time, the copy of Sarah Harris's death certificate arrived. I had completely forgotten I ordered it from the Alameda County records department. It didn't tell me anything new, of course, but seeing the cause of death—*lymphatic leukemia*—written in black and white, and holding physical proof that she was not my donor, still shook me.

Jane and I are now official high school graduates. Once everything calmed down, my parents took us out to dinner, along with Jane's mom, her stepdad, and the terror twins, who really aren't so terrible. They're squirmy and full of energy and exhausting, but they adore their big sister. I think she adores them too, even if she's always threatening to lock them outside when they won't leave us alone.

The two of us are on good behavior: instead of crashing parties and almost crashing motorcycles, we've been crashing in front of the TV at my house. My mom found me a therapist and, even though I can't tell her everything, it's helpful to be able to tell her some of it. Jane's cooled it on the partying for now. I'm helping her work on a portfolio so that she can apply to art school.

I also accepted my admission invitation from UC Berkeley—after everything, it felt like the right choice—but I'm deferring for a year. I might spend some time traveling. Surf somewhere where the water is warm. Climb the Eiffel Tower. Ride the subway in Tokyo.

Kai's heart, now mine, continues to beat.

Today, I get in my car, saying to myself that I just need motion. Speed. Wind rushing through open windows.

But I know where I'm going.

I head west, winding over golden hills and through valleys shadowed by tall, whispering trees. I turn off the Pacific Coast Highway at Bolinas. I drive under the canopy of eucalyptus trees along the lagoon, and make my way to the house that sits above the ocean.

I wonder if Kai's dad is even still here. It looked like he was about to move when I had showed up several weeks ago.

But he answers the door. Well, Ruby answers it first by practically knocking it off its hinges and greeting me with her dog version of "You are my favorite person in the universe."

Michael shakes his head. "Not one to call ahead, are you?" But this time, he doesn't seem upset that I'm here.

"I was close by and I thought I'd just . . . I'm sorry. I probably should have texted you first."

"It's okay." He opens the door.

"Are you leaving?" I ask as I step through the threshold. Inside, it's even emptier than it was. Most of the boxes are gone. All that remains: the old sofa, piled with blankets and a pillow, and Kai's board leaning against the wall like a ghost. The air smells of fresh paint.

"Yeah," he says. "The house is going on the market next week."

He doesn't offer any more information than that, but perhaps he doesn't want to live in a place that holds too many memories and too much sadness.

We both stand there for a moment, unsure of what to say. He is a quiet guy. Like Kai.

"I was just wondering," I ask. "Those photos you showed me. Of . . . Kai?" I almost can't speak his name. "Could you send me a few more?"

"Sure." He nods. "Of course."

Being in the same room with him now, several weeks removed from the shock of finding out his connection to Kai, I can't stop studying his face. In some ways they look alike, and in some ways they don't. While Kai and his mom shared a smile, and those dimples, he and his dad have the same jawline, same skin tone, and the same build—lean and surf-sculpted. Especially, I notice similarities in the way they move. I'll bet anything that they looked most alike when they were in the water. When they launched their boards off the wall of a wave, defying gravity.

And as soon as that thought enters my mind, an idea—maybe mine, maybe Kai's, maybe *ours*—bubbles up.

I nod toward the ocean, just like Kai would when he was signaling me to get a move on when the waves looked good.

"Want to go out?" I ask.

"Surfing?" Michael looks surprised. "You surf?"

"Yes," I say.

He shakes his head and laughs in disbelief.

"You have your board?" he asks.

"It's in my car. You just need to talk to my mom first, if you don't mind."

Dr. Ahmadi has cleared me for surfing as long as I go out with a partner who is experienced and knows to get help if I report *any* suspicious symptoms, like palpitations or short- ness of breath. I also have to keep a portable defibrillator in my backpack. My mom has additional conditions: I need to call her with my exact GPS location before I paddle out, as well as the name and number of my surfing companion; and I need to confirm afterward that I have returned, safe, to the shore. It's totally embarrassing but better than being forced to quit.

I was right about them looking most alike out here. Every move Michael makes is a mirror of Kai. It's uncanny. The way he paddles cleanly through the water. The way he pops up in a single, graceful movement. The way he pivots the board—Kai's board—as he moves across the face of a wave, keeping the ride going as long as he can, longer than seems possible, until he kicks out with ease and turns back toward the horizon to catch another.

I hold my own too, and afterward he tells me: "Someone taught you well."

"Yes," I say. "Someone did."

As we walk back up the path to the house, Michael stops at the top of the bluff, the ocean continuing its ceaseless cycle of motion below us.

"He called me six times that night," he says, looking out.

"The night he died?"

He's quiet for a while, and then: "Yes. Six times. And I didn't pick up. I knew Sarah was dying. I had gone to see her a few weeks before and it was . . . I thought I was prepared, but I wasn't. She was so tiny, so frail. I didn't want to believe it was her. Despite every shitty thing I did, every promise I didn't keep, I still loved her.

"She asked me to look out for him." That expression again. A grimace, as if he is in physical pain. "So when he called that night, I knew. I knew I should go to the hospital. I knew I should be there. It was way too much for him to shoulder alone. But I couldn't. I just *couldn't* see her like that again. I didn't know what to say to her, or to him. I froze."

He grips Kai's board, planted lengthwise at his feet, as if it's the only thing keeping him upright. "And when I finally did pick up the phone, it was the police. You don't know how much I have prayed that I could rewind and go back to make things right."

Maybe not in this universe, I think. But perhaps in another, there are other chances for him, other choices. I can feel him wanting to bang his head against the hard wall of regret he must be staring at, tall enough to block out the sky and sun.

He looks at me. "This is why I didn't want to meet you when you reached out. Because I wished—still wish—that that night had ended differently. If I had shown up when Kai needed me, he'd still be here. But then, maybe, you wouldn't. I didn't think I could face someone who would remind me of everything I had done wrong, someone who lives only because he died. You know what I mean?"

I nod, tears burning in my eyes. "I'm sorry," I say, "for not respecting your wishes. For showing up here —"

"No, don't be. I'm glad I got to meet you." He pauses, then says, "I know this may sound strange, but I kind of feel his presence in you."

It doesn't sound strange at all. Not one little bit.

"I feel it too," I say. If I could tell him how much, I would, but it's all too weird, too unbelievable.

The shrubs to the side of the trail rustle and shake as Ruby bursts out, tail wagging. As we walk back to the house, I finally get up the nerve to ask: "Did you visit my room that night? The night I got his heart?"

He looks at me with a curious expression and then shakes his head. "No. I didn't know where his heart was going after they . . . after they took it. Why do you ask?"

I can't tell him exactly why I'm asking. That it confirms that he wasn't crying in my room. He was crying over Kai. Yet somehow, *I* remember it.

"Sometimes I feel like I knew you even before we met," I tell him, explaining as much as I can. "Is that weird?"

He gazes out at the ocean and then back at me.

"I've heard of weirder things."

After I pack up my gear, I return to say goodbye to Michael. With his buzzed scalp and the neck tattoo, he's not a cuddly kind of guy like my own dad. But I hug him anyway.

"Thank you," I say again, catching him in a somewhat awkward embrace. He holds on tightly for a few seconds. Long enough to catch just a few beats of Kai's heart.

"Take care of it," he says, his voice caught on the words. "Don't waste a minute of the rest of your life."

"I won't," I promise.

It's a promise I intend to keep.

As I turn to leave, Ruby does her thing, weaving in and out of my legs and licking my hand. Then she rolls over in front of the door, offering her white belly, yet again, for a scratch. I wonder if maybe she's offering even more than that. This dog that chases balls and digs in the sand in my dreams.

In my memory.

In his memory.

It's worth asking.

"Are you taking the dog?"

Kai's dad looks at Ruby and shrugs. "I travel too much to have a dog but I can't just leave her," he says. "Not a lot of takers for a full-grown pit bull. Especially one with a scar."

I've got nothing against scars.

I rub her belly and turn to Michael. "Well, you only need *one* taker."

Ruby sits in the passenger seat and sticks her head out the window on our way back to my house, her ears flapping like flags in the wind. Before I left Bolinas, I texted my parents to let them know I was on my way home, and bringing a surprise.

# AGAIN

I no longer die in my dreams every night. There's no tunnel. No tree. No tires squealing on the pavement. Because now I know what happened. He died. I lived. In this universe, my universe, our orbits have moved out of alignment.

But every so often, I still catch a memory that I know is Kai's. A story. A scent. A song. An excellent ride at some spot that I've never been to but plan to visit someday. I see it through his eyes. Feel it through his heart. Instead of being spooked, I now look forward to these flashes. I reach out for one of his life's moments and hold it as long as I can.

It's nothing I can control. Just like I can't control the waves. Some days they cooperate. Some days they don't. But that's okay. Control is overrated, I guess. This is something I never understood before: Living, really living, demands that you give up on the belief that you're always in the driver's seat. You can do everything right, weigh every decision, mitigate every risk, and still nearly drop dead of a heart attack a few weeks after your seventeenth birthday. Or crash your motorcycle in a tunnel. Or get cancer. Or be sitting directly in the path of a flaming asteroid when it falls out of the sky. We are nothing but specks of dust that have settled, ever so briefly, on the vast expanse of everything. All it takes is a single cosmic breath to blow our way and we're gone.

But still.

And yet.

We get up every day. We go to school. We eat. We drink. We surf. We fall in love. If we are lucky, we grasp every moment we've got with both hands. And who's to say that the life here on this tiny planet, in this one of trillions of solar systems, in this galaxy among billions and billions of galaxies, in this universe that is one of multiple other universes that could go on and on and on into infinity—who's to say that this is our only shot? Maybe we do get to do it again.

And again.

All at once.

Over and over.

On and on.

Fate. Chance. Luck.

A roll of the dice.

Four: I don't get sick.

Six: I get a new heart.

Ten: Kai makes it out of that tunnel alive.

Is there a reality that allows us to meet under different circumstances? Where I don't get sick and he doesn't die, but somehow our paths cross anyway? Maybe. Perhaps there is a universe where, right now, right this very second, we are standing in front of a stage, listening to that band he wanted to see. Kai is behind me, his arms are around my waist, his chin resting on the top of my head. So close that I can feel the beating of his heart. And he can feel the beating of mine.

I've always thought it kind of sucked that the best weather comes to the Bay Area when you have to be in school. Summer, in the city and along the coasts at least, is often foggy and cool. And most winter breaks, it rains. But the fall is always glorious, with each day more brilliant and sun-kissed than the next. Days that, when I was stuck in school, would taunt me through an open window. But on this perfect, seventy-degree, clear-blue-skies-as-far-as-the-eye-can-see day, I don't have to be in school. I don't have to be anywhere in particular.

So of course I'm going to check out the surf.

I pull into the parking lot at a new spot: Ocean Beach. It's mid-October, almost one year to the day that I collapsed during track. One year since everything I thought I was sure about got shaken up, spun around, and put back in a different place.

I'm still going to college, but for now I am taking a break.

I have new friends, but I haven't forgotten the old.

I have adopted a silver-gray pit bull terrier with a scar above her eye.

I am back to asking *"Why?"* all the time.

But I'm working on accepting that there isn't always an answer for everything, no matter how hard I try to find it.

I have given up motorcycles.

But not surfing.

The water is sapphire-blue, glittering in the late-morning light. Ruby sniffs the sea air through the open car window and can hardly contain herself. She's ready to burst out the back door.

"Your dog is drooling on my neck," Jane complains.

"She only drools on people she really likes," I say.

"Well, she must like everybody then," Jane says. "Because she doesn't seem very discriminating, if you ask me."

Jane pretends that Ruby annoys her, but I know better. They are secret soul mates.

Jenna, the girl Tyler introduced me to at the party on Taraval Street, is meeting us here. We've gone surfing together a few times recently and, as a result, I may be able to claim a little credit for reconnecting her and Jane. At least I hope so. It seems like their story isn't over yet. I think Jane hopes so too because she's uncharacteristically jittery today. She tried on about twenty outfits before I had to drag her out the front door.

I'm lucky to have met Jenna—she's an incredible surfer. Better than me. Maybe better than Kai. And it's nice to have some female energy out in the water, because the surf community here is pretty much what Jane has dubbed it: a "dude fest." Jenna was telling me that even the local pro women surfers have to fight to be included in big competitions like Mavericks. And if anyone will make it there someday, it's her. Despite her sweet personality, she's a total badass—she surfs the biggest waves, often spraying the guys who shoot her the you-don't-belong-here look right in the face. I can't quite keep up with her yet, but I'm going to try.

Today the surf looks good. Rideable. The swells are big but not scary. There's a barely-there offshore breeze and the peaks sweeping to the right are clean and just about perfect.

Jane chucks a tennis ball for Ruby, who races back and forth on the sand as I make my way down to the ocean's edge.

I stand there for a minute. Feel the icy-cold water washing over my toes. Inhale the sea, the sky, the sun, everything.

I fasten the collar of my wetsuit.

Then I lift my board and run for it, pounding heart to pounding waves.

≈ ACKNOWLEDGMENTS ≈

I can't help but think of my own heart as I write these acknowledgments, and how full to bursting it is with gratitude for everyone who played a part, no matter how big or small, in helping to bring this book into being.

First, to my agent, Nicki Richesin, whose steadfast belief in my story from early on gave me the confidence to keep going. Nicki, I so appreciate your spot-on editorial instincts and your ongoing support in navigating all things publishing. Being a debut author can be overwhelming and even intimidating at times, and I'm thankful I can pick up the phone and call you anytime I have a question, an idea I want to brainstorm, or a worry on my mind. Thank you also to Wendy Sherman and the entire team at Wendy Sherman Associates, as well as to Jenny Meyer.

To my wonderful editor, Kaylan Adair. Where to start? Kaylan, I feel so lucky that this story brought us together. Thank you for all the love and attention you have given to this book. Your thoughtful ideas and insights, your kind encouragement, and your willingness to hop on the phone whenever I've needed to talk something through has truly enabled me to make *Everything I Thought I Knew* everything that I hoped it could be. For all of this, I am eternally grateful.

To the entire team at Candlewick Press: you all have been absolutely lovely to work with. Thank you to Matt Roeser for creating such a dreamy, beautiful cover. To Nathan Pyritz, for not only designing the super-cool interior art, but also for catching a very important motorcycling detail during the proofreading stage. And speaking of details . . . thank you, thank you to copyeditors Maggie Deslaurier and Debbie Sosin and to proofreaders Lana Barnes, Martha Dwyer, and Emily Quill. I am in awe of your eagle-eyed attention to every paragraph, line, word, and punctuation mark. I'm so grateful you all had my back! And finally, thank you to Anna Abell and Stephanie Pando in publicity, and to everyone in marketing and sales for your efforts in introducing this story to the world.

To Mindy Urhlaub and Dorothy O'Donnell, my longtime writing critique partners, who were there for me from the moment this book was just a germ of an idea. Thank you so much for everything—for reading multiple drafts, for talking through every possible idea, for running away with me on writing weekends, for being there through every up and down of trying to finish a book, and most of all for your friendship. I couldn't have done this without you.

Thank you also to Richard Kenvin, my friend Dorothy's

brother and a longtime surfer/author/surfboard historian, for giving my surf passages a read.

On the research front, I'd also like to thank the following authors, whose nonfiction work inspired and informed me as I worked:

Joshua D. Mezrich, MD, author of *When Death Becomes Life: Notes from a Transplant Surgeon*.

Rob Dunn, author of *The Man Who Touched His Own Heart: True Tales Of Science, Surgery, And Mystery*.

Brian Greene, author of *The Hidden Reality: Parallel Universes and the Deep Laws of the Cosmos*.

Thanks also to *Scientific American*, where I turned for inspiration around parallel universes/quantum mechanics. Thank you as well to countless surf blogs and research hospital websites. Hopefully I've been able to build a believable world—at least as believable as possible for a work of speculative fiction—and that my readers will be forgiving of anything I missed.

I'm so glad to have met so many talented and generous writers through the #Roaring20sdebut group. A special thanks to early readers Jenn Moffett, Liz Lawson, Shana Youngdahl, Tanya Guerrero, Andrew Sass, and Anuradha Rajurkar. Your kind words have meant the world. Thank you to Shannon Doleski for helping me with graphics and social media advice and for inspiring my son to build a cool submarine during the pandemic lockdown. Jenn Moffett, it's been so great to share work and conversations with you, and I hope by the time you read this, we will have made that trip to NYC.

To all of my dear friends and family, who have cheered and

supported me as this book has taken shape: the Shahs, Hunts, Blauvelts, Landes, Yanaris, Julie Maples, the Kickstart crew and, last but not least, my Lucas Valley village. (A special shout-out to Kala, who introduced me to my agent, Nicki, and to Nimish, for checking the math in my tutoring scenes!) I couldn't be luckier to have such a great group of friends—some of whom read early chapters (Hi, Mer!) and all who have celebrated every milestone with me and listened to countless updates about "the book." It's finally here!

To my mom and dad, who've always encouraged my love of reading and indulged my creative pursuits, even when those pursuits might have been a little half-baked. I love you both with all my heart.

And finally, to the three most important people in my life. Scott, you are my biggest champion. Thank you from the bottom of my heart for never once questioning why I wanted to write a book in the first place—you just found ways to help me make it work and believed in me every step of the way, even when I sometimes doubted myself. Love you. Emi and Evan, being your mom is the best thing that's ever happened to me. Thank you for keeping me grounded, for making me laugh, for giving me lots of hugs, and for never letting me forget what's most important: the here and now. You both make me so proud.

One more: to my readers—thank you for choosing my story. I hope you enjoyed it!

≈≈≈